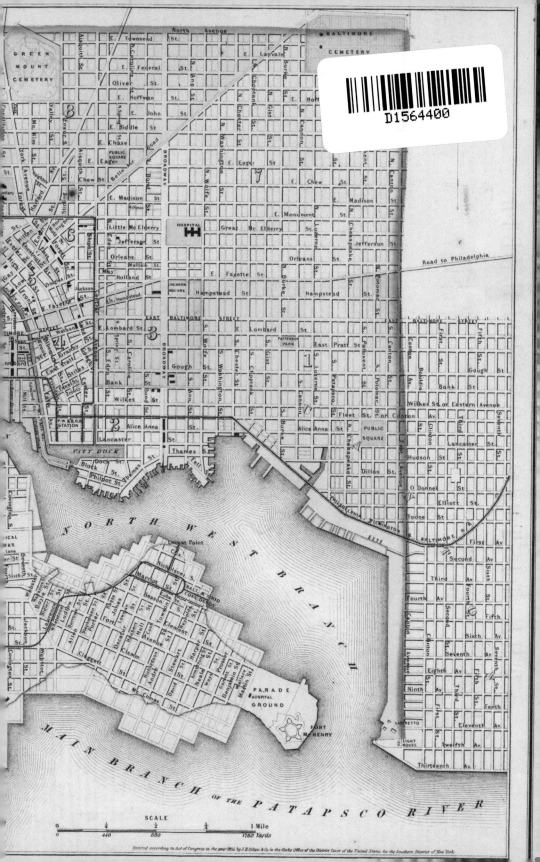

Plug Ugly Ball

A Mobtown Tale of Bullies and Baseball

To Larry,
Hope you enjoy my TALE of OLD
Baltimore

John Thomas Everett

Plug Ugly Ball

A Mobtown Tale of Bullies and Baseball

A Novel

By John Thomas Everett

The Baltimore Bookworks, LLC
Baltimore, Maryland

ISBN: 978-0-615-91415-2

Library of Congress Control Number: 2013954276

First Edition, First printing, 2014

Printed and bound in the United States of America by
United Book Press, Inc., of Woodlawn, Maryland.
Set in Georgia type by Absolute Service, Inc., of Towson, Maryland.
Portraits by Shayna Hardy Photography, Inc., of Baltimore, Maryland.

The Baltimore Bookworks is committed to the environment and proper management of our natural resources. This work is manufactured and packaged using environmentally friendly processes and recycled products.

Some scenes and descriptions in this book contain violence and language and are intended for a mature audience.

Any names, places, or events are property of their respective owners.

www.baltimorebookworks.com

Table of Contents

Part III: Civilized Substitution

Acknowledgments

I would like to thank all of those who have provided me encouragement and support in the creation and writing of this story. I have been humbled by the kindness and patience shown to me throughout the project.

Foremost among those offering assistance is my loving wife, Marge, whose advice on my female characters breathed more life into the story than I ever could have imagined when I started. If Bernadette and Jane show strength, it is in fact Marge of whom I am writing.

I am also blessed with a close, articulate, and well-read family that was regularly besieged with requests for opinions and help in solving problems. They never failed me and I'd like to thank them for that. Specifically, I'd like to acknowledge my late mother, Jane Devlin; my brothers, Christopher and Timothy Everett, and my sister, Kate Warr. My son, John Tier Everett; my daughter, Emily Hunyadi; and my son-in-law, Steven Hunyadi also were invaluable to me.

A number of formal and informal editors have had significant contributions to my thought process and the writing itself. They include: Paul Mueller, Dan Strodel, Mike Ricigliano, Dick Todd, my nephew Matt Everett, and my colleague and friend, Dr. Roger Kashlak.

I am indebted to my publisher Baltimore Bookworks and its owner, Scott Hipp. Scott not only operates the business, but also is the author of superb works of history, focusing on the American Civil War and Maryland's particular role in the conflict. I recognize and appreciate the risk he took in stepping outside of his historical roots in taking on a new author of fiction and mentoring me through the maze that is the business of publishing.

Stephanie Smith, the illustrator of the book's cover, its interior sketches, and its street map, should also be recognized certainly not only for her artistic talent, but also for taking on what was a very unusual project for her. While nationally recognized for a wide range of illustrations, Stephanie worked closely with me and did her own research in order to capture the tone of the times. The results speak for themselves.

I would also like to thank Steven G. Heaver and Rob Williams of The Fire Museum of Maryland. These gentlemen are the real experts on the history of firefighting in Baltimore. The work they do at the museum and the education they provide for thousands of visitors each year is not nearly recognized to the degree it should be. Anyone interested in supporting the museum and its mission can find Steve and Rob at www.firemuseum.org.

My understanding of the history of White Sulphur Springs, West Virginia, and The Greenbrier Resort comes from time spent with the resort's historian, Dr. Robert S. Conte. Dr. Conte is a natural storyteller whose love of his subject is as compelling as the beauty of West Virginia itself.

I would also like to thank David B. Stinson, author of *Deadball*. Mr. Stinson's novel is not only great fun to read, but it is also a wonderful source for the feeling of the old ballparks and the passion of the early players. Interest in these subjects may be further satisfied by accessing Mr. Stinson's website: www.davidbstinsonauthor.com

I would like to appreciate the help given to me and the kind and extraordinary service rendered by Jim Gillespie, director of The Johns Hopkins Peabody Library. Mr. Gillespie repeatedly went beyond expectations in securing and scanning the 1857 Colton map of Baltimore, which is used on the inside cover.

I would like to recognize the scholarly work of Mr. Tracy Mathew Melton, author of *Hanging Henry Gambrill: The Violent Career of Baltimore's Plug Uglies, 1854–1860*. Mr. Melton has painstakingly researched and written the definitive work on the firehouse gangs and their activities of the period. His book is not only rich in detail, but also is eminently readable and fascinating. It was Mr. Melton's work that sparked the idea for this novel and served time and again as a primary source document for the history employed in it.

Finally, my thanks go to all of those who have been of great assistance at The Maryland Historical Society, Library of Maryland History. The organization is often the lifeblood of researchers and writers, including myself. Without their resources, patience, and general helpfulness, this novel could not have been written.

*Only gods make true order out of chaos.
Human beings are not gods, but we aspire
to be and often pretend we are. So, we strive
to make our own order out of chaos. In the end,
what we achieve is civilized substitution
and even that is only temporary.*

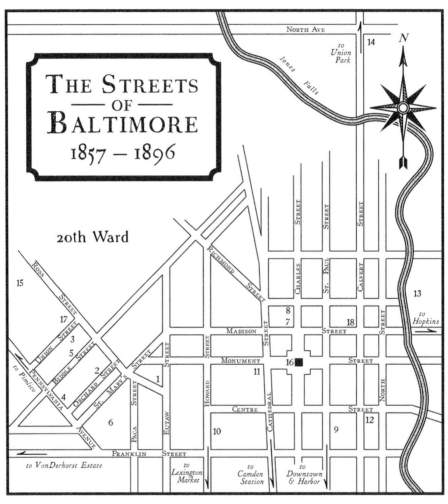

THE STREETS
— OF —
BALTIMORE
1857 – 1896

20th Ward

NORTH AVE

to
Union
Park

14

N

Jones Falls

RICHMOND STREET

STREET
STREET
STREET

CHARLES
ST. PAUL
CALVERT

ROSS STREET

15

17

UNION STREET
BIDDLE STREET

3
5

2

1

4

6

ORCHARD STREET
ST. MARY'S STREET
PACA

to Pimlico

PENNSYLVANIA

AVENUE

FRANKLIN STREET

to VonDerhorst Estate

8
7

MADISON STREET

STREET
STREET
EUTAW
HOWARD

MONUMENT

11

CENTRE

10

CATHEDRAL

16

STREET

18
STREET

STREET

STREET

9

STREET

NORTH

12

13

to
Hopkins

to
Lexington
Market

to
Camden
Station

to
Downtown
& Harbor

1. Morgan's Oyster House and Bar
2. Morgan's House
3. English's House
4. Black Horse Tavern
5. Mt. Vernon Hook & Ladder Fire Company
6. St. Mary's Seminary
7. Enoch Stanton's Mansion
8. Enoch Stanton's "Back Door"
9. Morgan's Rented Rooms (1882)
10. The Diamond Tavern (1896)
11. The Mount Vernon Hotel
12. North Central Railroad Depot Lot
13. Maryland Penitentiary and Jail
14. Eagle Brewery and Malt Works
15. Union Protestant Infirmary
16. Washington Monument/ Mt. Vernon Square
17. The Pig's Eye Tavern
18. St. Ignatius Catholic Church

Prologue

Baltimore
July 1899

The old gentleman sat by himself and watched younger men in derbies throw away their cigar butts in disgust as they filed out of the old ballpark. The Orioles had just dropped a close one in the ninth to the hated Beaneaters of Boston. McGraw had waved at a smash down the third base line by Collins, driving in Duffy. The run proved to be the winner since Kid Nichols then fanned Robinson, Brodie, and Jimmy Sheckard in order to end the game. It was just another game; but, like the old man, the Birds were clearly missing the fire of earlier days.

He waited patiently for the carriage that would take him home and gazed out over the raked base paths and the broad green field of Union Park. The second deck of the old beams and boards ball yard rose behind him; its shadow already covered the mound and was inching its way out to second base. Black men sweated in their effort to unfurl a tarp rolled up along the third base line. Others, way out beyond the center field fence, worked the lines that brought down flags and pennants that hung limply on whitewashed masts. Sweepers and trash boys swore at each other as they worked the bleachers to the right and left of him. From nowhere, in the still afternoon, a hot gust arose, filling his nose with the stale aroma of a ballpark after a day game.

The old gentleman's thoughts were about that afternoon's contest and baseball in general. He liked it because it gave him things he had very little of in his life—pace, structure, predictability. But if he were to be really honest, what he liked the most about baseball was closer to some of the things he had perhaps too much of over the years. The game still could produce surprise, excitement, and, occasionally, anarchy. That was particularly true about his beloved Orioles, who in years past, reveled in pushing the rules to the limit and beyond.

The world certainly had changed. It wasn't difficult for him to recall times in his life when there were no rules. They were hard times.

At least these days, as odd as it sounded, there was order to the disorder. Baseball was a perfect example. It was a little like Rome offering its citizens entertainment within the walls of the Coliseum as a proxy for the blood lust of war.

The old man sat contentedly and listened to hear the echoes of the day's crowd and those crowds of years past that seemed to permeate the wood of the now vacant park. But his reverie was shattered suddenly by the cracking voice of one of the young ushers who was standing a few rows above and behind him. The boy was yelling up into the out-of-town press box.

"Mr. Murnane! He's still here! There's the guy you want to talk to!" The boy pointed a sweaty, earnest looking fellow in a straw boater down through the rows of box seats to the old man.

"Pardon me, Mr. Morgan. Do you have a few minutes to talk to me? I'm Timothy Murnane of *The Boston Globe*," the man said upon his arrival in the lower deck. He extended a damp hand.

"I don't believe I read your paper," responded James Morgan in a voice that was like #4 grit sandpaper. "What can I do for you?" he growled, ignoring the man's wet paw.

The newspaperman took that as an invitation to sit. He chose a seat close to the old man and removed his hat. His head was large and clammy. An angry red ring left by his hat encircled his skull like a devilish halo.

"Sir, I understand that if anyone knows Harry Vonderhorst in this town, its you. I'm doing a story on him and I'd like to get to know the man who decided to gut the Orioles of Ned Hanlon, Willie Keeler, Hughie Jennings, and Joe Kelley. How does a native Baltimorean trade off maybe the best team ever to the Brooklyn Superbas?"

"Mr. Vonderhorst is a complicated man in a complicated business," offered the older gentleman mildly. He was not going to rise to the man's opinion offered in the thin guise of a question.

"He must be, if he can wring out the hearts of Baltimore's cranks without so much as a fare-thee-well. Doesn't his beer make him enough money already?"

It sounded as if the reporter was an Orioles crank himself, but that was not likely given his Boston credentials. Probably needs a story to meet a deadline on tomorrow's edition, thought the old gentleman.

The sportswriter was soaked through and not suffering the balmy Baltimore weather very well. A hankie appeared and the scribbler swabbed the deck of his broad forehead. Morgan felt sorry for the visitor to his fair, but muggy city.

"Well, Mister. . .ah," Morgan had forgotten or not heard the newsman's name.

"Murnane. Tim Murnane, Mr. Morgan. Please call me Tim," suggested the reporter.

"Well, Mr. Murnane, you have to think a little broader. Harry Vonderhorst loves baseball and he loves Baltimore; but he is also a businessman. And he did what he had to do to keep a team here. Attendance wasn't what it was back in '96, even before The Big Four were broken up. Harry went into the syndicate with New York as a means of keeping the Baltimore team afloat. The trade-off you mention was the price of that."

"It's a dear price if it means throwing away Baltimore's season by fielding a team of leftovers and has-beens."

At least he knows the team, thought the old man. Just the same, they were his Birds and he wasn't going to let an insult pass from some Boston clown.

"No season is lost as long as there's a game, son. It's still baseball and it still can be unpredictable. McGraw, Brodie, and Robinson can play and McGinnity has promise. There will be a lot of games worth watching this year even if the pennant race is a fantasy. But I thought you wanted to know something about the man, not his team."

The newsman realized that he was not talking to some rickety old fool, a bit antique in his feelings about the game perhaps, but no fool. And Murnane certainly wasn't going to be the one to attack the game itself—it was the hand that fed him.

"Yes, yes, of course you're right, Mr. Morgan. My apologies. I just get steamed when crass business decisions intrude on the integrity of the game."

Morgan looked at the reporter. "Mr. Murnane, you are talking out of both sides of your mouth. First you suggest that not winning the pennant is 'throwing away the season,' then you talk about business intruding on something you call 'the integrity of the game.' By the way, I never said anything about integrity. Are you really suggesting to me that there is an *integrity* to this game? How much do you know about professional baseball?" he asked the perspiring writer.

Murnane needed to start again. Somehow he had lost control of this conversation very quickly. Kindly old gentleman would not fit this ancient blue crab.

"Mr. Morgan, this is not really what I'd like to talk to you about. May I start again?" asked the writer.

After a shrug from the old man, he pulled out a note pad, placed it on top of his hat, and asked, "How long have you known Harry Vonderhorst?"

"I knew him as a boy, since my Plug Uglies days, back in the '50s," responded Morgan.

"You were a member of the Plug Uglies?" The reference to the notorious Baltimore firehouse gang had thrown the reporter off his focus once again.

"Yes, I was. But Harry was pretty young in those days. I knew his father, John, better. He built the Eagle Brewery and Malt Works, just over there on Belair Road, above North Avenue." The old man pointed out over the left field fence.

"His father paid for this place, didn't he?" The writer indicated the well-used confines of Union Park.

"No. John financed a large part of the original Oriole Park. And Harry built this ball yard in '83. His father did pay a lot of the early bills; that's true. But that was long after my first associations with the Vonderhorst family."

The old man noticed the reporter looking over his shoulder at one of the ramps leading down from the owner's box and the concession deck. The writer stood, holding his boater in one hand and working the hankie with the other.

Down the ramp came a distinguished lady, trim, tall, in her forties. She was dressed fashionably in what *Harper's* called "an easy, tailored, outdoors look." She wore a long, white, flowing skirt, caught at the waist by a wide black belt. Her blouse was a pleated gray stripe with a row of ivory buttons that ran up to a wide black ribbon around a high collar. Her jacket was short, made of black silk and sporting puffed shoulders. She carried a straw hat of her own. She looked cool, despite the summer weather.

"Jamie, I see you have a visitor," observed the woman with a smile, as the reporter gave her a slight bow.

"This man is writing a story about Harry. He thinks I may know a thing or two." Morgan smiled back at the woman.

"Not another story! Well then, I will leave you gentleman to your conversation. Jamie, I'll wait for you in the Owner's Lounge. Take your time." Without another word, and avoiding introductions, she turned and strode back up the empty ramp.

"Who was that?" asked Murnane, obviously impressed.

"That was Harry's wife, Bernadette," replied the old man.

"I'd like to talk to her as well," said the newsman, eagerly.

"That's not going to happen, son. You'd better stick with me," said Morgan. "Now, what can I tell you?"

"I don't know," said the younger man, still looking after Bernadette Vonderhorst, but realizing that the old man was willing to talk. "Just start at the beginning."

Part I
Aspiring To Be Gods

Chapter 1

Baltimore
April 15, 1857, Around Noon

The bar room smelled of sweat, cigars, and the rancid tang of yesterday's oysters. Hard men hunched over hard drinks or a pint of bitter beer. A low buzz was punctuated by the occasional drunken insult and its responding curse, which was nothing out of the ordinary for the place, even at noon.

James Morgan surveyed his clientele and sensed a different element in the air. Something was afoot. From his perch in the gallery above the bar, he surveyed the vaporous room. The regular sots continued the work of killing themselves. Exhausted shift workers, dressed in suspenders and stained Union suits, escaped the breweries, the slaughterhouses, oyster barges, and coal yards. Three young bucks, wearing grimy slouch hats on a slant, hunched over half-full glasses of foamless beer and waited with sharp, yellow eyes for that one chance to make their name. An off-duty city watchman sat by himself with his back to the door, staring into a cup of cheap rye, his topper on the floor. A couple of local firemen spat at a distant spittoon and dared with their eyes anyone who might take offense that the floor and wall was getting the worst of it. He knew them all, the usual volatile mix. But there was an added anticipation in the room, like the smell of smoke just before the firehouse bell sounds.

In the big booth in the corner, away from the window, John English sat among the tight group of bullyboys calling themselves the Plug Uglies. Morgan had known English since they were boys playing in the streets of the Twentieth Ward. As young toughs, they fought and worked together as pipemen for The New Market Fire Company's suction engine. Over the last four years, however, their bond had been sealed in bruises and blood while running with the Mount Vernon Hook and Ladder crew. Ironically, Mount Vernon had evolved into the chief rival of their former house, the hated New Market.

English was the originator and driving force behind Mount Vernon's militant wing, a necessary asset in Baltimore's patchwork of rival volunteer fire companies. Competing to put out a fire—often one they started themselves—was what they did. At any fire, the sound of gunshots was as prevalent as the cracking and popping of burning timbers. In recent years though, things had gotten more complicated. The firehouse gangs had fought and sometimes killed each other since the '40s, primarily for pride and revenge. But recently, a new element had been added: politics. And as the gangs began to choose sides based on party affiliation, they also began calling themselves *social clubs*. This charming title served as thin disguise for the mayhem they brought out into the streets. More importantly, the term worked to soothe the miniscule consciences of certain city and state politicians. These were the amoral men who sought the type of street-level alliance that would generate the right kind of votes and discourage the wrong kind, come election day. The social club operating in the Mount Vernon area of northwest Baltimore was home to John English's American Club, better known as the Plug Uglies.

Morgan's saloon and oyster cellar had become the center of the Plugs because of his ties to English. This was certainly good for business and, with advanced warning out of the precinct house, he could usually avoid problems associated with the occasional showy raid. Hell, there were days when he couldn't tell whether the cops were coming in to bust someone or just looking for a drink. He often joked that his back door was used more often than the front. Still, as he got older, he began to wonder how much longer it could last. He worried too about the escalating violence that he saw in his friend, English.

"Goddamnit, they broke two teeth and busted my lip! How do you want me to feel? It was them New Markets and I swear I'll going to kill me one of them sons-of-bitches."

The drunk was loud and deadly serious, teary with anger. He reached down into the leg of a filthy boot and, in a practiced motion, had a stained jackknife open. He jammed it into the scarred table.

"I was just getting some fish from the Lex for the old lady. The Market's firehouse was two squares away! The next thing I know I'm eating alley apples! Well, someone's going to pay," the man concluded with force, stabbing the table again.

"Shut up, Mouse. We'll take care of it; just button it." The man sitting with the drunk hunkered over the table and spoke quietly to him. Then, he peered over his shoulder to the corner booth.

"No way in hell I'm going to take it. I know where I can get me a pepperbox pistol. I saw who they were."

This was said with a rising pitch and Mouse's drinking partner noticed that the conversation at English's table had stopped. At that, he kicked back from the table with a scrape, walked over to the bar, threw down a few coins and disappeared through the front door.

"Where you going? We've got to think about this," whined the drunk. "Okay. The hell with you. I'll do it myself. I don't need you!" The man was shouting now, and the rest of the bar had grown quiet.

Morgan had stood during this rant, descended from the gallery, reached behind the bar for the axe handle stashed there, and stepped quickly to Mouse's table.

"Time to go, Mouse," said Morgan.

"Jamie, but look what they did to my face," whined the man. "I can't go home, now. My old lady will go nuts. I won't get tagged to work the docks tomorrow! That means no rent money. I'm gonna make the New Market pay in blood!"

"You're going to do no such thing, Mouse. What you are going to do is get your ass out of here."

Morgan laid the axe handle on the table; then, as if lifting a cat with the mange, he grabbed the drunk by the scruff, yanking him up out of the chair. With his other hand, he swept up the knife and, in one motion, flung it into the wall where it stuck, quivering just off the middle of an Eagle Beer sign.

The man's boots left a trail through the floor's sawdust and filth as Morgan dragged him backwards toward the front door. Pushing it open with Mouse's head, the barman flung the lush out onto the scarred cobbles where the wheel of a beer wagon abruptly stopped his progress.

As Morgan was performing this house cleaning, he saw English nod to David Houck. Houck stood, waited for Morgan to return to the bar, and then slowly walked through the front door to the street.

The bar quickly returned to its normal surly drone, hardly noting the minor disturbance. English leaned in over the table in the booth and spoke to the three men remaining with him.

"The west entrance to the Lexington Market is where we meet. Get the boys to come in twos and threes from different directions. There will be about twenty of us. Everybody gets there at midnight, so there's no standing around. Then, we move directly up Howard Street to the firehouse, do what we have to do, and then disappear the same way we came. I've clued in the beat cop. He and his pals in blue won't be around. Houck and I will bring the tools. Any questions?"

"Yeah, John, I got a little present from my brother the other day and I'd like to see what it can do. Mind if I bring it along?" Dickie Harris was a particularly active member of the club. He was also a frightful specimen. His jaw was apelike and it sat atop a pair of massive, dock-hardened shoulders. He had long, ropey, tattooed arms and huge hands that were knotted and scarred from years of using an oyster knife. These endearing attributes led his bravest friends, in his absence, to claim him as the source of the name "Plug Ugly." He didn't need English's permission to carry the pistol; he was just showing off.

"Bring it, but keep it in your pocket. Use it if you have to," said English. "You won't be the only one there carrying. Just be sure to bring that sledge of yours too. Anything else?" After a brief look around the table, he said, "Okay, then, get out of here. Remember, we meet at midnight sharp."

With that, the three men rose and left English alone in the booth. Morgan moved to join his friend, stopping when he saw Houck come back through the front door and walk over to English. They exchanged a few words, then Houck left again through the back way, nodding at Morgan as he moved past him.

Morgan reached behind the bar, pulled out the bottle of single malt with his name on it, took the top two glasses from the pyramid, walked over to English in the booth, and sat down.

"What's up John? My nose itches," started Morgan, as he pulled the cork and filled the squat glasses halfway.

"Better not say, Jamie, my friend. Leave your nose out of this one," said English. "You've been getting nervous lately."

"You're going to hit The Market, aren't you? And, it's not nerves, John. The operations have been getting messier. The Mayor and the Reform Committee's up in arms again. That guy Houck you're spending a lot of time with, and Harris too, they're in it for the sport. No purpose other than the shear joy of it. I don't like it," commented Morgan.

"You don't have to like it. You're not in it. I'm running this event. J.W. is with me this time. Look, you and me and Gambrill, we're tight and always will be. We've had each other's back since before Mount Vernon, before the Plugs, before the bleeding politicians sniffed votes and money in the streets. You want out because the stakes are higher, because Mayor Swann gave one of his mealymouthed speeches? Okay, I get it. You're out on this one," English growled.

"John, you know I'm with you. I just think some of these boys are out of control," said Morgan.

"It's the goddamned Market who's out of control!" stormed English. "I saw it. I saw them shoot the Cuddy boy and bust up a couple of other Plugs. We were working the fire just fine when they showed up."

"You set the fire and it was on Clay Street. Their turf," observed Morgan.

"Damn! See, that's why I'm not asking you in here. I don't get this crap from Gambrill. You don't get it anymore, Jamie. Houck and Harris are just tools. The kind of tools I need to answer dicks like The Market and the Regulators. And, somebody's got to stop the goddamn Democrats; they're running wild! If I don't, there will be no neighborhood for our families, no Plug Uglies, no American Party, no John English, no Morgan's Bar and Oyster House. You want some Irish son-of-a-drunk running Baltimore?"

English was getting that little bit of crazy in his one good eye that Morgan knew well. There was no changing his view of the world. His view was an eye for an eye, yes, but also an ear, an arm, and a leg. It was also the nativist view of America for Americans, not the garbage that was unloading onto the Pratt Street docks every day or the arrogant freed slaves walking Baltimore's streets. Morgan had this conversation with English before.

"Okay, John, settle down. I know what you're doing and why you're doing it," Morgan said, trying to avoid English reaching that low boiling point of his.

"Don't tell me to settle down, Jamie! I'll bust this place up if I want to," threatened English. "I don't care if it is you. I said you're out, so you're out—for now."

English gave Morgan a hard look, stood abruptly, pushed his John Bull down on his brow, and slammed his way out of the bar without a look back.

The Plug Uglies controlled the northwest section of Baltimore, mapped out as the Twentieth Ward. The neighborhood started below the city line at North Avenue, then ran south, spreading out along Pennsylvania Avenue.

The Twentieth Ward, sometimes known as the west end, was a smoky grid of dirt alleys and cobblestone streets. Along its passages, grimy, warped-wood structures alternated with the occasional run of two- or three-story brick businesses and row homes. The houses were stained dark by the area's furnaces, but, like a coalminer's ragged smile, many sported gleaming, white marble front stoops.

There were a variety of cheap bars, oyster cellars, and commercial storefronts shaded by awnings in a variety of colors and stripes. Dilapidated boarding houses were many, accommodating neighbor-hood locals and the occasional county farmer in with his produce. Increasingly, the alleys were filling with makeshift hovels. Squatters, mostly threadbare immigrants fresh up from the docks, crowded available space. The neighborhood was dotted with rusting machine shop yards, tumbledown stables and pens, noisy slaughterhouses, and a stinking tannery as well. In other words, it was much like any American city ward.

Despite its stained pedigree, the neighborhood was not without its pride or affluence. The trades were well represented and the big tinware factory, the cotton mills, and the sheet iron foundry all were running two shifts and employing the neighborhood. There was work down on the docks, as well, and the Twentieth's men fought their way into all of the maritime trades, from shipbuilding and repair to shucking and canning oysters.

This was the province of the Plug Uglies. Little of interest moved in or out of the tight neighborhood without them knowing, approving, or working to get their share. For drinking money, the occasional street robbery was popular. For amusement, the gang would scour the alleys for runaway slaves or harass the German and Irish immigrants seeping into the city. The really serious business, however, was the settling of grievances with the other fire companies and their street soldiers, the social clubs.

Some of the Plug Uglies had a trade, ran a small business, or worked in a mill, in a factory, or on a dock. Others with connections infiltrated the police, became watchmen, or took patronage jobs with the city. English himself, at various times, was both a policeman and a watchman. Many were married with families, leaving the raising of their brats to the manure-splattered, cobbled streets. They were men of the world, but that world was a small, mean one.

Despite its hard urban life, or perhaps because of it, the Ward also had a spiritual side. While it was difficult to imagine any of the Plugs fearing anything but a pistol pointed at them, most people feared the Lord and remembered to thank him every Sunday for the things they had. As a result, the neighborhood could boast its share of the church spires that defined the city, soaring arrows offering obvious proof of devotion. Even the neighborhood's least spiritual would brag of the huge, brick-walled compound that was St. Mary's College and Seminary on Paca Street. Hardened thugs would crow of the institution's founding in 1791. And, despite a general hatred for Catholics, these same toughs would drop their voices in reverence as they described St. Mary's best-known inmate, the saintly Mother Elizabeth Ann Seton.

Feuding between the fire companies in Baltimore began long before the rough-and-tumble clubs formed. A network of volunteer companies was the city's firefighting solution coming out of the eighteenth century. However, fuzzy boundaries, scarce equipment, neighborhood pride, and high levels of youthful testosterone combined as ingredients in a very unstable concoction. And that explosive mix was regularly sparked by the standard insurance company policy of only paying the fire brigade that arrived first at the scene. It was no mystery why a spike in arson coincided with this frugal corporate decision.

Soon, firehouses began to develop human muscle to assist in territorial disputes, as well as pulling suction engines and hose carriages. In the '50s, these firehouse gangs emerged with names like the New Marketers, the Regulators, the Double Pumps, the Rip-Raps, the Blood Tubs and the Plug Uglies. This evolution occurred about the same time the clubs' interests expanded into power politics. As a result, party affiliation became yet another layer of friction among the firehouses and their informal adjuncts.

In 1856, Baltimore City added mayhem to the national and local political process. Each firehouse and social club decided its allegiance between the Democratic Party and the American Party. The Plug Uglies, the Rip-Raps, the Blood Tubs, and their respective fire companies believed in a nativist philosophy and were staunch members of the American Party, backing Millard Fillmore for president. These supporters were labeled the Know-Nothings in a slight by the Democratic press. Democratic candidates, aligning them-selves with James Buchanan, were supported by the likes of the New Marketers, the Regulators, the Calithumpians, and the Empire Club.

Elections were always anticipated by the clubs for the lucrative opportunity that voter intimidation offered. But politics wasn't just a matter of money. More than that, it was an avenue for the clubs to define what they thought America and Baltimore should be. For the American Party and the Plug Uglies, it was well defined: no Catholics, no Jews, no Irish, no Germans, and no abolition.

At the bottom of it all, in the firehouses, in the saloons, and on the streets of the Twentieth, there was real fear. It was a fear that their lives would change for the worse. Those who had just recently risen from the jobs that slaves or freedmen normally did were particularly fearful of going back to that hell. Pressing them as well was the rising tide of Europeans into the city. Caught between the two forces, men sought solutions. And politics offered a dam against the flood.

Battle lines were drawn along streets like Clay, Howard, and Biddle—appropriately named for war heroes and firebrands. The fight for control of the city also presented ample opportunity to mete out lessons where lessons were owed or to administer them by those who were just entertaining themselves. Violence and murder could be random, but were often strategic. In Baltimore's recent election, the strategy of anarchy was highly successful. The adversaries were emotionally and politically well defined; and, therefore, Election Day itself was an all-out war. Because polling places were often located within the firehouses around the city, they became flashpoints and scenes of siege, revenge, and bloodshed.

The American Party and its supporting clubs were particularly well organized and active in the fall elections of 1856. Plug Ugly or Rip-Rap bullies drove hundreds of naturalized citizen voters away from supporting Democratic candidates. At one point, American Party supporters won control of the ground around the New Market Firehouse, blocked voters from the poles, and smashed down the doors of the engine house. The streets of Baltimore rang with running gun fights, guerilla warfare, and the occasional pitched battle.

Those stalwart Democratic souls who fought their way into the polls to cast their identifying striped vote more than likely came away bloody for their trouble, often bleeding from multiple awl punctures. This nasty leatherworking tool happened to be the weapon of choice of the Plug Uglies. The Blood Tubs, on the other hand, preferred the revolting practice of dousing Democratic voters with chicken blood as they attempted to vote.

Democratic social clubs supporting their candidates were not asleep either. The noxious practice of *cooping* was a regular tool. This trick involved groups of men, plied with drink, and held against their will in a dank basement or an obscure warehouse often for days at a time. Once Election Day arrived, these unfortunates were herded like disoriented sheep from poll to poll and forced through violent persuasion to cast multiple votes for Democratic candidates.

Any given gang's signature methods were not really unusual for any of the city's social clubs. The tactics were a la carte: threat, intimidation, extortion, organized thievery, battery, riot, arson, and murder. Rioters used fists, bricks, cudgels, awls, a variety of knives, pistols, and the odd musket. During one melee, one of the Democratic clubs mounted and fired a swivel gun at its enemies, another dragged a cannon out of a firehouse and fired into a group of brawling American club members.

These groups operated openly, with little fear of retribution. Cozy relationships were formed with many of the city's police and watchmen who had become used to supplementing their incomes with kickbacks and bribes. The gangs often developed a type of police adjunct status, working with the cops against rivals when it suited them. In recent years, political debts had even opened some positions on both the Force and the Watch.

Baltimore's judicial system was mired in street politics too. The clubs maintained cozy relationships with judges, rewarded enterprising clerks who mishandled paperwork, and showed appreciation to overworked investigators who cut corners. Arrests rarely resulted in conviction, even when they could find witnesses. Even then, many would either melt away or stay and perjure themselves.

Governors, mayors, and even minor officials ran and won on platforms of social and legal reform while using hellish tactics in the process. In the 1856 mayoral election, it was hard-nosed B&O Railroad executive, Thomas Swann, who defeated Robert Clinton Wright, former president of the Baltimore and Susquehanna Railroad. These were men with skewed moral compasses who prepped for office by constructing brutal businesses out of steel and rock, and operating them on the backs of half-starved workers. Once in, these kind of men appointed prosecutors and judges in return for favors, accepted bribes for everything from dock space to building contracts, supported cronies, and ignored atrocities committed against immigrants, freedmen, and slaves. Each of these public servants said they wanted to preserve Maryland and Baltimore for Americans. That aegis allowed them to straddle two parties while never really having to define who or what an American was.

Like the flotsam washing up against the piles of the Main Dock, reform groups formed and met without any seeming impact or conviction. Scathing diatribes were written on bales of paper, but never acted upon. And when the occasional, nervy newspaper printed a broadside against the gangs who had turned the city into a mob town, offices were burned and editors beaten. Clubs like the Plug Uglies reveled in the politics and power of their name and dared anyone to challenge them.

The firehouse gangs' political activities, while costly to their paying connections, were very lucrative for the clubs. Politics was seasonal work though. So, a steadier income was needed. That often came from catching runaway slaves, thanks to the Fugitive Slave Law of 1850 and Maryland's pivotal position between the North and South.

Baltimore was just as dangerous a place for freedmen as it was for those seeking freedom through the Underground Railroad. The city's population of black freedmen was the largest in the country, and as many as fifty thousand lived within its boundaries. Unfortunately, these new citizens soon found out that those pursuing slaves were quite often indiscriminate in their efforts.

The Kansas-Nebraska Act was only a couple of years old; blood was being spilled in Lawrence, Kansas in support of slavery; abolitionism was gaining momentum; and a South Carolina congressman caned one from Massachusetts on the floor of Congress over the issue. Southern sensitivity and defensiveness was at an all-time high and the battle between Buchanan and Fillmore for Maryland electoral votes added to the poisonous atmosphere.

As a result of all of this, the American Party made considerable headway in securing city and state offices in 1856, as disorder held sway. With the Governor dithering, the Mayor refusing action, and the social clubs gaining strength and nerve, the coming municipal elections of 1857 promised more of the same.

Chapter 2

Baltimore
April 15, 1857, Near Midnight

The New Market Fire Company was one of the oldest firehouses in the city, established back in 1806. Its white, Georgian bell tower rose above surrounding roof tops and stood as testimony to its power and influence. Its members were proud, tough, and good at what they did. What they did was put out fires, support the Democratic Party, and protect the neighborhood and their reputation, not necessarily in that order.

The Company could boast a brand new gallery engine, a suction engine, a spouting engine, and several hose carriages and reels. All of this was thanks to their street-level political efforts in previous elections. They had well over three hundred trained firefighters and at least fifty young toughs who assisted the company in the odd, dirty jobs associated with fighting fires in Baltimore. Because of its proximity to the preeminent Lexington Market, this social club had become known across the city as the Market. They were clearly at the top of the heap and had the will and wherewithal to stay there.

Augustus "Bully" Albert was New Market's president. Bully called the tune for firemen and street soldiers alike at the west side house. His men were a direct reflection of Bully himself: hard, unforgiving, and relentless. Some of the young studs had even begun to sport his trademark bushy handlebar.

Despite the fact that it was around midnight, Bully and five or six of his fellows were standing on the gas-lit, concrete apron of the firehouse. Some were leaning against the building's iron facade, admiring the new engine, and passing a bottle.

"Where's Georgie tonight, Bully? I wanted to ask him about the Clay Street fire," asked one of the drinkers.

"Better leave that alone, Dick. Your man's upstairs sleeping it off with the boys on call. He didn't get much shut-eye in the lockup with all of the whores screaming and the rum-bums off that Indies schooner talking their trash," growled Augustus Albert.

"I just heard that he got in a few good licks on them Plugs and I wanted to hear it from the horse's mouth," pressed Dick.

"Boy, you got the wrong end of the horse. Georgie's a fool for putting a hole through that Plug's leg. I told him not to bring that piece. Hell, I spent all evening convincing the magistrate that it wasn't Georgie. Good thing we got friends," observed Albert.

"C'mon, Bully. Them Plugs had it coming. That was our fire. It was beautiful how we stole it right away from them," commented another of the young thugs as he took a pull from the bottle.

"You boys shut your holes. Let it be. I advise you to forget it, see?" The president fixed them with the fish eye until their smiles faded. Then, he released them with a derisive chuckle and said, "Now, this here's a thing of beauty."

The fireman ran loving hands down the side of the new John Rogers suction engine, over its gleaming pipes, its polished oak pump handles, its brass fittings, its piston tower, and its silver pressure equalizer. He stopped his fondling when he reached the painted picture of Tecumseh and the silver plaque beneath. The plate's gold scrollwork spelled out the name they had picked for the fire engine, The Chief.

As Bully admired the beautiful complexity of the apparatus, he looked up and beyond the carriage's big holding tank. His smile faded. A knot of dark figures was moving fast toward him and the firehouse. This did not look good.

"Get this inside, you assholes. Now!" screamed Albert.

But, it was too late. The group's reaction was slow, unaided by the rotgut they had been drinking. Before they knew it, the dark figures were on them. Immediately, two of the Market's men were down, felled by three or four clubs at once. Albert, protected behind the pumper, left it and sprinted through the double doors of the house. The remaining Marketers fought back briefly before they were overwhelmed, taking blows from all directions. Some of the attackers continued to cudgel the fallen. Another group moved to the new machine and began to lay into it, one of them using a heavy maul. Others began to throw kindling, hay, and other flammable debris against the building's clapboard side.

Albert, gaining the pull for the alarm bell in the Market's watchtower, began to yank it, while howling like a man possessed. The alarm, the president's bellowing, and the growing noise of battle outside shocked those dozing in the firehouse into rapid motion. They mobilized like a kicked anthill, just as they had been trained to do.

"It's the Plugs, you bastards. They're busting us up. Get your ass outside. Grab that axe, Butchie! Break out the hooks!" Albert ordered.

As the New Market firemen began to arm themselves, Albert sprinted back outside. He pulled up short when he saw one of the attackers throw a Lucifer match into the pile against the building.

The aggressors began to back slowly away from the fallen, nodding at their handiwork, and looking for more prey. Then they came on again in a rush as firemen and club members began to boil out of the building.

Albert ducked what looked like a pickax, then swung the heavy shovel he had grabbed. He felt it smash the back of someone's head with a loud clang. As he moved quickly to the burning pile, he jumped over one of his boys on the ground. The man was curled around a knife or an awl or something in his gut. The flames began to grow, licking at the vulnerable wooden wall of the firehouse and the stables behind. Using the shovel, Albert scattered the flaming debris, tossing burning pieces behind him into a knot of fighting men.

The sound of shattering glass split the air as bricks found the windows on the first and second floors. Men were fighting all around him. A Plug took a fire hook in the backside, where it stayed, its long handle hanging down and bouncing on the street's cobbles as the man swung around, trying to remove the embedded barb. Other wounded were crawling away to dark corners. There were a number of bodies lying still in inky pools on the pavement around the ruined engine. He saw with little satisfaction that at least the odds seemed even now.

As Albert booted the remaining embers away from the wall, he heard a pistol shot and immediately felt a stinging along the top of his ear. He turned to see a huge man not five feet away, cursing and lowering a single shot, Derringer pistol. Reacting, he rushed the attacker with shovel straight out, catching him just under the jaw and snapping his head back. As the man staggered, Albert moved in and brought the edge of the shovel down in a broad arc where it imbedded itself in his attacker's skull. Albert left it there and turned at the sound of his name.

"See you in hell, Bully," snarled John English, as he pulled the trigger of a Colt pocket model pistol and watched his rival's face explode and his body slam against the side of the firehouse, leaving a long, bloody smear.

Chapter 3

Baltimore
April 16, 1857, Midmorning

*T*he *Baltimore Sun* called it the worst riot in the city's history. It wasn't, of course, but the editors were going for outrage. The newspaper detailed the six dead and fifteen severely wounded. It lamented the damage done to the New Market firehouse and its equipment. It emphasized the cost to the city. *The American News* called for immediate and concerted action from Governor Ligon and Mayor Swann. It decried the fall of social order and the powerlessness of the city's police force to do anything about it. *The Gazette* pointedly called the city prosecutor inept and corrupt, even hinting that the gangs of ruffians who ruled the city financed his big house on Charles Street. It scoffed at the lack of witnesses and demanded that the perpetrators be brought to justice. All three newspapers were very careful, however, not to name names or point a finger at any particular band of rioters.

John English sat in the corner booth in Morgan's and scanned the three papers. Satisfied that no direct mention of the Plug Uglies was made in connection with the previous night's activities, he called for two dozen Chincoteagues and a pitcher of Eagle. Setting aside the cigar he was chewing, he shoved the papers onto the floor as the oysters arrived. He filled his glass, took a long pull, and watched Houck approach the table.

"Sit down, David, my man. Have some. Nice and salty," English offered expansively. He extended a fat, gray blob dripping off the end of an oyster knife.

"Not me. I hate those things. Tear me up. The primes are the worst," said Houck looking at the thing with disgust. He carefully eased himself into a chair.

"What's wrong with you? You look like hell and you're walking like some old lady," English observed, making a sucking sound as an oyster disappeared.

"Nothin'. Don't ask," mumbled Houck. He didn't want to talk about the hook that tore one of his rear cheeks the night before. "I just wanted you to know that I took care of that little extermination problem we had. I set a mouse trap and. . ."

"Good," cut in English. "Keep it to yourself."

"Okay, fine. Forget it," Houck shrugged. "Too bad about Harris though, huh?" probed Houck.

"Who? I don't know what you're talking about. I don't know no Dickie Harris, get it?" snapped English. "Now beat it. You're disturbing my lunch."

English's good mood didn't last long and Houck knew it wasn't going to get any better. He pulled himself out of the chair, gave English a wounded look that was ignored, and turned to go as English threw the wet lump into his mouth.

But Houck wasn't going anywhere. Through the front door pushed William L. Barton, the toughest, nastiest cop in the city and another foul son-of-a-bitch from the Biddle Street neighborhood. Behind him were a lot of others in blue, wearing stars and carrying truncheons.

Houck turned to exit through the back door, but a tall, broad-shouldered man in a bowler and a vested suit stepped through it. The man shifted his weight to the balls of his feet and slammed a set of brass knuckles into Houck's nose, dropping him like an admiralty anchor.

"Going somewhere, asshole?" the man asked belatedly. Then he addressed the room, "Nobody moves. I'm Thomas Kent, U.S. Marshall. The District Attorney wanted me to stop by and pay you beauties a little visit. You'd be amazed at how many people watched the entertainment last night."

With that, he swung his hand up and pointed a huge '51 Colt Navy at the bartender. "Come out from behind there and leave whatever you're reaching for right where it is."

The barman's arms shot up and he tried to look stupid. The patrons in the half-full bar stiffened, pushed back from their tables or stood against the wall. They were careful to show their hands, sucked in their breath, and waited for the hammer to drop.

John English froze too, oyster still in his mouth. The first thing he did was check the gallery over the bar looking for Morgan who was not there. Damn, no cover. At the same time, he eased his away-hand under the table to check his belt for his new pinfire revolver.

Barton was sharp though and he was eying English closely. Stepping quickly to the corner table, he put his Dragoon to English's head. "Go ahead, Johnny-boy, save us all a lot of trouble," Barton suggested with the empty smile of a predator.

English slowly put his hands on the table, turned to look at Barton, and said, "Well, lookie here. The big turd has floated back to the old neighborhood."

With that, he spit the oyster onto the badge on Barton's chest. His grin was only half formed when the cop's other hand flashed and a sap connected with a sick, wet smack. English sensed a bright white, then nothing at all.

James Morgan watched the police from up the street. He saw them jam some losers into a barred van, including Eisenhart, his bartender. Then they carried two bodies out and threw them unceremoniously into a flat bed dray. Drivers and guards climbed up onto the two vehicles, got the horses' attention, and clattered off. They headed not for the local station house, but toward Monument Street and the bridge across the Jones Falls to the City Jail and Penitentiary.

Morgan waited as the cops milled around the front of the Oyster House. Then he saw Big Bill Barton walk out. He was talking to some dandy in a suit who was casually waving a large Colt as he gave instructions to Big Bill.

Damnation! One of the bodies was English and the other was maybe Houck. Morgan hadn't heard gunfire so maybe John was still alive. He edged over to the newsstand, bought a *Sun* from a nervous little man who was in a hurry to bring his striped awning down, and stood against the wall of the Empire Paper and Print Shop, peering over the newspaper.

Gawkers began to gather. Those trying to peer through the door of the bar got shoved back roughly, one stumbling and falling awkwardly out onto the cobbles of Eutaw Street. As he picked himself up, the unfortunate had to extract his hand from a fresh deposit left by the morning's equine traffic. The cops found this hilarious. They were still laughing when they nailed a couple of boards over the bar's front door and tacked up a "Closed" notice.

Morgan watched Barton and the suit get in a hansom and head downtown. The last of the cops strolled off after them on foot, swinging their billies and talking of boxing. He waited until they turned the corner at Paca Street, then sprinted across the street, tore off one of the boards, and ducked inside.

The cops had enjoyed themselves and the damage was considerable. But Morgan needed to move. He climbed the stairs two at a time, spun around a carved post and into a shabby office. The bulls had screwed with his safe but couldn't open or move it. He spun the tumblers, stuffed the cash, account books, and his Webley into a burlap sack and leapt back down the stairs. He checked the cash box under the bar, but of course it was empty. The cops had to live too. He turned for the door but then doubled back, stuffing the good single malt, a bottle of Monumental Rye, and what was left of the box of Ambrosia Claros into the sack. Taking one more look around, he moved quickly over a puddle of warm oyster stew, shot out the back door, into the alley, around a jumble of reeking, stacked pallets, and left Morgan's Oyster House and Bar behind as fast as a determined walk would take him.

Chapter 4

Baltimore
April 16, 1857, Late afternoon

Hattie Simpson English had been a beautiful, sweet-tempered girl and now she was a beautiful, sweet-tempered woman. Morgan had met her at the neighborhood Grand Christmas Ball back in '55. She captured his heart immediately. When she smiled at him, his breathing stopped. When she spoke to him, there was a roaring in his ears. When they danced, his legs became wooden. It was wonderful. Later, he lay alone thinking about what could be and making plans for the future.

Because of one rare and wonderful night, however, those plans never came to be. Their budding love affair was short-lived, once Hattie met John English. The handsome, patch-eyed leader of the Plugs offered her the security she sought and simply swept her off her naïve feet. Was that how it really went? Or did he just let her go? He really couldn't remember, or didn't want to. Those thoughts he kept deep inside, well buried. It just seemed that John English got his way more often than not.

Now, Morgan stood on the stoop of the modest redbrick home Hattie kept with his friend and wondered what he was going to tell her. John talked very little about his wife to him. Morgan had no idea how much she knew about her husband's life or even what kind of man the Plug's leader really was. He didn't know if they were close or not. He did know, however, that there were a lot of nights he never even bothered to go home to her.

"Jamie Morgan, what are you doing standing out here?"

Hattie had opened the door suddenly. She stepped back and ushered him inside.

"We don't often get a visit from you. It's nice to see you. John's not home. I'm not sure where he is. Wait, he said he was going to be with you," she recalled at last.

Then, looking at Morgan's face. "Something's happened, hasn't it? What is it, Jamie? Where's John?" She peppered him with questions.

"Now, Hattie, I think John's okay. He's had a little trouble, but I think he'll be okay. I sure could use a cool drink. Let's go sit in the kitchen for a bit."

His deflection did nothing for her worried look. But she led him to the back of the house, pushing a few loose strands back into the chignon that every woman in Baltimore seemed to prefer. She truly was beautiful, but there had been a change. A big change. Her protruding middle spoke of an expansion of the English family.

"Jamie, why are you here? I want to know right now," Hattie demanded as she reached for a glass and filled it from a sweating stone pot near the back door.

"John's been arrested and they were none too gentle about it. They're holding him in the big lockup over on Truxton. It's pretty confused right now and I haven't found out yet why they took him. Something about that mess down on Howard last night."

Morgan was dissembling and he hoped Hattie didn't realize it. As he spoke, he watched her closely. It was obvious that the late pregnancy was hard on her. It wasn't just her wince as she eased herself into a chair opposite him. She didn't look well. Her normal color was gone; her face was the tone of old ash. The dark patches under her blue eyes only emphasized her pallor.

Hattie had begun to cry. "Is John hurt bad?" she asked. "Can I go to him? I've got to go to him," she said and began to rise.

Morgan reached across the table to her hand and gently brought her back down.

"He's okay. A doctor is with him. Big Bill hit him pretty hard, but John's going to be okay." Morgan knew he had to be careful here. He knew what English expected.

Earlier that day, after slipping down the alley behind the bar and stashing the sack at his place on Orchard, Morgan had gone immediately to the office of Jackson W. Stokes, the city's man for the

Twentieth Ward. The gofer also ran the occasional errand for the Plug Uglies.

A balding file clerk stammered that Stokes wasn't in. Morgan stiff-armed the man, knocking the desk, the neat piles on it, and the clerk's comb-over out of kilter. A well-placed boot to the inner office door left Morgan staring at the ward boss who was sitting with his feet up on his desk, popping pimples in a lady's handheld mirror.

"Christ, James, can't you knock?" whined Stokes, whipping the mirror down.

"Jack, get off your ass and get over to Truxton Street. That bastard Barton has taken English. Busted him up good too, as far as I could tell. I need to know what's going on and I need to know now," demanded Morgan.

"Now Jamie, settle down. I've got some information on the bust, but I wasn't told everything," Stokes said in a patronizing way.

Morgan struck like a snake. He had Stokes' neck in one hand and his crotch in the other. He lifted the political parasite and pinned him against the framed picture of Mayor Swann hanging on the wall.

"You mean you knew about the raid?" Morgan snarled menacingly.

"No, Jamie. No. The beat cop just stopped by a few minutes ago. He was coming off his shift and told me what he knew. I wouldn't hold out on you and John like that. I wouldn't," choked Stokes.

"You're lying to me, you fat slug!"

Morgan looked around for something sharp, found the hand mirror instead, and smashed it against the side of Stokes' head. He had to stay in control though, knowing that he needed Stokes to do some nosing around. He also knew he couldn't trust the prick and he wanted to put the fear of God into him. A few lacerations should help.

"Get your hat, Jack. You're on your way to the jail. I need to know how John is. I need to know that they're not killing him as I speak, and I need to know what the charges are. You have two hours. I've got to find Gambrill, pass the word, hire a lawyer, and pry English away from those sadists. Meet me at The St. Clair over on Monument. Three o'clock, sharp. If you're not there, Baltimore won't be big enough to hide you. Go. Now!"

Morgan released Stokes, jammed a bowler from the rack against the wall on his bleeding head and shoved him toward the door. The clerk had disappeared.

Morgan found his friend John Wesley Gambrill where he knew he could, in a vacant lot on Oliver Street near the North Central Railroad Depot. Gambrill was the star pitcher for the Lord Baltimores, one of the growing numbers of amateur baseball teams in the city. As he approached the field, he could see that the game was in suspension due to a wrestling match going on in the dirt around second base. One of the wrestlers suddenly stood and began stomping and kicking his opponent. Morgan assumed that it was Gambrill delivering the beating until his buddy walked up behind him and said, "That umpire stinks. He deserves a good thrashing."

"J.W., there's no time for this nonsense. We've got big trouble. John's been taken by the cops. Got him over at the City Jail. Bill Barton and some U.S. Marshall came into my place and beat him and Houck good."

Gambrill's response was loud and profane.

"I knew there were too many eyes on us," he finally observed. "They'll need a new engine at the New Market though."

"Small potatoes now, J.W. Bully Albert is dead. And the cops like John for it."

"Man! Bully Albert! That'll be real trouble on the street. Okay, what'd want to do? Probably could use a lawyer, now."

"He needs a doctor, too," said Morgan. "Look, J.W., I need you to pass the word in the Ward. See what leverage we have at the jail and start to stir the neighborhood behind John. We need to get him out of there before they kill him. Too many enemies there. Watch your back, too. The Market must be crazy over this."

"What are you going to do?" asked Gambrill.

"I've got Jack Stokes nosing around, but I've got to go see a lawyer now. Ever heard of Henry Winter Davis?"

"Just be sure to check your purse when you leave."

"They've closed the Oyster House so I'll meet you later tonight at the Black Horse."

With that, the two men split up, each moving fast.

Morgan had never gotten directly involved with English's downtown connections. He already knew more than he thought was healthy. Last year's mayoral elections and the vicious fighting around the Orleans Street polls made a real name for the Plug Uglies and the other American Party supporters. It also gave the Know-Nothings control over the city for the time being. The former B&O man, Swann, was elected mayor by nine thousand votes and he, and a number of others, owed it to the street tactics of John English and his allies. Now it was time to cash in.

He recalled his conversation with English almost six months ago, just after the election. They were in the tavern, standing at the bar.

"Jamie, we've got some cover now. It wasn't pretty, but it got done. We had a lot to do and the damned Democrats were standing in front of us. They're licking their wounds now, though," said English with some satisfaction.

Morgan sipped his whiskey as English continued, "Swann will make some key appointments, and our boys are in line. Hell, I'm thinking about doing some police work myself. Might come in handy when it's time to roll a Big Six."

English laughed out loud at his joke in reference to one of the Plug's Democratic archenemies, the Big Sixes. Morgan had laughed too and raised his glass to his friend's wit.

"Look, Jamie, I'm serious about this though. It's getting big. You know that asshole congressman of ours, Henry Winter Davis? He was a Whig when that suited him, now since they're dead and the American's on the rise, Davis is moving to catch the updraft. Buchanan's got the White House and he's a Democrat, but Davis is a drinking buddy of Fillmore and good ole Millard and the American Party ain't done yet in Washington. Meanwhile Baltimore's solid, thanks to us. Means we've got some wiggle room."

"John, you know I don't truck with politicians, and don't want to. Those buzzards circle with the fair wind, just as you say. You can't trust them. All we can trust is ourselves," said Morgan as he signaled Eisenhart behind the bar.

"Jamie, I don't trust them. But I'm sure as hell going to use them for all they're worth. I did Swann and the others a big favor. They owe me and they don't want anyone to know it. That puts us in the catbird's seat."

English leaned in close, elbow on the bar. In a gesture of both vanity and intimidation, he adjusted the black leather patch that covered the scarred right eye, damaged by a gunshot when he was a boy. The man's good eye peered hard at Morgan.

"Here's what it means, plain and simple. We do what we have to do with the Market, with the Regs, and the other clubs, with the Democrats, with the Micks, and the Krauts. We do what we have to do to keep this country American and to keep our neighborhood safe for our people. We did what we had to do during the election, and now we have a hammer."

Morgan nodded through English's litany of hate, arrogance, and self-imposed responsibility. He wasn't in complete disagreement, but he was struggling with his friend's vision of the Twentieth Ward. And he wasn't so sure that all of the blood spilt in the streets gave the Plugs the freedom English thought it did.

"John, Swann's in, sure, but he's not everybody. *The Sun* was talking about the formation of a citizens' committee, high-hats and reformers from all over the city. They're getting fed up," Morgan observed.

"Fed up? This is our city not theirs! Fed up?" The color on English's neck had risen. "These reformers in their silk ties and their Charles Street mansions are about to get some real feeding!"

English glared at Morgan with a single, blistering eye. Then he slumped and let out a sigh.

"Jamie, why do I always have to have these conversations with you? You're always looking at the down side. Haven't we done well up to now? Haven't you, J.W., and I always done what we wanted to do? Now, I know you're not a stupid man, but I'm going to tell you something plain and simple and I want you to listen closely."

There were times when English's patronizing tone was about all Morgan could take. He often wondered what would happen if he and English really went at it. He had done his share of close, bloody work and he was afraid of no man, including the leader of the Plugs.

"Here it is," began English. "You're the number one when I'm not around. But if I ever get in such a jackpot that you or the boys can't get me out, I want you to contact John Hinsley. You know him, he's that sporting man that hangs with the Rips. The bail bondsman. He's our in with certain people. Tell him I need Henry Davis.

"If you have any trouble with Hinsley, Davis keeps a big law office down on Saratoga. Tell him who you are and what you want. He'll take it from there. If he gives you any guff, just remind him that we have long memories when it comes to his election to that soft seat in the District. I've got more cover than you know or need to know. Okay?"

English looked at him in earnest to be sure he had gotten it. He had gotten it all right. Davis was his safety net.

So it was that Morgan, after first making sure Stokes was headed in the right direction, jumped a cab and headed for Saratoga, east of Charles. He wasn't going to bother with the go-between, Hinsley. He was going straight to Davis. He didn't like this, but he had little choice. John needed to cash in a few chips, fast.

The law offices of Henry Winter Davis were a pretty nice place to hole up, Morgan thought, as he pulled the doorbell next to two polished oak and brass doors. A very black man, dressed impeccably in a cutaway morning coat and tie, answered the door. Morgan stepped past him into the vestibule and said, "Mr. Morgan is here to see Henry Winter Davis on behalf of John English. It's urgent."

The servant bowed, took Morgan's soft-crowned hat, indicated a leather chair, and disappeared through another set of doors.

After what seemed like more than enough time, Morgan stood and strode to the inner doors. He reached for the ornate brass knobs, but as he did so, the doors were opened from the inside. A very tall, thin, young man stepped out. He was sporting a bushy set of muttonchops and wearing a brocade vest under a formal frock coat. Morgan could see a busy office scene over his shoulder as he pulled the doors closed behind him.

"My name is Cooke, I'm Congressman Davis' personal assistant. May I be of some help?" the man said as he took Morgan's measure.

"I asked for Henry Davis, not his assistant," Morgan said with a sneer.

"Yes," the young man said, "but the Congressman is very busy at the moment. I am an attorney and I assure you that I am highly capable in matters of the law."

"Does he know that this is about John English and that it's urgent?" Morgan responded, showing some restraint, which seemed necessary for navigating in these unchartered waters.

"The congressman received the message, Mr. Morgan, and he asked me to talk to you until he could get free from a meeting. He's with some highly placed gentlemen at the moment."

Ignoring the young stiff's emphasis on the word *gentlemen,* Morgan stepped up to the man.

"Tell Davis that English has been arrested. He's hurt and in need of legal assistance immediately. They have him in the hole up on Truxton Street. Tell him that the chickens have come home to roost. Tell him English wants him now."

Morgan was nose to nose with the attorney, his fist balled in the man's lapel.

"This may be the most important decision of your life, son. It might be Davis' as well. Don't blow it."

With that, Morgan shoved the startled lawyer away and strode out the door.

Fifteen minutes later, Morgan was sitting on an omnibus bench across from Davis' offices. He watched two men emerge hurriedly from the law office. One was the thin man with the chops, the other was a short, portly man carrying a thick, leather portfolio. They climbed into a waiting cab, gave orders, and sped east on Saratoga then turned north at Calvert in the direction of the City Jail.

Morgan was about to pay Henry Winter Davis a second, more personal call. But before he could rise, the law office disgorged three more men. Two immediately perched stovepipe hats on their heads and buttoned frock coats. They nodded seriously and shook hands with the third man. One walked briskly around the corner to Charles Street. The other first stroked a well-waxed mustache, and then did the same to a blond goatee, as he waited for a hansom to come up. Then he was gone as well.

The third man Morgan recognized as Congressman Henry Winter Davis. Despite English's condescending explanation, Morgan had actually heard the man speak on two separate occasions. Powerful in delivery and theatrical in his appearance, Davis drew people to him. A fastidious man, the Congressman dressed and cut his hair in a way that emulated his good friend, the Baltimore actor, Edwin Booth. Davis too called for a cab, then rode down Saratoga in the direction of the mayor's office.

The St. Clair was a large, clean, well lit, three-story brick hotel and tavern just a block off Mount Vernon Square. It was favored for the occasional business lunch, a respite from touring, or even a family dinner. A room could be rented for a night or two, upstairs from the ornate dining room. Off and on, Morgan found himself upstairs with a woman he liked, or in the dining room, splurging on dinner with his sister, Anna, before she died. He chose it for his meeting with Stokes because it was as neutral a place as he could find—no cops, no clubs, no riff-raff.

Before entering, Morgan automatically ran hands through his hair and brushed at the short jacket he was wearing. He followed a waiter to an inconspicuous table for two, then ordered an Eagle.

Morgan scanned the room while he waited. He was a few minutes early. The wait staff was between shifts and the tavern was not crowded. Its few patrons were absorbed in their own worlds and paid Morgan no attention. As the beer arrived, so did Jackson Stokes. He was sweating and nervous.

"Jamie, I'm glad you're here," said Stokes as he sat down quickly and waved the waiter away.

"I can't stay long. I've got to go." Stokes shifted his chair so that his back was not to the door. "Things are bad. The cops are pissed and so are their bosses. Something's going on that I don't understand." The ward boss was fidgety and speaking rapidly in a hushed tone.

Morgan leaned over and grabbed Stoke's wrist and squeezed, hard. As the man yelped, Morgan said quietly, "Shut up, idiot. Calm down. You're here until I get answers. What are you afraid of?"

"The cops, they're all fired up. One of them punched me in the kidneys and all I did was ask about English. They were ready to take me in the back when these lawyers arrived. That fired the cops up even more. There was a lot of yelling until the deputy high constable walked in and took them into his office. That gave me a chance to disappear down the hall."

Good. Davis' man is on the job, Morgan thought.

"Well, what's the situation with John. Is he all right?"

"No. He's in bad shape. They'd been wailing on him ever since he arrived. The only thing that stopped the bastards was the fear of the state's attorney. He arrived a little after I did. I found out from this clerk I know that he personally stopped the beating. Said he needed English alive. Even got him a doctor. Put English in isolation."

"What are the charges? Did you find that out?"

"Yeah, it's murder. They want him for the Albert killing. Say they have witnesses who will testify." As Stokes said this, he glanced at the tavern's front door.

"Oh, God," he breathed.

Morgan looked up and saw two hard men step in. They eyed the room and found Stokes, then they spotted Morgan. After a hair's hesitation, they backed out of the tavern—two men who had changed their minds.

Morgan knew them and they knew him. One was a particular Democratic hard-on by the name of George Konig out of the Fells Point waterfront; the other's name he couldn't remember. They were Double Pumps, the social club that controlled the Second Ward, blood brothers to the New Market House. He needed to move. He rose.

"What are you going to do, Jamie?" asked Stokes, practically crying. He wasn't worried about Morgan; he was worried about his own skin.

"You're not going to leave me here? It was me they were following."

Checking for a rear exit, Morgan said, "Stay here. They were following you to see who you were nosing around for. I'm the prize. You got a gun?"

"Jamie, are you crazy? I don't carry a gun!" Stokes was panicky.

"Then stay here. They won't come back in. Not here. I'm going out the back," said Morgan who threw some coins on the table and walked rapidly to a curtain covering the entrance to the kitchen. Stokes snatched up the untouched beer and took a long pull, slopping a good bit of it down his front.

While pushing past a sputtering man in a vest, Morgan realized that the back door would be covered. So he demanded, "Where's the stairs to the roof?"

The man, cowed by the menace exuding from his questioner, pointed mutely to a set of wooden service stairs. Morgan took the stairs, up two flights and down a narrow hall to a heavy door that groaned but opened when he threw his weight against it.

Morgan crouched and ran across the tarred surface to the edge above the alley. A quick look over told him that the man whose name he couldn't remember was there against the wall and covered, behind a pipe running from the roof and into a large rain barrel. He watched the thug check his pistol.

Turning, he looked for something heavy and found a half-full, leather tar bucket. The tar in it had hardened. He walked to where the Double Pump man hunched, intently staring at the hotel's back door. Morgan aimed and then let the bucket drop. There was a dull thud and he could only see the ambusher's shoes jutting out from behind the barrel at odd angles.

Morgan sat holding Hattie's hand. It felt warm and right, but he knew that if John were there at that moment there would have been hell to pay.

"Hattie, it'll work out. I'm sure of it. It always has. There must have been a mistake." Morgan wasn't sure what he would do if Hattie lost control.

"What happened, Jamie? Tell me the truth," pleaded the woman.

"Well, I wasn't there, but as far as I can tell, Barton and some hard guy from the states attorney's busted into my place, grabbed whoever was there, and shuffled them over to Central. John must have said something that set Barton off because Big Bill hit him hard and laid him out cold."

"Oh my God!" cried Hattie, her hand flying to her mouth.

"Now, hold on. They got him a doctor and he's in a room by himself. The cops will leave him alone now. I hear he's a bit beat up but nothing he won't come out of, just as he always has."

Hattie had had enough. She wasn't processing what Morgan was saying. John was hurt and she was not there. There were things she didn't know about John and though their marriage wasn't great, he was all she had. That was what counted. She was going to him. She stood in a rush, took a step toward the door, and collapsed.

Chapter 5

Baltimore
April 16, 1857, Evening

In a large brick mansion, just off of Monument Square and within the shadow of the huge memorial to the Father of Our Country, a group of well-appointed, well-whiskered men pushed back from a lavish dinner and followed each other into an ornate, paneled library. As the black, liveried servants poured French brandy and offered hand-rolled cigars, the men found seats, leaned against the marble fireplace, or otherwise found a means of letting their heavy meal settle. Several undid the buttons of their waistcoats with audible sighs. The meeting of Baltimore's Reform Association was coming to order.

The agenda was a full one and the relaxed, torpid gathering wasn't likely to either complete the evening's business or even make a dent in it. As with most meetings, the discussion would consist of an occasional spewing forth of rhetoric that was answered with a chorus of "Hear, hear!"

The Reform Association had been around under different aliases for a number of years. It was an informal gathering of Baltimore's policy makers, merchant princes, manufacturers, churchmen, and legal wizards. Their stated mission was to solve city and state problems and make recommendations to the governor and mayor for improvement and change. They were an ex-officio body but not without considerable power, potentially.

The Association's aim was objectivity, purged of prejudice, and focused on the greater good. In practice, too many of the Associations' current membership saw their own, personal good as the greater good.

Mayor Swann was a regular member. So was the National Bank's C. J. Jamison, the B&O investor and merchant Johns Hopkins, the philanthropist George Peabody, and Elijah Stansbury, the grand chancellor of the Masons. The room was filled with names like Garrett, Baldwin, Watts, Pratt, and Warfield. It was Baltimore's top layer.

Two men stood together at the fireplace and shared a match. They were of a like mind and showed it in their bored attitude toward the latest opinion being forcefully shared. At least the topic was actually on the agenda—the formation of a municipal fire department that would replace the present volunteer system that operated in the city. It was always on the agenda.

The speaker provided a litany of familiar heroics of the brave men who served as volunteers, concluding that this alone was proof that the volunteer system works just fine. This was received with less than total enthusiasm. Half of the room was appalled at the man's logic and the other half would follow the man into hell. Henry Winter Davis was not a logician; he was an orator. And that's a calling that uses logic, but uses it sparingly.

As Davis moved to his next favorite subject, the two men studied their ash. The tall, thin one spoke quietly. "This can't last. Davis is losing the argument over the volunteers. His opposition is gaining leverage every day, thanks to his nasty friends. We need to be ready when the tide turns and the bloodshed creates a backlash so great that change is a demand, not an option."

The change was about winning the war in Baltimore's streets. The change was also about winning the war in Maryland's hallways of power. Severn T. Wallis, attorney at law, was expert in the field of political gardening. And he understood the importance of getting to the roots to kill weeds.

Wallis' companion was almost as tall but sturdier, especially through his chest and shoulders. This gave the man a dignified, Prussian bearing that was magnified by his precisely groomed blond mustache and goatee. John Vonderhorst was a stark contrast to Wallis' impersonation of a gaunt, Presbyterian minister. But they were together in their opinion that Henry Davis and his pack of wild dogs had to go. To do that, the firehouses had to be separated from the politicians, then the gangs had to be separated from the firehouses.

A municipally owned and run fire department was a start, but it wasn't enough. The rats had to be exterminated if the streets were to be safe.

Vonderhorst made and sold beer, a lot of it. He also played power politics. Further, he was no dummy. He'd sell a beer to whomever had five cents, but while riots and murder might be good for certain candidates, they were not good for business. What's more, his foreman at the Eagle Brewery up on North Avenue recently just managed to put out a suspicious fire. The blaze somehow started after Vonderhorst refused to buy a block of tickets to a Plug Ugly Ball. It made him very angry in a way that needed satisfaction.

"Wally, we may have an opportunity here. Did you know that they arrested John English for murder this afternoon?" asked Vonderhorst.

"Is the bastard still alive?" responded Wallis, not sounding like a minister.

"Not by much. Cops beat him to a pulp. Seems Albert had a lot of friends on the Force, all Democrats. Some other scores to settle too. Meade Addison, the U.S. district attorney, had to step in to save his life."

"Save his miserable life? For what? He is the embodiment of the devil!" Wallis said with volume, now beginning to sound more like a minister.

"This is the opportunity I mean," said Vonderhorst as he stepped a fraction closer. "I met with Davis today almost as the arrest was happening. He knew it ahead of time. Didn't try to stop it though. He has to walk a fine line."

"You were with Henry Davis today?" asked Wallis, surprised. "He didn't try to stop it?" Then he immediately followed with, "What's he want?"

"Addison is fired up over this killing. Augustus Albert was some relative of his. He's getting calls from everyone. He's got witnesses. He's a Democrat and he wants to lower the boom. Davis wanted to meet with him and I was the go-between. As it turned out, I was there for another reason as well. Davis wants to deal; English for major financial support in the fall elections. I was the major financial support."

"Nothing was agreed upon," Vonderhorst continued. "We were interrupted with the word that English was in such a bad way that he may not survive. Davis moved quickly and so did Addison. They managed to save him, but just."

"Look, he's a pretty big oyster," the blond man went on. We could put him on display in a very public trial. Then hang him. It'll give the clubs a face, something the voters can vote against. The district attorney is definitely interested," said Vonderhorst more quietly.

Wallis looked at his friend. The possibilities began to emerge for him. He was sincere in his efforts to drag Baltimore into some sort of civilized state out of its present chaos, but if he were to manage it, he had his own profile to raise as well. They'd need ready money. The two men's eyes met. They would make a few visits to the right offices and be back in touch in a more discreet place.

Chapter 6

Baltimore
July 1857

The last three months had been beyond his imagination in their brutality. He never dreamed that his life could be so full of pain. One blow followed another—too many to be able to think. For a while, his life was a series of convulsions. But, slowly, his thinking began to clear from the first days. The piercing headaches were subsiding as well. But the damage done to his knees led to his doctor's belief that he would never walk again. This was an idea that was rapidly becoming a reality for him, given the anguish that standing brought. His jailers, however, told him not to worry; he would have help getting up the gallows steps.

His misery was doubled by the loss of Hattie. She was his, no one else's. He felt robbed and violated by her death. Now all he had was the primal scream that welled up during the lonely, painful night. When he screamed, it emerged not in full throat but in a muffled, anguished groan inhibited by a wired jaw, swollen lips, and a broken nose.

Hattie had died in childbirth. The attorney from Davis' office had told him little else other than James Morgan had managed to get Hattie to the Union Protestant Infirmary up on Division Street. There, Hattie gave birth to a baby girl, but the mother never survived the ordeal. Hattie was gone.

English saw few visitors, only Davis' toady, the prison doctor, and an occasional stop-by from someone with a score to settle. The scant information on Hattie created a million questions in his mind. So, the baby had come. What did that mean? Where is she? Who's got her? At one point, the lawyer said Davis was taking care of it. What did that mean? And why was Jamie with Hattie? He saved the infant's life, but why was he with her in the first place? And where was goddamned Gambrill while all of this was happening? His answers to these questions flew around his head in a batlike frenzy until he felt the scream begin to build.

He was caught in a mental grinder. But he needed to stay in control. So, he focused on what he didn't know and then went on to what could be. It gave him a compass of sorts. There was a price for this though. His sanity was being torn away in big ragged hunks by the *could be* side of his reflections.

Morgan had reopened the Bar and Oyster House, but it took him a month and had cost him a heavy fine. The judicial process got its take, as it always did. They said this time was different though. That basically meant more expensive. He and the bar were linked to English and English was bad news. The place was practically empty.

Morgan and the other Plug Uglies were not happy that the normal channels had failed. Even Henry Davis had made little or no progress in getting John released. Who or what was driving the district attorney so hard? And who the hell was this man, Vonderhorst? A brewer from up on North Avenue. Since when did the Reform Association develop a spine? Every day the papers carried a new quote that slammed John, the social clubs, or the firehouses. Morgan himself was named in a list of bad apples. One bold *Washington Star* editorial in June said that the Plugs were "as pestilent and scrofulous a brood of scoundrels as hell itself could vomit from its vilest crater." It was obvious that there was a lot more at play here than Morgan understood and that made him anxious and edgy.

He had also heard that his friend was now both physically crippled and despairing over Hattie's death. Morgan had wondered how the Plug's leader would take it; he also wondered what John thought about him being with Hattie when she died. And then there was the baby girl.

Despite the loss of their leader, the Plug Uglies never missed a beat. From May to July, the Gambrill brothers and their bullies kept things lively on the streets. Political demonstrations and parades were a staple of both parties as elections drew near, but the nativist gangs often turned them into scenes of bloodshed and murder. In fact, revenge and hatred flowed freely between the American Party social clubs and their enemies whenever the opportunity arose. And when the opportunities didn't arise, the social clubs found ways to create them.

At one point, after a particularly pointed attack on the clubs by *The Sun,* the Plugs had taken it into their head to stop the editorial barrage. In the very early hours of a hot July morning, a dozen drunken men gathered loudly at the paper's offices on the southeast corner of Baltimore and South Streets. The party included a number of Plug Uglies and some toughs from the allied Black Snakes and Rip Raps. There, they attempted to batter-in the front doors. Failing that, primarily due to disorganization and their level of inebriation, the mob threw buckets of pig's blood all over the front of the building. Then the rioters began to smash the long windows along the street level, until they were driven off by the arrival of police armed with muskets.

The mob's energy was not spent, however. It re-formed, picked up more supporters, then moved north to the Eagle Brewery. At the sprawling facility, the attackers again ran into resistance. Vonderhorst had been expecting them for days. The brewery's entrances had been barricaded, windows boarded up, and armed men stationed on the upper floors. Even the stable fences along the rear of the carriage house were protected by hired muscle. The rioters shouted anti-German epithets and called for Vonderhorst's head. They then began to launch bricks, stones, and other loose missiles at the windows. Once a window was broken, burning faggots were hurled at the openings and men inside could be seen scrambling to douse the fires. It was then that the order was given from within the brewery to open fire. Immediately, three rioters dropped, then two more. Instead of deterring the mob, the resistance seemed to incense it. In response, scattered pistol shots were added to the siege. This phase of the battle continued for a while, then devolved into sniping from the buildings' surrounding streets until dawn when a contingent of police finally arrived.

The Democratic camp was not idle either. The New Market men took their revenge for Augustus Albert's murder, even as they waited for Maryland to hang John English. In May, someone walked up to a Plug Ugly lieutenant from behind and put a ball in his head. That same month, two other Plugs had been wounded in a shootout with some firemen from the Mechanical House. Several Twentieth Ward bully-boys found themselves the victims of large groups of men patrolling Clay Street, an unspoken boundary between the Plugs and the New Marketers. A well-planned riot broke out over a mysterious fire on Saratoga at Eutaw that saw the Mount Vernon Hook and Ladder boys once again chased off by musket fire that killed two bystanders. The Rip Raps told of similar incidents occurring in the Fourteenth Ward.

Another election was only four months away and the Democrats had learned a few lessons in '56. That meant the American social clubs had to be more organized, better armed, and more creative to maintain the upper hand. It was time to finalize plans now and English's absence was bringing things to a head among the Plug Uglies.

"What's the latest on John?" asked J.W. Gambrill, leaning on the corner of the bar next to Morgan who was counting the chits and the cash in a moneybox. It was late, the bartender and the kitchen help had gone. The two friends were having one more before they threw the last few bar flies out.

Gambrill had been with English and Morgan since their early days in the New Market Firehouse. He was tested and bloodied. With English out of touch, and Morgan working other angles, he had reluctantly begun to fill the role of leading the Plugs.

"Trial date's been set for the end of this month, but that's not new. That weasel Davis can't or won't answer my questions. His errand boy tells me that John's still alive and that Davis is working on his defense and building support. They say they'll be ready," spat Morgan.

"I hope they're ready. Have they talked to you? They sure as hell haven't talked to me and I was there on Howard Street. In fact, I don't know anyone they have talked to. I'm not feeling good about this," commented Gambrill, looking at Morgan with some expectation.

"Goddamnit, J.W., what do you want me to do?" snapped Morgan. "I'm kicking in Davis' door now. I'm calling in markers and giving away free drinks to try to get a message to English. I spent a week talking to Swann's election committee, reminding them of the coming November vote. I've kissed enough ass down at City Hall to last a lifetime. You tell me what else to do, you bastard."

What Morgan did not tell Gambrill was that he also buried Hattie and talked the small group of sisters at St. Mary's into caring for English's newborn daughter. He was not fond of the nuns or Catholics in general for that matter. But he knew they would take good care of her until John got free or Morgan could figure something else out. He had kept it all to himself. Using St. Mary's would infuriate English, so except for telling Davis, he kept his own counsel on the matter.

"Look, Jamie, I've been trying to hold the club together. Christ knows it was hard enough when John was out on the streets. You were next in line, not me. Now, I'm taking more crap than I'm used to. Some of the Plugs listen to me and some don't. What's really chaffing my ass is that a lot of the younger guys are starting to follow Houck," said Gambrill with a sneer. "I hate that son-of-a-bitch."

"What's the matter, J.W., don't like competition?" said Morgan, turning back to the moneybox, more interested in his own problems than in his friend's.

"No, I don't. Especially from him," said Gambrill with some heat. "Houck's stupid and unstable. Drunk most of the time too. I wish the judge had never bailed him. The idiot was calling me out over at the Black Horse a couple of nights ago. He doesn't know who he's foolin' with."

"My guess is that he doesn't. But, you're going to get a chance to school him very shortly," said Morgan with a rueful grin. "Here he is now."

As Gambrill pivoted to check the door, Houck and three young toughs made a noisy entrance. They chased a table of tired mill workers off and sat down, scraping chairs and yelling for whiskey and oysters. Morgan nodded at the waiter and went back to counting change.

Houck noted the owner's signal to the waiter and said loudly, "Better damn-side serve me in this dump." Then, looking at Gambrill, "Looks like they'll pour any neighborhood loser a drink in here." Houck's companions laughed and voiced their agreement in the assessment of the status of the Plug's reluctant leader.

"Did you hear that, Jamie? He just sent a message to you," observed Gambrill.

"Did he?" asked Morgan casually. "That sounded like a message for you, J.W. The only message I got was a customer wants to pay for some oysters."

Gambrill leaned against the bar and looked at David Houck. His subject noticed, frowned, and then stood. His companions rose with him, their hands moving inside their shirts and vests. The few drinkers in the bar scraped back their chairs and quickly disappeared through the door.

Grinning, the younger man said, "John Wesley Gambrill. Giving me the stink eye, like some kinda real man. Why aren't you at home playing with the wife and kiddies? Streets and bars are no places for someone your age."

It looked as if Gambrill hadn't moved a muscle. From his angle at the bar, however, Morgan saw a slight ruffle of the man's cutaway coat. Houck was bigger, stronger, and drunk. That made him foolhardy, so he moved in close to Gambrill, breathing cheap rye.

"I asked why you aren't at home playing with that luscious wife of yours," said Houck, leering into Gambrill's face.

The movement was swift, forceful, and deadly. A long, thin blade of about ten inches rose up from below the bar rail, entered the cleft between Houck's jaw bones, continued up into his brain and made a little, hairy mound in the top of his skull without poking all of the way through. Houck's companions started, then seeing Morgan's Webley pointed at them, backed away slowly as a group. They had made a mistake, backing the wrong man.

Gambrill, leaving the shaft in place, supported a wide-eyed Houck until Morgan grabbed him under the arms. The two men dragged him back behind the curtain into the back kitchen. Morgan threw open the back door, stepped out into the empty alley, and checked for witnesses. He kicked over a rain barrel and rolled it to the kitchen door. The men hefted the body into the big container, bending the legs to make the tight fit. Morgan went to find a lid, a hammer, and some nails. Gambrill left to find a horse and cart.

Chapter 7

Baltimore
Late July 1857

The trial went badly from the beginning. Several witnesses to the murder of Augustus Albert, president of the New Market Firehouse and unnamed leader of its particularly vicious social club, were either dead or missing, by accident or by intention. The Plug Uglies, the Rip Raps, the Black Snakes, and other clubs with ties to the Know-Nothings had been busy since spring.

Henry Winter Davis also had been busy. Certain newspapers focused avid readers on the excruciating details of John English's notorious life. Other papers, fed by Davis, discovered that Albert's own checkered past was a mirror's image of the accused. Reformers equated punishment of English with stopping the street violence. Countering, the defense isolated the English–Albert relationship as a private feud between like individuals. When Democrats howled about American attacks, Davis parried with a litany of offenses, reprisals, and indignities heaped upon American Party supporters.

Jurors were scarce and came mostly from the county. They were sequestered and guarded. The three weeks of the trial had been hell for them. Long deliberations in an enclosed room during a sweltering Baltimore July were bad enough. But mostly, jurors spoke of their fear of sitting in the courtroom, on display for the rabble that filled the seats beyond the rail.

District Attorney Addison was eloquent, thorough, relentless, and fearless. His life was threatened during the trial twice. Each time, he took immediate action, arresting the offenders and splashing incidents and names in the newspapers.

U.S. District Judge William F. Giles ran a tight ship, clearing the courtroom on several occasions as the testimony got heated and nerves began to fray. After marshals managed to disarm a screaming man with a knife who rushed English's defense table, the judge emptied the room, added more officers, and required pat downs in order to enter the building at the corner of Lexington and Calvert.

The trial played out in the streets as well. Assault and battery was up sharply. Roving partisans skirmished with their opposition. Barrooms substituted for the courtroom. As a result, the informal deliberations and the inevitable objection were settled by gunshots in more than one instance.

John English's halting testimony, delivered from a wheeled chair, made him the lead actor in the production. But the trial saw several players emerge to take their place at center stage. Prosecutor Addison was building a following. Henry Davis was at his rhetorical best in defense, but his strategy of obfuscation and misdirection was even better. Severn Teakle Wallis, supporting the district attorney in the prosecution, brought his blue-nosed pedigree, expensive education, and community outrage to the proceedings. Wallis became the man with a new vision of Baltimore.

Without any particular authorization or, for that matter, objection, John Vonderhorst spoke for the Reform Association. Newspapers needed to feed a ravenous readership, and the German-born brewer, banker, and social reformer was more than willing to accommodate them. His message was simple: if the city was going to move forward, John English and those like him had to go. That meant the volunteer firehouses had to go. Others in the association, however, stayed quiet. This included Mayor Swann who was unusually silent on the trial, refusing to comment or answer direct questions.

In the end, the lack of credible witnesses, the roiling political landscape, and the physical condition of John English doomed the prosecution's case. Shaken jurors refused to decide and two hung juries resulted. Judge Giles mistrusted the district attorney's motivation and kept him on a tight leash. No one believed English to be innocent of the murder; many would have convicted him on past offenses alone. But the judge, recognizing a failed prosecution effort when he saw one, ended the trial, acquitting English of all charges.

Henry Davis wondered whether his dealings with John English were worth it in the long run. The trial had taken a great deal of money, energy, and resources and still English wanted more. He wanted cash, he wanted medical care, he wanted protection, and he wanted his baby girl. Dealing with the devil, even if it meant reelection, was a fool's game.

What Davis did know was that he had to make his client disappear, at least for a while. English's life was at risk and he was in no shape to defend himself. In addition, Davis didn't want him around to expose their extracurricular dealings. He especially wanted to avoid the Plug Uglies' leader learning of his deal with Vonderhorst, his financial angel. Vonderhorst himself was now a problem too, given the fact that English had walked. Davis' intent was to put up a good court fight, but to fall just short in his defense of the gang leader. He had not expected Judge Giles to end the trial so decisively and quickly. He wondered whose pad the judge was on.

So, upon English's release, the first thing Davis did was to wheel him out of a side door and into a closed hansom. The driver had instructions to follow a large party of heavily armed men on horseback east along Madison Street, up the York Road, and out of the city. He told no one their destination.

Speeding north, Davis could see several plumes of heavy smoke arising out of the neighborhoods in the west and south. The reaction to the trial's conclusion had begun quicker than he had anticipated. He knew for certain that the Democratic gangs had made contingency plans when the horsemen and the carriage came under fire near the Greenmount Cemetery, then again at North Avenue. His men were well chosen though. In military fashion, both times, they screened the carriage, drew their Navy Colts, and fanned out to discourage the snipers. Davis himself found the floor of the cab but left English as he was, slumped in the corner. The laudanum Davis had given him had done its work.

Vonderhorst sat at Barnum's mahogany bar, raised his glass of Baker's Pure Maryland Rye, and looked in the big mirror that reflected the lobby of the city's most prestigious hotel. He was philosophical about the trial. True, they had lost the effort to hang English; he had known for some time that they would. But, the trial had accomplished his primary purpose and he could eat his strudel without icing if he had to. They had succeeded admirably in bringing the issue of the volunteer firehouses and their street thugs to a boil. The plans to form a municipal fire department would now sail through. Purging the streets of the likes of John English would just take a little longer.

Over the rim of his rye, Vonderhorst watched his friend Severn Wallis walk into the lobby. Wallis spotted him through the bar's marble arch and approached with some agitation.

"I just left Meade Addison," said Wallis as he sat down, indicating Vonderhorst's drink to the barman. "We were threatened by a couple of bullyboys. One opened his coat to show me the butt of his revolver. Addison went crazy. They eventually walked away, but not before suggesting that we were lucky that English walked. We all need to be very careful."

"If I was going to be careful, I never would have allowed my name in the papers," replied Vonderhorst. "The bastards attacked my business and wounded my foreman. My son, Harry, was there. Bullets were flying. Thank God, he wasn't hurt. Believe me, I'm not finished yet with these street scum. And this time, I may not take my shots through editorials," smiled Vonderhorst grimly, showing his friend the butt of his own revolver.

"Just watch your back, John. We made a lot of nasty enemies on both sides," observed Wallis. "Have you talked to Davis since the trial?"

"I did. But you never know when that bastard is lying and when he's telling the truth. He wishes he were rid of English, the Plug Uglies, and the entire American Party. Evidently, he owes a political debt and he's finding the interest pretty steep. He was whining about how much the whole mess has cost him. He asked me again for support. I reminded him that he was supposed to help nail English. He pointed out that we had gotten what we wanted, conviction or no conviction. I told him that my support was limited to the fall elections and had no intention of helping him to pay-off English."

"What he wanted the money for would have likely gone to the gangs anyway," observed Wallis. "Man, he must be in deep."

"He is. He was even crabbing about having to find a place for English's new baby in St. Vincent's, " threw in Vonderhorst.

"I almost felt sorry for English when I heard his wife died in having the girl," said Wallis. "I hope the baby's not unlucky enough to know him as her father."

"I've been thinking about that," said the brewer bitterly. "I owe English and his gang one and I'm the wrong man to cross."

Before Wallis could explore Vonderhorst's comment, the attorney checked his Waltham pocket watch and downed the remains of his drink.

"I've got to meet Swann. We're counting votes on the municipal fire department. We're not quite there yet and I don't trust 'His Honor' as far as I can spit."

With that, the men shook hands and Wallis was gone.

Vonderhorst thought about the situation with English's baby. Davis or someone had stashed her at St. Mary's over in the Twentieth Ward. He wondered if there wasn't some way he could take advantage of the situation. He felt no compassion for English, his dead wife, or the baby. He was going to exact punishment for the attacks on his livelihood and his scared son. True, Harry shouldn't have been at the plant that night and he wasn't hurt, but he could have been. That was the point and he would not let that pass. He had friends in Baltimore's Child Welfare Association and they had ties to Judge Giles.

Chapter 8

Baltimore, Maryland
October, 1857

Morgan had not spoken to John English since before the arrest back in April. He had not even heard from the former leader of the Plugs after the trial. That was almost three months ago. The baby was still with the nuns and they were making noises that it was time for the child to find a home. During one of his recent visits, the suggestion had become a demand.

He left the Oyster House in the bartender's hands and headed along Pennsylvania Avenue to St. Mary's. After three months, he really didn't mind going by the convent. In fact, he was fascinated by the changes he saw in the baby each time he saw her. He had decided that he would find a suitable nanny and take the child in himself until John got back. He was sure he would hear from his confederate soon. It wouldn't be for that long, the house on Orchard was big enough and he had always kept it clean. He would do it for Hattie.

Making his way to the college and the sturdy door embedded in the long red brick wall on St. Mary's Street, he moved onto the cobbles to avoid a knot of dirty kids. The brats were playing some sort of game by bouncing one of Mr. Goodyear's rubber balls off the wall and catching it. The kids stopped their play to watch Morgan pass. He was well known and well respected in the neighborhood and he could hear his name in hushed tones as he ignored them. The baby aside, he never had much interest or like for kids. They all grew up to be punks. Just like he had. Maybe if he had a wife. Maybe if Hattie had chosen him.

The door was opened shortly after his knock and a fat nun whose habit could have sailed a schooner ushered him in. She smelled lye soap as he moved past her into the mother superior's office, a required stop before being allowed to check on the baby. He had gotten to know the head of the small contingent of sisters over the past few months and he would have avoided her when he visited the baby if he could have. She was unpleasantly officious and surprisingly political. She knew the neighborhood and she knew of its players, including English, Morgan, and Gambrill. This did not create warmth in their relationship.

"Please sit down, Mr. Morgan," directed the nun, indicating the hard, wooden chair in front of her desk. She had a raw-boned, manly face for a woman and peered out at him mercilessly through ugly, wire-framed glasses. The sister sat with gaunt rigidity behind a monstrous, mahogany desk. Morgan stared past her to the huge, grotesquely carved crucifix on the wall. The thing hung away from the wall so that it looked like it was leaning out over her shoulder. It always reminded him that some ways to die were worse than others.

The nun took immediate charge of the conversation. "I'd like to speak to you, and Bernadette has a visitor at the moment."

"Bernadette? Visitor?" asked a surprised Morgan.

"Yes, the baby needs a name. You didn't see fit to give her one and we couldn't keep calling her 'the baby,' so we named her after the saint on whose day she was born," the mother superior informed him.

Raising a flat palm in his direction, she continued, "Don't start telling me about the father's rights, or your rights for that matter. I know the situation better than you do. The only important thing here is that baby girl, her survival, and her soul. And all of that's going to be taken care of shortly."

Morgan was in no mood to take on this formidable woman, but he would be damned if he was going to let her call the shots.

"Look, Sister, I appreciate what you have done for me, but I don't much care what you think, what you have planned, or what you call the kid. I'm taking her with me now."

"You ass," the mother superior raged, rising from her seat. "I wouldn't lift a bead for you, you moron. I did it for the child!"

Morgan was stunned by her vehemence and venom.

"The visitor I spoke of, he's here with a police officer. He'll be taking custody of Bernadette immediately by Court Order. They showed me the papers twenty minutes ago and Sister Agnes is getting her ready to go now."

The blessed woman stood back after her series of salvos and gave him the kind of smile that gets people killed. Before Morgan could react, however, the door opened behind him and through it came Big Bill Barton. On his heels was a finely dressed, tall man wearing a blond goatee. Morgan knew the man immediately. John Vonderhorst now was known to all of the social clubs in the city.

Barton was a real red flag. Contact with him was best to be avoided. It was like being in a small, hot room with a dog that has a history of biting. He gave Morgan the same look a dog would give a man in that situation.

"Mr. Vonderhorst, this is James Morgan, Number Two in the Plug Uglies. Or is it Number One now, Jamie?"

Morgan ignored Barton, stood and spoke to Vonderhorst. "Show me the papers. I want to know what's at play here. The law cuts both ways, as you well know."

Morgan's instincts were to seriously disable Bill Barton and deal with this pompous German in a way that would get his attention. But he understood the need to avoid complicating the situation. He also felt a dawning sense of relief that he didn't want to admit to.

"Mr. Morgan, it was not my intent to do this with you here," Vonderhorst began, as he opened a leather folder and laid out several official documents, signed and sealed. "I understand that you have taken responsibility for the child since the disappearance of Mr. English. I admire and thank you for that. However, I am carrying out the specific orders of Judge Giles. The Court, with the advice and concurrence of the State of Maryland's Child Protection Agency, has decided that neither John English nor yourself is fit to be responsible guardians of the child. In accordance with that decision, Bernadette English will be taken into custody by Officer Barton and given over to me, pending adoption proceedings. The baby will be well placed, she will be well taken care of, and as she grows, she will be given a chance of a far better life than she ever could have realized in the streets of the Twentieth Ward."

James Morgan was exploding inside. How far did they think they could push him without a reaction? He moved quickly toward Vonderhorst, but stopped when the barrel of Barton's Colt interposed itself between them.

"Now, Jamie, that's another reason why I came along today. Tempers have a way of flaring in this neighborhood. Why don't you just sit and calm down a bit?" With the revolver, Big Bill guided Morgan back to the front of the nun's desk and sat him in the chair.

"I suppose you have made this as legal as possible," said Morgan to Vonderhorst, "but that baby has a father and I'm responsible for her until he returns or there is proof that he's not coming back. This is not right. It needs to wait until I can get a lawyer. It is not for you to decide the kid's life. This will not stand."

"If I do not do it, Mr. Morgan, who will?" reasoned Vonderhorst. "English? You? These good sisters? Be practical. This is an opportunity for the girl."

Morgan sat in his kitchen on Orchard Street. In front of him was a half-empty bottle of Glenfarclas single malt and a tin cup. He felt like he had failed. At the same time, he wondered, not for the first time, what he owed John English anyway.

J.W. Gambrill's face appeared at the window over the stationary tub that looked out into a narrow backyard. Morgan rose to let his friend in, wondering what occasioned the visit.

"We just heard from John," Gambrill began. "He wants us to meet him."

"Great," answered Morgan with little enthusiasm. "Where is he?"

"I don't know exactly. Somewhere up in Baltimore County. I was coming off my shift with the Hook and Ladder and this odd-looking bastard, wearing farmer's britches, walks up to me, hands me this note, and waits for me to read it. Gambrill slid a grimy piece of paper across the table to Morgan. The note was unsigned and simply said that "a friend" needed to see him and Morgan as soon as possible. They were to follow the directions of the man delivering the message.

"It's got to be English, all right," observed Morgan. "What's this all about?"

"You now know as much as I do, except that the messenger gave me directions to a house about twenty miles north of here. John's laying low for a number of good reasons. This town doesn't forget."

"J.W., we need to talk to him, so I guess I'll go. But I need a couple of days." Morgan was not going to talk to English without fully understanding the situation with the baby girl. He needed to see Henry Davis and slow down the custody process.

"I'm pitching in a big game on Sunday," said Gambrill. "So, I'm heading up there in the morning. I'll be back in two days. I'll catch him up on the election situation. What do you want me to tell him about you?"

Morgan was relieved to have finally heard from English, but he was not happy about being summoned to appear out in nowheresville without some explanation. He knew that he had done all he could for him. Still, he was nagged by a sense that somehow he had let English down. He also felt a growing conviction that Vonderhorst was probably right about what was best for the baby. And, as always, there was his own ego that resisted orders from anyone, even English.

"Tell him I have some things to wrap up here and that I'll see him in a few days, as soon as I can," replied Morgan.

After passing on the directions, Gambrill finished the scotch in Morgan's cup, stood, and left the way he came in. Morgan splashed some more whiskey into the cup and sat staring at a woodcut hanging on the wall. The picture captured Chesapeake watermen, frozen forever in the brutal business of tonging for oysters—another reminder that there were some really bad ways to die.

Chapter 9

Cockeysville, Maryland
October 1857

Gambrill traveled on horseback through the chill, colorful, October countryside over rutted roads to a small village buried among a series of small valleys. He had come almost twenty miles due north to the town of Cockeysville. There, sitting in a very welcome tavern, he learned that he was to head east about a mile to find the Beaver Dam Road. A local also told him that he would find marble and limestone quarries and the Potato Irish who worked there.

He rode into an enclave of worn clapboard houses and a few decrepit buildings perched on the lip of a former limestone and marble quarry. If the place had a name, it was not mentioned in the tavern. There was a steepled Catholic church, but little else of note. The few residents he passed, the ones the barkeeper called Potato Irish, glared at him out from under dark eyebrows and thick black hair. Evidently, they had come to this hardscrabble place to cut marble and to escape the famine at home. To Gambrill, it didn't look like they had succeeded in reaching their promised land.

When he asked for the Beaver Dam Road, a disheveled woman of indiscriminate age sullenly pointed to the far end of the hamlet. Unsure whether the woman was giving him directions or just telling him to leave, he followed her bony finger until he passed an open warehouse surrounded by rusting machinery and the detritus of cut stone. It looked played out and content to settle under a hoary layer of dirty gray dust. Just beyond, however, he found the road matching his directions from English.

Gambrill was not looking forward to talking to his old friend, John. So much had happened since the trial and there were more questions than he had answers to. He had taken over the leadership of the Plugs and the planning for the November elections. With Houck at the bottom of Baltimore Harbor, and Morgan seemingly uninterested, he had held the social club together and the Plugs had given as good as they got on the street.

Despite this, Gambrill had the uneasy feeling that he was being summoned to explain himself. He fought down the memory of being called before his vicious father, an experience that invariably ended with a bloody nose and bruises to go with it. A sick feeling rose from the pit of his stomach and poisoned his thoughts. Recognition of the similarity of the two situations also made him angry.

His horse followed a dirt track rather than any kind of real road and, if at one time there were beavers in the area, they were long gone now. The overgrown lane wound along the rim of the marble pit, up a hill, and into woods overlooking the town.

In passing the quarry, Gambrill had craned over the lip. The cavity was full of inky water, smelling of decay. Soggy leaves floated in coagulating patches like ugly, angry blotches on a stonecutter's chest. They would eventually grow together until the big, black pool was covered over completely. It looked deep and dangerous.

Eventually, he found a clearing that held a battered, frame house. As he approached, he could see an elderly man sitting on the covered gallery of the decrepit structure. Both the house and its resident clearly had seen better days. The place looked held together by nothing more than the lack of a good breeze. The codger himself appeared held together by shear will, as he sat with a shotgun on his lap, awaiting the rider's approach.

Gambrill was about to ask for John English when he recognized his old companion. He was so stunned at the deterioration of the man that he could say nothing. Both he and English were thirty-four but this man looked more than twice that. There was something like a smile from English, then an indication to come join him.

With his eye on the weapon, Gambrill tied off the horse, climbed the rotting steps to the porch, and extended his hand in greeting. English raised his own, but it was done with effort and the hand held out suffered with a palsied shake. Gambrill took the dead thing uncertainly, and English croaked, "John Wesley, it's been a while. Jamie?"

"It has been some time, John. Jamie's coming. He said he had some things to take care of. He'll be here in a couple of days," responded Gambrill. "You and I have a lot to talk about," he began. This was not the man he had expected to see, so all planned social niceties had been forgotten.

"Time enough for that," wheezed English, "Inside the door. A jug. Get it." It was plain that talking was difficult for his friend. The jaw was not quite right. It was also plain that moving around was painful. The cops had really done their brutal work well. English was still a mess and would be forever.

Gambrill found the jug of corn whiskey. He handed it to English who took it expertly with his bent hand, raised it slowly on his forearm, took a pull, and let it fall to the floor with a thump. Gambrill was not offered a taste. He looked around for a seat, found what looked like a rusty, overturned cauldron, and sat on it.

"I miss Baltimore," managed English. This was said in such a broken way that Gambrill was forced to fill in missing and garbled syllables. "Election coming."

"Mobtown. That's what the northern papers are calling us. Hot as a two-dollar pistol at the moment and it's going to get hotter come November," replied Gambrill. "I've been working with our contacts in Baltimore and Annapolis and I've put some plans together for controlling each of the legitimate polls."

"I love the fall," said English, looking around at the fiery reds and yellow-browns of the surrounding trees that had begun to sway with a building breeze. When he spoke, he turned a bit toward the visitor and so did the muzzle of the shotgun.

"John, I have to tell you that things are different than when you were running the Plugs. More organized, now."

Gambrill couldn't tell if English had picked up on the transition that had occurred in the social club. In fact, he couldn't tell if English had heard him or was ignoring him. He made no response. His watery eyes reflected the red of the trees, but he just continued to stare out at them.

"John, did you hear what I said?" asked Gambrill.

English sat very still and continued to gaze at the autumn splendor before him. After an eternity, he spoke clearly, "I heard you, J.W." Then, "Hattie is gone. The Plug Uglies are gone. My plans are gone." Then, turning full to Gambrill, he said, "I trusted you."

With that, the shotgun roared and John Wesley Gambrill flew backwards, smashed into the wall of the house, and slid down its flaking exterior to the floor of the porch in a bloody heap.

English showed no emotion, staring with empty eyes at his one-time friend. Over his shoulder, he spoke to a man in overalls who had appeared in the doorway of the house.

"Zachariah, it was just as you said. This one goes to the bottom of the quarry."

Chapter 10

Baltimore
Late October 1857

It had taken Morgan a week to see Henry Winter Davis. The attorney had been in the District of Columbia on party business. His assistant, Cooke, had offered to talk to him, but Morgan would only deal with Davis. The legal system maze around custody and adoption was only half of the problem. It was the son-of-a-bitch's connections that he needed as well.

They sat in the congressman's oak paneled office, frustration evident on both men's faces. The realization that he was not going to get the help he was seeking was quickly turning Morgan's dissatisfaction into anger. At the same time, Davis was struggling to contain his annoyance with his visitor's persistence, but he also knew what his visitor was capable of doing when crossed.

"James, I don't know how else to say this. I do have powerful friends, but this situation has gone far beyond my influence. The Court has already ruled and the child is off limits. Vonderhorst has the upper hand, a lot of money, and his own powerful friends. I'm hearing that he is considering adopting the child himself."

Morgan's irritation was not just being driven by Davis' unwillingness to act. It was more a matter of not knowing why he wouldn't act. With English in exile and Gambrill missing, Morgan had stepped reluctantly into the leadership of the Plug Uglies. The November election was a week away, the clubs had been active on behalf of the American Party, and plans were set for controlling the polls. He knew Davis was getting what he paid for. Morgan also knew that the attorney had protected English, had gotten him away, and probably was paying to keep him away.

Davis, on the other hand, would have liked nothing better than to be done with John English. The man had practically bled him dry. A sizable percentage of the funds Vonderhorst had provided for the election went to English. If the German ever found that out, there would be hell to pay, maybe worse. Now Morgan wanted him to step in on English's kid. Davis weighed the risk of alienating the source of his finances against continuing to support the needs of these street goons. He had had enough. He was not going to do it any longer.

"James, we are not going to win this one. You and John are going to have to let this go."

As Davis tried to bring the discussion to a close, he also checked the pistol in the open drawer of his desk for the third time. He was taking no chances with the Plugs' boss.

Morgan was no fool and he could see that Davis was juggling unknown factors. In truth, Morgan's own resolve on the matter of the baby had begun to wane. He wasn't sure now what English would have wanted him to do. What's more, Morgan was convinced that Gambrill would have returned to play his baseball game, if he was at all capable of doing so. That was not a good sign and he wasn't going to travel to meet English until he saw Gambrill again.

"This is a dangerous decision you are making, Congressman. It's not my child, it's English's. I have done what I can. You'll have to deal with him when he returns. And we both know he will be back."

"James, please. I'm not making any decision. You need to believe that our hands are tied here." Davis stood to bring the conversation to an end.

Morgan sat looking at Davis for a moment, making the attorney nervous. Then, he rose and left the office with no further comment.

The Bar and Oyster House was well lit and packed. As men wedged past each other in and out of the front door, the bar maintained the equilibrium of a sardine can. Teenage punks with ratty, high silk hats tipped down over their eyes to give them that sharp look stood outside on the sidewalk in the light of the bar's windows, like moths drawn to a flame. A swarm of younger brats skipped and danced around out on the cobbles, punching each other, swaggering and swearing like the adults they mimicked. Ever wise, the street kids stayed just out of the reach of their older brothers in the high hats.

Morgan pushed past some drunks sharing a brown bottle and blocking the mouth of the alley next to the bar. Wading through the garbage and trash, he turned at the back door, kicked a cur dog away from a pile of oyster shells, and entered the kitchen. He moved quickly through the black shuckers whose hands and wrists moved with a speed and grace worth watching. He slid around bulky men changing the tap on a keg. Signaling the bartender, Eisenhart, he climbed the stairs to the office.

"Swede, who's in here tonight?" Morgan asked his longtime bartender, now partner.

As the election neared and Morgan took control of the social club, the bar had once again become the center of the Plug Uglies' world. Business was booming at a time when he was juggling a lot of balls. John "Swede" Eisenhart was the perfect partner and Morgan wished that he had thought of it earlier. He needed someone to run the place and the big man was ideal. The only way he could get Swede to do it, however, was to give him a piece. So he did.

"Everybody's in here, Jamie. Even Raz Levy from the Raps. He and some of the boys are sitting at the corner table. They're waiting on you."

That was another thing that had changed with the absence of recent leadership. A new cadre of lieutenants quickly emerged from the Twentieth Ward's streets. Morgan knew them all and it was his reputation that drew them. He had them now, but he knew at some point a challenge would come. It always did.

"How are the receipts? Need me to do anything?" Morgan asked half-heartedly.

"No, no, Jamie. I've got it under control. We're doing great. I'll show you later. I had to kick some ass among the waiters, but the shuckers really know their business. Oh, yeah, I changed the beer over. No more Eagle, as you said. Vonderhorst can go to hell."

"Swede, I've got to talk to Raz. Is that bottle of Baker's still under the bar? Any cigars?" Morgan rose, patted Eisenhart on the shoulder in thanks, and went back down the stairs to work.

XXXXXXXX

"Raz, thanks for coming up here to talk to us."

Morgan sat among his young chiefs and poured the visitor a sizable snort of the rye, then passed the bottle. He reached over with a Lucifer and put the flame to Levy's claro.

Then he said, "I've seen the plans to work the polls and I'm good with them if you are. The timing of events also works for me, but I think we need to bring in more clubs from the east side when we hit Howard Street. The Snakes and the Tubs have their own parties planned, but the New Marketers remember last year too well and they're reinforcing."

Levy savored the whiskey, set it down, then took a long pull on the smoke. As he shot a plume of blue smoke into the air, he rocked back in the chair, settled his fat bulk, and grinned at Morgan.

"Jamie, I been through a lot with you and John, but I never thought I'd hear you say that your girls here needed help." He looked evilly at the sour faces around the table.

"Raz, you know that my debutants could kick your delicate queens' assess up and down Lombard Street any time we took the fancy," replied Morgan in a heavy cloud of smoke aimed at his friend and ally. He almost laughed watching the young toughs at the table nod and straighten their shoulders.

"Well, Jamie, we might find the truth of that one day, but not today. You're right about reinforcements. They have the weapons too. I hear they got hold of a swivel gun. Have any experience with artillery?"

"I'm not worried about that. Those idiots will probably blow a hole through three of their horses firing that thing. I'd like to ask you to talk to the Blood Tubs about Howard Street and I'll talk to the Snakes. Okay?"

The men were in agreement and they moved on to cover other details of the coming days. Off and on, over a few hours, Morgan would send one of the Plug Uglies out of the bar with a message or to make some additional arrangement for Election Day. At around midnight, the meeting broke up. Morgan checked that Eisenhart would lock up, pulled the Webley from under the bar, then pushed through the remaining hard core to the street.

He turned the corner at Orchard to head home. As he passed the alley a few doors down from his own, a huge Norwegian rat bolted out of the dark passage. In an instant, the thing ran at Morgan's legs and did a full, confused turn around him. It then sped across the street and through a hole in a wooden fence. The dance with the rat surprised Morgan and threw him off balance to where he staggered against a lamppost. With that, he heard the echoing blast of a big pistol. A good-sized chuck of brick immediately flew off the corner of the house just beyond him. He had seen the flash out of the corner of his eye somewhere off to his right. He dove down, behind the post. As he pulled the Webley, he heard running. He focused on the sound, then leapt up and tore after it.

The assassin was pelting down Madison Street at a high rate and Morgan was not going to catch him. The runner passed under a gaslight and Morgan couldn't see much, but he thought the man was dressed like a farmer.

Chapter 11

Baltimore
Mid-November 1857

The year 1857 had been one of transition and turmoil in America. The states' rights argument resurfaced as the South's agrarian interests ran headlong into the burgeoning industry of the North. A devastating financial crisis in August and September crippled both economies. The struggle over whether new states coming into the union were to be slave or free was played out in graphic detail all of that year in Bloody Kansas, where zealots from both sides traded massacres. The aisles of Congress were not spared physical violence over slavery and property ownership. Chief Justice Roger B. Taney rendered his incendiary decision on Dred Scott's status as a human being, putting additional fire in the belly of the growing abolitionist movement. President Buchanan's partisan appointments literally put the Democratic Party in revolt. Eastern port cities continued to swallow thousands of immigrants, cramming them into tenements and alleyways, forcing appalling living conditions, and incubating hideous diseases. The country was very sick in many ways.

Maryland and Baltimore had it all that year. Fault lines could be seen between southern and northern sympathizers, between slave owners and antislavery advocates, between the Democrats and the American Party. Other fissures existed between social reformers and the firehouse gangs and between newly franchised Americans and everyone else. The political world in the Old Line State was a large, crazed jug, leaking severely and about to collapse.

In the November elections, seats were open for the congressional delegation, the governor, the House of Delegates, judicial officers, and the Baltimore City council. With that much bait, the sharks were in the water. The phrase *early and often* not only applied to those voting, but to those attempting to intimidate those voting. As a result, the free election process was a travesty. Anarchy ruled and turned the streets red with blood and rage. Taking the brunt of it were the recently arrived Germans and Irish. Attempts to exercise their newly won freedom were punished. Delivering the punishment were the stalwarts of the American Party ideal. One irreverent newspaper observed that, "In some precincts, there were more dead and wounded than votes for Democrats."

The plans made ahead of time and coordinated among the Plug Uglies, the Rip Raps, the Rough Skins, the Blood Tubs, the Black Snakes, the Tigers, the Mount Clare Boys, the Thunderbolts, and the Wampanoags all paid off. And so did the winners of seats.

When the polls finally closed and all ballots were tallied, the strategy of the American Party street thugs proved to be so effective that it was embarrassing. The Know-Nothings won nineteen of twenty wards, garnering eighty-seven percent of the vote in those precincts. In the neighborhoods where the Plug Uglies and their allies held sway, Democrats failed to even nominate candidates. Those who did run were thoroughly threatened, if they were lucky. The Democratic City Council candidate in South Baltimore had his nose shot off. In other wards, Democratic candidates withdrew for a variety of other health reasons.

This sham, of course, was national news and Baltimore's reputation as the last bastion of the gasping American Party was solidified. Even with the election over, the city continued to suffer as revenge and retribution produced seven murders in the days immediately following. "A Dying Party in a Dying City" was the newspaper headline in one rival East Coast urban center.

James Morgan could not forget the baby he had come to think of as Bernadette. Even as the election raged around him, he would wonder about the child. It wasn't even a matter of English anymore. He couldn't quite explain the responsibility he felt. He knew that Vonderhorst was probably right about her welfare. On the other hand, he didn't like being manipulated the way he had been. He didn't like things being taken away, regardless. So, he determined to have one more go-round with the German brewer. That meant paying him a visit at the Eagle plant up on North. Morgan was hoping that this would allow him to reconcile Vonderhorst's high-handedness. At the same time, he hoped to purge himself of the feelings for the child that were so foreign to him.

The Eagle Brewery and Malt Works started as a large, four-story brick edifice and that aging structure still housed the main brewing operations. In recent years, however, the business had added a warren of smaller brick buildings and wooden frame structures radiating out from the original site. Everything seemed in a state of disrepair. Even the new construction going on added little to the place's image. Sales of the German lager had grown steadily over the years, but the physical plant always seemed to be playing catch-up. The facility expanded, but only in fits and starts and then, only when John Vonderhorst was absolutely forced to do so. That was only one of the reasons his hired men privately referred to him as Cheap John. Wages were another reason. A third was the German's penchant for using slave labor and freelance construction workers to build the place.

Morgan strode through the front gate of the brewery and past an armed guard who looked at him oddly but did not attempt to stop him. He was immediately assaulted by the pungent odor of malt and horses. Morgan stopped a filthy black man who was pushing a barrow of horse manure out of the ground's carriage house, a dilapidated wooden barn. The man pointed him across the plant's central yard, past the haphazard scaffolding of new construction to a small redbrick office.

He dodged brewery workers and loaded drays moving quickly to whatever tasks they were about. As he ducked under the scaffolding and edged his way through a group of slaves carrying hods of new brick, he eyed the work going on. He thought he recognized one of the construction workers, but before he got up to him, the man had climbed out of sight.

Past the work, Morgan honed in on the small office and picked up his pace. The crash of wood and metal falling from a height and the angry curses of those on the ground made him look back and up to the scaffolding. When he did, he was sure that it was Crab Ashby looking down at the pile of debris that had fallen.

Ashby was a particularly unstable, former member of the Regulators, but now active with the Black Snakes. Morgan knew he was no bricklayer; hell, for that matter, he never knew the man to work a day in his life. Ashby flipped his middle finger to those on the ground, and then noticed Morgan staring up at him. The silly grin retreated from his face and he disappeared back into the bowels of the construction.

This was very curious. What were the Black Snakes doing on Vonderhorst's property? The German was no friend of theirs and he had proven it during the recent election. In an interview with *The Sun*, he had spoken for the Reform Movement, naming the social club and several of its leaders as employers of "knock downs and drag outs" in controlling the Eleventh Ward polls. This particularly barbaric tool of firemen and the gangs was a simple shaft with a lump of iron on one end and a hook on the other. It was very effective when persuading Democratic voters to the Know-Nothing way of thinking.

Before Morgan could puzzle out what he had just seen, the door to the brewery office opened and John Vonderhorst walked out with a young boy in tow. The two men stared at each other. Then Vonderhorst pushed the boy behind him and spoke rapidly to someone inside the open door. Two very large men with clubs stepped out.

"How did this man get on the premises?" Vonderhorst asked with a distinct edge. "What the hell do I pay guards for?"

As the two brutes moved to Morgan, the Plug Uglies' leader snarled, "Vonderhorst, unless you tell your dogs to back off, you'll be paying funeral bills as well." His Webley appeared and he let it hang loose, pointing to the ground. The men stopped.

"Papa, what did that man mean?" Then, "He's got a gun!" said the startled little boy.

"Harry, I want you to run over to the carriage house. Tell Moses to get the Spindle Seat ready. We're going home."

"But Papa, he's got a gun!" The boy was alarmed.

"No need to worry, son," said Morgan. "I've just come to talk to your father. I mean no trouble."

"Go, now, Harry" said Vonderhorst calmly, but firmly, brooking no further protest from the boy. "I want to talk to this gentleman."

Harry took off at a run, looking back at the men and wearing a worried expression. The brewer waved the guards away and gestured to Morgan, inviting him to walk with him to a quieter place.

"Look, Morgan, with what you and your thugs managed to do over the last couple of weeks, I have no mind to talk to you at all. Do you have any idea what you have done to this city, to this state?" began Vonderhorst.

"Yeah, I do. We saved it," replied Morgan, in no mood to deal with the German's arrogance. "But spare me your sanctity, Vonderhorst. I'm here to talk about Bernadette."

"Bernadette?" said the brewer, obviously surprised. "I thought you might have come to your senses on the child by now."

Morgan wasn't quite sure that he had come to his senses because he wasn't quite sure he knew what his senses were. It didn't make any difference though because the scream of "Fire!" ripping through the yard demanded all attention. Morgan had heard something else as well: pistol shots.

A breathless, sweating man in overalls smashed into the two men in his haste to escape the blaze around the new construction. From where he stood, Morgan could see that the carriage house was also billowing smoke. Vonderhorst could see it too, but just as the terror began to rise, he slumped at Morgan's feet. A red blossom was rapidly forming around his stomach. Morgan dragged the German to the step of the office where the two guards found enough brief courage to step out and lend assistance.

James Morgan barreled toward the carriage house. He skirted the blazing scaffolding and wooden framing behind it, feeling its intense heat. He could hear men shrieking for help, caught on the new upper floors. He also saw two bodies sprawled in the dirt of the yard.

The carriage house was now burning. Instead of men, the screams belonged to horses. Three black men were in the building, running around with their arms flailing, silhouettes against a backdrop of flame, working to drive panicked horses out the door. Wagons and carriages were going up like dry leaves one by one as the fire rapidly burned through. It was there that Morgan looked and found the little boy hunched in the back of a smoldering buggy. It had run close, but he had gotten to him.

Morgan carried the boy out into the yard and, hunching against the heat of the blazing scaffolding, made his way back to the brick office and John Vonderhorst. The brewery's foreman was there and, despite a nasty wound along his neck, seemed to be in control.

Orders were being issued and men were running with purpose. Vonderhorst lay propped up, ashen and unconscious, but breathing. Morgan handed the child to the startled yard boss and walked out.

He looked for an exit away from the two fires, now forming a wall of flame between him and the front gate. He found it by following one of the foreman's messengers out through a small, barred door. As he stepped through it, he could hear the volunteer fire companies responding. He also could see a large, dark knot of men about twenty yards to his left. They were treating the messenger none too gently. Morgan began to edge away to his right, but it was too late. He had been spotted. He pulled the Webley and began to move faster.

"You! You, there! Stop where you are. This is the police!"

The order came from the middle of the pack and the collection of men began to spread, then run. Morgan ran too. The man issuing orders stopped, aimed his Colt, and fired. The ball tore through the brim of Morgan's slouch hat, tipping it forward but leaving it on his head.

Morgan halted, turned, and returned the fire. He heard his assailant grunt, but did not see him fall. This stopped the pursuit momentarily, giving him time to disappear down an alley, over a fence, and through the back door of a busy laundry.

He bolted past steaming vats, drying lines, and startled washerwomen on his way to the front door of the business. Freedom was short lived, however. Just as he scrambled out onto the cobbles, he was forced to pull up in front of four more of Baltimore's finest.

Morgan fled back through the laundry. Clearing himself of wet clothing and sheets, he again had to stop short. Facing him with a gun in one hand and using the other to press a bloody rag against his side was the man he had just shot, Big Bill Barton.

"Jamie, you put a hole in me," observed Barton almost matter-of-factly as the muzzle of his Colt moved up.

"Yeah, Bill, and here's one for the English family," replied Morgan as he swiftly raised the Webley and put a ball in the big cop's forehead.

Simultaneously, Barton's weapon fired but sailed wide, tearing a hole through the drying laundry and finding a mark in the leg of one of the pursuing officers. When the cops ducked for cover, Morgan turned and fired two wild shots in their general direction, then bolted out the back door and over the fence.

James Morgan sat looking through his reflection to the dark southern Maryland countryside sliding by the window of the B&O train carrying him away from Baltimore. He thought about how it had all come crashing down. He had stumbled into an ally's plans to deliver retribution to its enemy. What the hell was he doing there anyway? He had no place for a baby. They'll probably try to pin the German's death on me too. Christ, Big Bill would have killed me, sure as hell. At least I had no choice in that.

Morgan felt a sense of relief to be away from the craziness, but the look on his face was one of sadness. He wasn't sure whether he would ever see Baltimore again.

Part II
Making Our Own Order

Chapter 12

New York City
September 1882

Bernadette Vonderhorst stood at the rail of *The Liberty* and watched the sprawling, energetic scene of the Port of New York crawl past. She thought of her father and how excited she was to see him again. She thought of the boring Clive back in Hyde Park and how happy she was to escape his cloying marriage proposal. She thought of her dear friend, Emily Thorne Vanderbilt, now Emily Vanderbilt Sloane, whose grandfather, Cornelius, had built this port and many of the east's railroads.

Bernadette smiled to herself as she recalled Emily's most recent letter. Her friend had explained that, while everyone talked about Vanderbilt's locomotives, it was this harbor and the boats in it that her grandfather loved the most. He would tell her exciting stories of plying these waters in some of the first steam-powered skiffs. Emily loved her irascible old grandpapa and Bernadette was sorry that she couldn't be with her when the commodore died just this past January. She had even missed her best friend's wedding, almost eight years ago now. Bernadette thought about all she had to tell her childhood soul mate after so much time away.

It seemed that she was always away somewhere. So much so that it was difficult to decide where home was. She guessed that in her twenty-five years she had lived and gone to some sort of school in at least four different cities: New York, Paris, Rome, and Barcelona. She assumed that she was born in New York City where she had spent her first sixteen years. That's where she and Emily, five years her senior, had become close. The young Vanderbilt had been more than just a friend; she was Bernadette's big sister as well, the only family she had, really, with Papa being so busy and traveling most of the time.

Bernadette still remembered that awful day when her father said she was sailing to France for "rounding out." She had been lonely and scared to death. He had visited her off and on over the ensuing years, of course, but thank God for Mrs. Cooper.

Jane Cooper had been her chaperone and tutor back then, but after all their years together traveling, she had become much more. In fact, Bernadette thought of Jane as her surrogate mother and she could not love her more than if she were her real mother. The two were now returning to the United States at the request of her father whose letter mysteriously mentioned that they were going "home" to Baltimore, a southern city of which she knew nothing.

"It won't be long now," observed Jane, as she joined her charge at the rail. "Your father will be waiting for you on the dock."

The trim, dignified woman threw a shawl around Bernadette's shoulder who accepted it gratefully, glad to have something to ward off the stiffening breeze coming out of the Hudson.

"I'm nervous, Jane," said Bernadette, using the name she had just recently begun using in place of Nanny, the endearment adopted so long ago. "It's been two years since he visited us in London and I've changed so much. Do you think he'll still like me?"

"Bernadette, your father loves you. Always has. Hasn't he taken good care of you? Given you the best?"

"Yes, he has and I love him, too. But his letter was so curious. I don't want to go to Baltimore. I know no one there and I want to see Emily."

"You'll have a chance to catch up with your friend, I'm sure," said Jane, reassuring Bernadette, as she always did.

When Jane Cooper first met Bernadette, the girl was a rambunctious, five year old. Her father was looking for a top-rate governess, explaining that the child's mother had passed away during delivery and that the toddler had been with a series of wet nurses up to that point. Jane was twenty-two at the time, young certainly. But she had been classically raised and had earned a degree in fine arts from the New York University at a time when women graduates were very rare.

The recent loss of both her parents to typhoid left her in sizable debt and in need of work. Her father had been a respected estate manager and gamekeeper on one of the Vanderbilt's larger properties. Over the years of hunting and fishing together, he had become close to both the commodore and his son, William. So that's where she went for help. It was fortuitous that, at the same time, William was courting a southern investor who was in need of an au pair. Through these connections, Jane met John Vonderhorst.

Vonderhorst and Cooper bonded immediately. She thought him very impressive in an old world sort of way. It was plain that he loved Bernadette, cared about her happiness, and would put his considerable resources behind his plan for achieving that. Vonderhorst found young Jane to be pleasant, levelheaded, sophisticated, and moral. And, even if she wasn't exactly the belle of the ball, her solid English stock gave her passable good looks. Regardless, her no-nonsense personality was just the sort he was looking for to take charge of little Bernadette. As a result, he spent a considerable amount of time explaining to her his plans for his daughter's development. They talked about expected responsibilities, finances, and a wide range of other details, including Jane's traveling persona. She would now be Mrs. Cooper, a much more suitable, although fictitious, title for a governess and European traveling companion. They quickly came to an agreement and Jane never looked back with regret at her decision to take on the job. In fact, Bernadette had become her life.

"Jane, I just can't wait. I have so many things to ask Papa. What do you think he meant when he wrote, 'We would all be together, finally'? What do you think he has planned?"

"Bernadette, I'm sure he was just expressing his hope that the two of you would be able to spend more time together. Don't read more into it than that."

In fact, Jane thought Vonderhorst's letter drawing them back to the States was indeed curious. It was not like him. He and Jane had developed a steady correspondence outside of his letters to Bernadette. Nothing very personal, but he wrote regularly to check on the progress of the education of his daughter. He also kept up a steady flow of news, all the way back to those terrible days of the war among the states. His writing style was clean, direct, and informative. His latest set of pages, however, had been a departure. It was almost as if he had something important to tell Bernadette, but he wanted to do it face to face. Jane had as many questions as Bernadette did.

"I didn't realize how much I've missed this country," commented Jane, looking at the colorful crowd on the dock as *The Liberty's* crew worked to bring the steamer parallel with the quay. "I've missed this city, too. There's a life here, a spark that is decidedly not European."

"I feel it too, Jane. Look! There he is! He sees us! Wave! Wave!" shouted Bernadette excitedly over the noise of the crowd and the deep, heart-thrumming blast from the ship's horn.

John Vonderhorst spent a lot of time in New York these days and maintained a very respectable set of quarters at a very respectable Park Avenue address. It wasn't home, though, and it never took very long for him to begin thinking about Baltimore. Over the years, he had had more than a casual hand in building the dirty port city and he would never leave it for very long.

The Monumental City had survived the war; had even survived the brutal ensuing years of Johnson's and Grant's plans for rebuilding. His town had emerged from an epidemic of political and social diseases—deadly power struggles within the incumbent Republican Party, invading northern scalawags, and the hate on horseback that was the Ku Klux Klan.

Black faces had appeared in Annapolis and in City Hall, no longer shining shoes and pushing brooms, but wearing shiny shoes and pushing buttons. The crushing panic of ten years earlier and its deep, ensuing financial depression saw a number of prominent Baltimoreans flounder, sink, and hit bottom, leaving concentric rings of debt and little else. The firehouse gangs were gone, of course, with so many young men taken in places like Manassas, Chancellorsville, Shiloh Church, Sharpsburg, Gettysburg, and Petersburg. But, through it all, the sooty, muscular town had survived.

Now, Baltimore was a city of rolled-up sleeves. It was a city that produced. Vonderhorst's town had moved beyond oysters, beer, and riots to produce coal, steel, petroleum, manufactured goods, building materials, paints, chemicals, silver goods, and much more. Its rail yards and expanded docks worked twenty-four hours a day, sending the fruits of American prosperity across the country and out to the world. The Chesapeake Bay, Baltimore's private pond, continued to be one of the most productive bodies of water in the world.

The city's denizens also had changed. Its citizenry was no longer dominated by Anglo surnames. Or, if a name was Anglo, it might just as well be appended to a black man as a white one. The German, Irish, and Catholic communities had survived the hate and bloodshed of earlier days and were large and thriving. Ethnic and religious festivals, foreign foods, and accents were prevalent, but distinctly American and, in particular, Baltimorean.

Much to Vonderhorst's satisfaction, all of this success seemed to make the city's residents very thirsty. Hell, they seemed to be thirsty regardless. Even during the dark economic times of the early '70s, Eagle sold. It seemed that when people start to need, the one thing they need the most is a little comfort from the storm. For many, that meant drinking. For the neediest, that meant beer. For Baltimore, that meant Eagle. So, the Eagle Brewery and Malt Works rode high on the waves of the tempests that blew through the city and picked up speed and distance in the good times, making the Vonderhorst family very wealthy in the process.

As lucrative as beer was, it was Vanderbilt's railroads and Vonderhorst's investment in them that made the real money. The collapse of southern railroads and the push to expand east to west and west to east created opportunity that men like Vanderbilt, Jay Gould, and Leland Stanford did not miss. The wealthy Baltimore Brewer was caught in the draft of the New Yorker's steam-powered growth. That engine pulled Vonderhorst along just as fast as *Old No. 119* and *The Jupiter*, rushing at one another to join the Atlantic with the Pacific at Promontory Peak in Utah, not so many years earlier.

Now, as he sat in the Landau town coach with his arm around Bernadette, they maneuvered around and through the New York traffic. He couldn't be happier. His plans had succeeded far beyond his imagining. She was a stunning young woman, a poised, sophisticated lady now. Her professors, one after another, had been loath to give her up, describing her as "brilliant" and hoping to employ her sharp, focused mind in their own research. Jane Cooper too had been a coup, a godsend really. The woman had become family in ways he may never be privy to but could easily see in Bernadette's eyes when they spoke or even looked at each other.

Vonderhorst also thought about what he had to tell his daughter. He probably shouldn't have let it go this long, but the time never seemed right when she was young and he didn't trust his letters to convey the love he felt for her. He knew that what he had to say would shock her, and Jane too for that matter. But none of that could be helped now, and the time had come.

Chapter 13

Baltimore
October 1882

T he hired men worked steadily unloading the fourth freight wagon that had come from the Camden Yards Station. Unlike the three loads of household goods before it, this wagon was full of expensive leather and wooden trunks, cases, and wardrobes. The latest tenant in the exclusive neighborhood along Madison, west of Charles, just off Mount Vernon Square was filling a four-story brick mansion with the things that could only be acquired by the very wealthy. Early evening strollers speculated on their new neighbor and craned to see what was being carried up the marble steps, past the scrolled, brass-topped iron railings, and into the wide oval atrium of the building. Some stayed long enough to watch a large, black, enclosed Barouche stop at the Madison Street address. The coachman climbed down, sprinted to open the street-side door, removed his hat, and offered a slight bow. Out of the carriage came a well-dressed, well-built man in his forties. He was a dark, hard-looking sort who gave short, harsh orders to the driver. The coachman quickly replaced his high hat and clambered back to his seat. He took the reins in hand and looked straight forward, awaiting further instruction.

The man leaned into the cab, spoke to a second passenger, then surveyed the street. When he caught the eyes of the curious, he stared rudely, long enough for them to look away and go about their own business. When foot traffic along Madison slowed, the dark man opened the carriage door, removed a complicated contraption that, when unfolded, became a wheeled chair. He placed the chair at the top of the mansion's flight of steps, then reached back into the closed cab and extracted an older gentleman, heavily wrapped in a shawl that covered most of his face and all of his gnarled legs. With little effort, the companion lifted and placed the man in the mobile chair. The two then disappeared quickly into the mansion.

Shortly, the valet returned to the carriage, removed a long, leather gun case, and gave the coachman his orders. Looking up and down the street one more time, the sturdy man reentered the house, closed a massive oak door, and threw a bolt with a heavy thud.

"You've done very well, Zachariah," observed the bent man as he was wheeled into a large study, lined with books, furnished richly, and dominated by a huge desk of ebony. "Please draw those curtains and light the lamps. Behind the desk will do, I have some letters to write and some reading to do."

The valet said nothing, but went about the business of getting the gentleman what he needed and settling him in his new quarters. He had come from Chicago several months ahead of his charge to arrange the move and ready the arrival. There was still much to be done, but the man thought nothing of it. No task or request was too big or too small for Zachariah. He offered his employer and patron total dedication and loyalty for all of the things he had done for him over their years together.

"Oh, and remember, Zachariah, my name is Enoch Stanton. We are new to Baltimore, never been here before. We've come from the south and I'm in oil, rail, and shipping. Our business has brought us to the city. We know no one here and I am a very private man."

"Of course, Mr. Stanton. I understand, just as we have discussed. Is there anything more you need at this point?"

"Yes, bring me copies of the Baltimore newspapers, especially *The Sun*. Is the research I asked for here? I need to relearn my old town all over again. The streets are the same but much has changed in twenty-five years."

"It's all there, sir, just as you asked. I have not completed the work on the city's orphanages, though. But I should have that soon enough."

"Good. That will be all for this evening," answered the man.

It had been a quarter century since John English had been in Baltimore. Now, he was back under a different name. The place was full of memories for him, but it was also full of unfinished business. And this was business that he would finish.

Utah
October 1882

James Morgan rode into the town called Eureka, just as early snow flurries began to swirl around him. He was leading a mule loaded with well-worn mining equipment. He was filthy, tired, cold, hungry, and very thirsty. He was also glad to have gotten out of the mountains ahead of the merciless winter storms that raged in the high country. Morgan headed for the only livery stable in the one-horse town.

"Take the jenny and the horse and store my equipment for me?" he inquired from a massive blacksmith with biceps like cannon balls, hammering away at a horseshoe.

Without looking up, the sweaty smith asked, "How long?"

"I'm leaving tomorrow," replied Morgan.

"Six bits," said the man.

"I didn't say a week," grumbled Morgan.

"Six bits," repeated the man.

"Feed?" Morgan asked.

"That'll be another four bits," said the man, delivering a heavy blow to the iron.

Morgan opened his long duster, dug the coins out of a pair of grimy Levi's, and tossed them on the anvil. The blacksmith scooped up the coins, paused long enough to peer closely at them, then resumed his banging.

Seeing that the man was not about to stop, Morgan led the two animals to a back stall in a worn barn, unloaded both, brought in some fresh hay, and mixed some mash he found. Morgan brushed the horse and the jackass down while the two devoured the feed.

He slung a pair of heavy saddlebags over his shoulder, dug his Colt Navy out of the pack, and walked across the street. He ignored the stares of a couple of raggedy cowboys and entered a frame building marked with a fading sign that read "Baths 10¢, Shaves 5¢." He emerged an hour later, feeling better, but hungrier and thirstier now.

Back across the street, he spotted the lone hotel, The Rose. A painted panel running down the side of its front door advertised rooms, steaks, and beer. Like the rest of the town, the hotel was a bit ratty, but he had never been all that choosey. He pulled his coat closed against the sharpening wind, walked past a set of windows that looked like they had never been washed, and entered the lodging house. He paid for a room for one night and moved into the saloon, passing under an arch decorated with a set of moldy elk antlers with several of the points broken off.

The place was half-full, a fact that surprised Morgan, given that the town's glory days had long passed. He walked to the bar, ordered a steak, well done, and a glass of something they were calling beer.

"Welcome, mister. Take any table that's free. We used to have whiskey, but we ain't seen any in awhile now." The bartender spoke with an annoying lisp. He put a chipped, glass mug of goldish liquid in front of Morgan.

"Gotta pay for the beer 'for you drink it, house rules."

Morgan picked up the beer and drained the glass in one long draught. "Another," he demanded.

The bartender, with a small hesitation but without a word, refilled the glass. Another pull and the second mug was half empty.

"That hat you're wearin', mister. Cavalry?" probed the barman.

Morgan said nothing, but turned and surveyed the room. There were scattered tables that contained a few unenthusiastic poker players; some farmers; three gray miners negotiating with a working girl; a sleeping man; a little, bald clerk-type in a vest working in a ledger; and the two men he saw outside the baths. Whatever this group was doing, they were just as interested in him. Some tried to mask their curiosity, others stared openly. This must be a boring town, thought Morgan.

"Lose that arm in the war?" asked the bartender, indelicately.

"If I say I did, does it get me a free beer?" answered Morgan.

"Maybe. If you were fighting on the right side," said the man, getting flippant.

"What side would that be, asshole?" Morgan snapped, turning back full to the bar and glaring at the man. At the same time, his right arm moved across his chest, flipped open his coat and reached under his left armpit to adjust the holster and revolver that hung there. Stamped clearly on the leather were the letters: C.S.A.

"I asked you a question," pursued Morgan, now facing the man who held his hands up in self-defense.

The bald man in the vest rose quickly from his table and moved to the bar.

"Now, mister, Chauncey don't mean nothin'. He lost some kin at Chickamauga, and sometimes he runs his mouth when he shouldn't. I'm Arthur W. Koon; I own this place. Chauncey, get the soldier another beer," ordered the short man.

The barman snatched the glass, sloppily refilled it, jammed it down in front of Morgan, and then moved quickly down the length of the bar.

"And don't forget the steak," said Morgan to the bartender's back. Then, looking down at the owner, he said, "I never said I was a soldier." With that, Morgan threw some coins on the bar, grabbed the beer, and walked through his audience to an empty table in the corner.

A few more beers and a tough steak later, James Morgan found himself graced with the presence of the lovely Lorna. At least that was the name she gave him. He doubted that she was worth the price she quoted him, but he had been a long time out in those mountains.

"You got a room, yet, honey?" she asked him.

He lay content under a rumpled sheet in a jangly brass bed, and watched her get dressed. She was a talker but she had a nice ass, he thought. She was saying something about how rare it was to get paid without the usual hassle.

As she edged closer to his saddlebags, he said, "Now, don't spoil this wonderful evening by getting too nosy, sweetheart."

Lorna whirled away as if she had no idea what he could be talking about, picked up her remaining things, and walked to the door.

"Thanks again, soldier. Let me know if you decide to stay longer, maybe we could get together again," said the businesswoman.

She offered a wan smile and went out the door. But the door never closed because the two loitering cowboys pushed past her and into the room with pistols trained on the man in the bed.

"Bucko, we're here for them saddlebags of yours. We know you been doing some digging and we're bettin' you ain't empty handed."

Both sets of eyes looked for and found Morgan's saddlebags and his Colt revolver hanging on a chair. The taller of the two laughed, pointed to the bulge in the sheet between Morgan's legs, and said, "Billy, it looks like our payday is ready for some more rogering."

The bulge under the sheet twitched and the roar of an old, but well-oiled Webley filled the room and a black hole appeared in the sheet. One of the cowboys flew backwards into the washstand, smashing the ceramic pitcher and bowl, and continuing his momentum, shattered the window that opened onto an alley. The body hung halfway out of the window. The remaining saddle tramp, dumbfounded, turned to watch his partner die. Another roar was heard and the man took a ball in the side. He then slumped in the corner of the room and began to bleed out.

Morgan rose and walked to the window to check his accuracy. It didn't take much to assist the thief the rest of the way through the opening. As he watched the corpse fall the two stories, he noticed that townspeople were starting to look cautiously down the alley. He stood over the crying, bleeding man and cocked his pistol. Hearing running feet making their way up the hotel stairs, he eased the hammer back. He pulled on his pants and his boots, threw on his shirt and coat, and reached for the Colt and the saddlebags. Fists began to pound on the door.

Morgan reloaded the Webley, then pulled open the door. The bar's patrons, led by the little man, cringed backwards in the hallway. He bulled past them as they rebounded to peek into the room, now filled with layers of blue smoke. Morgan strode down the stairs, out through the lobby, and headed for the livery stable. He guessed he wouldn't get to sleep in a bed this night after all.

Morgan left the mule and the mining equipment in the stall, saddled his horse, and rode hard that entire night. Once again a fugitive, he was headed due east to pick up the Price River. When he hit the river, he would find the Central and Southern Pacific Railroad that would spirit him out of Utah. From there, the line ran over the Colorado Rockies, below Pike's Peak, and met the railroad running south out of Denver to Clifton, just over the New Mexico border. Once there, Morgan knew from his earlier travels west that he could jump the Atchison, Topeka, and Santa Fe and reach El Paso in a matter of days. In El Paso, he would find an assay office that had enough cash and would ask no questions. It would be a relief to be able to put down the saddlebags. The Texas cow town was also the terminus for the Texas Pacific Railroad that would carry him all the way to his objective, the city of New Orleans. In New Orleans, he would have a choice to make.

Chapter 14

New York
October 1882

Vonderhorst had made friends with the maître d'hôtel at Delmonico's, and the restaurant at #2 Williams Street had become his favorite. He loved the wine list, the steaks, the Maryland oysters, and ordering a la carte. It would be in one of the institution's private rooms that he would do what he had been putting off. But he would do it within the context of great food and a great celebratory wine, a 1876 Perrier-Jouët Brut champagne.

The party included Bernadette, of course, but he had also invited Jane Cooper. Bernadette had begged to allow her close friend Emily Sloane to come as well. His second son, John, was away in California and would not be here tonight. But he had managed to pry his oldest, Harry, away from his responsibilities at the brewery and the pleasures of Baltimore that he was so fond of pursuing. Vonderhorst had been able to convince his eldest of the importance of the dinner in New York without telling him exactly why. Harry was running late, of course. This was not surprising; in fact, Vonderhorst had planned on it, hoping for a few minutes to prepare Bernadette for what he had to tell her.

The group was settled with a flurry of laughter and anticipation in the small, but sumptuous room. Vonderhorst of course was dressed formally in a dark tailcoat and trousers with a dark waistcoat, topped by a white bow tie and a winged collar shirt. The ladies were the height of fashion. Mrs. Cooper was stylish, but more demure than the younger women. She wore a high-necked black satin costume, trimmed with beaded French *passementerie*. Bernadette reflected her European taste and upbringing, wearing royal blue. She showed a fitted bodice with a low point in front. Her skirt was cutaway in front and hung over a gored skirt with ruffles. Daringly, like younger teenage girls, she wore her skirts just above her ankles. Emily was equally as striking in peach silk, corseted, bustled, and wearing her hair swept up to the top of her head and feathered along her forehead in the way that all of New York was wearing it.

The chilled wine, waiting in an ornate silver bucket, was opened and poured. John Vonderhorst began to raise a glass in toast when Bernadette interrupted him.

"But, Papa, wait. There's an empty chair here. Are we waiting for someone? A mystery guest perhaps?" Bernadette teased. "Shouldn't we wait for him? Or is it a her?" asked the young woman with a wink at her friend.

Between Emily and Bernadette, they had speculated on the obvious announcement that was to take place that night. They were positive that the group was going to be introduced to someone very special to the elder Vonderhorst. After all, he had been alone way too long, they reasoned.

Bernadette's mother, Henrietta, had died delivering her. So, other than Jane, she had never really had a mother. Anyway, it was about time, for her father's sake.

"There is someone else coming tonight, Bernadette, but all in due time, all in due time," said her father, smiling. "In the meantime, I think we have a lot to toast tonight and we might as well start now. Here's to your homecoming, sweetheart! May we never be parted again for long." With that, glasses were raised, hurrahs were heard, and that first, cautious sip of the delicious wine was taken.

"Now, Bernadette, I'm glad that you're surrounded by those dearest to you because what I have to tell you will come as something of a surprise. I gathered us intentionally because I want you to know and see how much you are loved when I tell you. First, I want to say that you have come home to a real family."

Encouraged by Bernadette's beaming face and her second sip of the champagne, he went on, "What I mean to say is that our family is bigger than you realize. In fact, it's bigger by two. You have two older brothers that you have never met."

Bernadette was really surprised. This was totally unexpected and a quick glance at Jane, then at Emily, proved them to be just as shocked. Before she could say anything, her father rushed on, "Before you start asking questions, one of them will be joining us tonight. Harry, your oldest brother, should be here any minute. John, two years younger, is in San Francisco and couldn't come east at the moment."

"Papa, I have brothers?" asked an astounded Bernadette. "Older brothers? Why didn't I know? Why didn't you tell me?" Bernadette was rapidly moving from surprise to confusion to annoyance as she tried to sort through the news and to understand its implications. She loved her father, so she was willing to give him the benefit of the doubt, but this was stunning. Emily and Jane sat immobile, gauging Bernadette's reaction and waiting to react themselves.

"Bernadette, believe me, there is a good reason I haven't told you before now. Allow me to explain," Vonderhorst began calmly. Just then, the door to the private room flew open and the space was filled with the larger-than-life presence of Harry Vonderhorst.

"So sorry I'm late, Papa. Please speak to Mr. Vanderbilt about the punctuality of his trains for me. It took forever to get up here," said Harry with a laugh and smile all around.

Harry Vonderhorst was a thirty-something version of his father, with the exception of his formal, bow tie that rode at an odd angle. Harry was a very handsome man. He was also well aware of this fact and his impact upon both men and women. Men immediately saw his vanity; women saw confidence. Men often found him frivolous; women found him fun. Men saw him as lumbering; women described him as athletic. Both realized quickly enough though that he was very sharp. They also came to realize that, even with all of his advantages, he was self-depreciating, never taking himself too seriously. This trait eventually broke down most animosity toward him, and as a result, he could fill a hall with those who considered him a friend.

"Well, we are so glad that you could join us, Harry. I know your social interests keep you very busy," said his scolding, loving parent.

"I'm happy to see you too, Papa. And who do we have here?" asked an amused and interested Harry who was surveying with obvious pleasure the three women in the cozy room. He graced Jane with a broad, toothy smile, gave Emily a gentlemanly bow with an impish twinkle in his eye, and stopped at Bernadette and stared, momentarily at a loss.

Bernadette had known men like this before. They were found in the hallways of palaces and summer retreats in France, Spain, and Italy. She also knew how to handle them, and that was none too gently, especially when they were so rude as to stare at her with such brash liberty. So, this dandy was her older brother.

"Harry, I'd like to introduce you to Emily Vanderbilt Sloane, the daughter of the man whose railroad you just insulted."

Harry tore his eyes away from Bernadette, gathered himself, and graciously bowed to Emily. "I am honored to meet you, Mrs. Sloane. I have heard a great deal about you and the family, of course. Please don't take my weak excuse for tardiness as an indictment of what your family has achieved," said Harry with an apologetic smile.

"Of course not, Harry. I find the steam ships much more reliable myself," joked Emily, returning him a warm, welcome expression.

"And, this lady is Mrs. Jane Cooper, a dear and trusted friend of the family," continued the elder Vonderhorst.

"Mrs. Cooper, a pleasure. I hope we can be friends as well," responded the younger man.

Then, turning to Bernadette in anticipation of the introduction, he resumed his interested gaze with even a bit more intensity. For her part, she was not about to be flustered by this man who seemed to think so much of himself. So she formed a calm, semiattentive look and awaited his unctuous comment.

"And this beautiful young lady is Bernadette, your sister, just now returned from Europe."

John Vonderhorst had thought about this moment for a very long time. Even then, he had no idea how it would go. A moment before, Bernadette had seemed shocked and less than enthusiastic to learn of her brothers. Now, he watched the dynamic between them with an unexpected nervousness.

The grin on Harry's face struggled to stay there as he processed the words of his father. Multiple emotions intruded and wrestled with each other across his face. His sister? His father had never mentioned a sister.

"I'm sorry, Papa, what . . . what did you say?" The stammer, reflecting his confusion and all too obvious disappointment, was the best he could do.

Seeing her new brother knocked off his pins, despite her own unsettled feelings, was so amusing and satisfying that it made Bernadette laugh out loud. Her reserve was forgotten and her laugh was true, with a hint of raucousness that spoke of her personality. It was the laugh that Jane said she should never let loose in polite company.

"What's the matter, big brother? Don't you recognize the resemblance?" Bernadette joked. She sensed that teasing him would not be taken badly, and it wasn't.

"No, no, I . . . it's just that. . . . ," struggled Harry. Then, recovering quickly, he said, smiling, "The Vonderhorsts have been missing something for a very long time. There are way too many men in this family. I just never dreamed that our feminization would come in the form of a sister, and a beauty at that."

"Save your smooth lines for the girls whose heads I'm sure you turn with regularity, Harry. Instead, come give your little sister a hug."

With that, Bernadette stood, moved around the table, and gave a nonplussed Harry a warm squeeze that told him she was pleased to have an older brother. Bernadette's reaction diffused the awkwardness of the startling revelation. The elder Vonderhorst breathed a sigh of relief, poured a sheepish Harry a flute of champagne, refilled the women's glasses, then raised his own in celebration of the union of family and friends.

As Harry settled into the party, conversation began to flow at a furious pace. There was a lot of ground to cover and to catch up on between the two new siblings. As dinner was served, they talked of each other, their interests, and their experiences over the past twenty-five years. They shared ideas, argued over Standard Oil's formation as a trust, and marveled at Thomas Edison's genius and the lighting of New York's Pearl Street Station with electricity. They even made plans to go to see Mr. Barnum's latest attraction, Jumbo the Elephant. They taunted each other and told amusing stories as they began to fill in the blanks.

In the midst of the conversation, John Vonderhorst sat back and fixed a smile on his face as he listened to his guests. He had not finished what he had hoped to finish and now it was too late. He listened to an animated Harry, holding forth in defense of his passion for bowling and drinking beer. He laughed and jeered with the women as his son bragged over winning ribbons for the two favorite sports of Baltimore's German community. He was not about to spoil the party with a second dramatic revelation, one that he knew now he should tell Bernadette when they were alone.

Chapter 15

New York
November 1882

By the time the Christmas season had begun, John Vonderhorst realized that he could put off the inevitable no longer. In three short months, Bernadette, with the help of Emily, had jumped into New York society with both feet. Her calendar was the envy of the most upwardly mobile daughters of the best families. She had her pick of invitations and her choice of beaus. She was welcome and becoming well known at opera openings as well as sporting events. She was a sought after guest at poetry readings, dress balls, and formal dinners. She could discuss John L. Sullivan's bare-knuckle technique as well as the merits of the British invasion of Egypt. In short, she was becoming the toast of a town that he knew he would leave soon, taking her with him.

Vonderhorst wanted to be home for the holidays and the joys of the season among his people, Baltimore's German–American community. New York could be wonderful at this time of year and it seemed that every door along the avenue was decorated with Edison's latest marvel, festive strings of little twinkling lights. But New York, as exciting as it could be, was not home.

Harry had returned to Baltimore a few days after that first dinner, claiming the need to oversee the production of the Eagle Brewery and Malt Works' first winter bock. His father suspected his son's motivation was more tied to interest in a young fräulein he had met at one of the many festivals held in the fall. Just the same, the elder Vonderhorst was quite proud of the way Harry had been managing the business in his absence. The senior Vonderhorst's time recently had been taken up with the consortium he had pulled together to create a new insurance company. That and his growing investments in Vanderbilt's empire inevitably had drawn him away from the beer business.

Harry had stepped in admirably, however, steadily increasing sales, overseeing the building of a new brewery in '75, and fighting the city's relentless, teetotaling reformers who would limit the sale of all alcoholic beverages. He had laughed heartily at his son's recounting of marching in protest against a new city ordinance banning beer barges in the harbor. Harry had led an oompah band right up to the door of City Hall with a hundred people behind him. His son was a scalawag, certainly, but he was a businessman too. In fact, Harry had mentioned briefly, just before leaving, that he was working on a new idea to sell more beer than Eagle ever had before. As a result of Harry's success, John Vonderhorst had planned a very special Christmas present for his son. With an interest going to his brother, John, Harry was to be given controlling ownership of the brewery. That was another reason he wanted to get home for the holidays.

"Papa, you wanted to see me?" asked Bernadette, walking into her father's study, rubbing her hands. She had just come in from a cold, windy day and immediately moved to the well-used fireplace where she began rubbing her arms as she smiled at the man behind his desk.

"Sweetheart, I have been putting off telling you something very important that I cannot delay any longer."

"Uh, oh," Bernadette mugged. "This is not going to be about moving to Baltimore is it?"

She had chosen not to raise the subject since her return to New York since her father hadn't. She had hoped that he had changed his mind.

"Yes, it is about going home, Bernadette, but there is more. Please come over here and sit down."

He now had her full attention and he moved from behind the desk to one of the two red leather chairs in front of it. Bernadette sat in the other.

Vonderhorst paused before he began, then, reaching out to her hand, sighed and said, "You don't know this, my dear, but Baltimore is your home as well. You were born there. Your mother's heart failed delivering you and I found you with the sisters at St. Mary's not long after."

The young woman sat very still, beyond surprised. She was once again bowled over by this man she thought she knew. Did she understand him correctly? She didn't know quite what to say, so she said nothing, afraid of what might come out.

The older man continued, "You see, sweetheart, I am your father and always will be, just not your natural father. I adopted you legally back in '57 and nothing will change that. You are my daughter and I could not love you any more than I do."

"Papa, I—" Bernadette started.

"No, wait. Let me finish. I have to get this all out. You must know it all and why I took you away from Baltimore until now. I can't keep this inside any longer," Vonderhorst said. "Your father was, plain and simple, an evil man with evil friends. He was in prison, on trial for murder, when your mother died having you. For reasons I cannot explain, your father, despite his obvious guilt, was acquitted of the charges. He disappeared immediately upon his release and has not been heard from since. That was twenty-five years ago. Since then, I have spent years trying to locate him, to no avail. Last summer, however, I received word from a reliable source of a man in Chicago on his deathbed who told a story of his life in Baltimore. The tale tracked closely with what I knew of your father. From that information, I could only conclude that he is dead and that it's safe to take you home again. That's when I wrote to you in London."

Bernadette was no child, but this was overwhelming. She sat stiffly, not moving, her adopted father's warm hand on hers. There were too many questions. All she could manage was, "You lied to me."

"I never lied," he swore quickly. "Perhaps by omission," he corrected himself just as quickly. "Bernadette, your mother did die in childbirth and her name was Henrietta. Hattie, really. Hattie English. Your father's name was John."

Vonderhorst was emotionally exhausted and felt the most he could do now was to answer her questions as best he could.

The young woman's world was shaken. Despite the assurances of this man who called himself her father, she was completely at sea. Her thoughts were scattered but she managed to conclude, "So, Harry and John are not my brothers? And you are not my father?"

"We are still your family, Bernadette. Nothing changes that," he said with feeling.

"But, you are not my real father. And Baltimore is not my home. It is your home, not mine. There is nothing in that dirty city for me. What if I choose to stay in New York? My life is here now. Emily and Jane are more family to me than the Vonderhorsts are," she observed hurtfully.

Bernadette withdrew her hand, rose unsteadily, walked to the door, opened it slowly, and closed it quietly behind her. John Vonderhorst sat and let the tears run down his face.

Over the next few days, as he made final arrangements for the move south, Vonderhorst saw little of his daughter. She spent as much time as possible away from the Park Avenue address and with her friend, Emily. He had had a long conversation with Jane Cooper who had been very understanding. In fact, her support of him in this situation was just what he needed. She had even begun to talk to Bernadette to ease her through the wrenching emotional turmoil she was experiencing. This was not going to be easy, but with Jane's help, he felt sure his daughter would remember the love shown to her over the years. He hoped she would begin to understand the decisions he had made and agree to join the family in Baltimore.

Over the next few weeks, Bernadette did come to acknowledge and appreciate her adopted father's devotion. At the same time, however, she developed a fervent desire to understand her beginnings and the parents that conceived her. Her decision to leave New York and join the Vonderhorsts in Baltimore was primarily driven by this passion. However, contributing to her change of heart was New York's high society itself. As soon as the word of Bernadette's humble roots began to circulate, the company that she had become so fond of no longer found her quite so acceptable. Although Emily Vanderbilt launched heroic efforts to rebuild her friend's status, the invitations that once were so plentiful had begun to disappear rapidly.

As she, Jane, and her father boarded the Pennsylvania Railroad train in Grand Central Station for the trip south, Bernadette was determined to find out all that she could about John and Hattie English. John Vonderhorst joined his daughter in the first-class car with decidedly mixed emotions. He could not be happier that they were going home together. On the other hand, he couldn't help but feel an uneasiness that was hard to define.

Chapter 16

Baltimore
December 1882

A portly old man sat awkwardly in one of the last pews of the dimly lit church. The final gray wisps of his hair formed a tonsure that he occasionally ran his hands through. He had adopted this habit as he focused on his conversation with his maker and away from the pain that was with him constantly now. He suffered from a variety of ailments and old wounds, but he thought of it as penance for some of the things he had done and some of the things he hadn't done in his life.

Early evening was a perfect time to visit St. Ignatius. This place and this time allowed him to be alone with his thoughts and his God. That was the way he liked it. He liked the smell of candles and incense clinging to the walls and wafting through the dim, stained glass light of the apse. He liked the muted colors of the terra cotta statues of saints. He imagined that the Virgin Mary, just to the right of the gleaming white marble altar, was smiling warmly at him, understanding him. He admired the courageous Loyola, offering his sword to God in another painting in the nave. When he looked straight up, he could see heaven and its residents looking down on him from the oval mural, high in the vaulted ceiling. And at this time of year, St. Ignatius was decorated for celebration of the Nativity, decked out in green, red, and gold floral arrangements.

This church had fought hard for a toehold in Baltimore as far back as 1852. At a time when Catholics were reviled, feared, and persecuted in Baltimore, this church had been tenacious. The Know-Nothings and their street gang auxiliaries had done their damnedest to drive the "papists" from the city. But the Jesuits were a hearty bunch, more resolute than their adversaries. They must have been, given the fact that they started this parish, and a college not long after, on the doorstep of the Plug Uglies.

W. Meade Addison had been a secret Catholic in those days and he was ashamed of that. He was ashamed that he had climbed the political patronage ladder to win the U.S. district attorney's office for Maryland at a time when no avowed Catholic was given a clerk's job, much less the powerful position he had attained. He felt guilty and prayed for forgiveness for not owning up to his faith.

After a while though, he felt better, and as always, he began to thank his Lord for the things he had and the positive things he was able to achieve in his time. He had actually been an important player in the reform efforts of those early days and liked to think that much of his work had made Baltimore a better place, more civilized.

As he sat debating whether his thoughts were worthy or simple hubris, he sensed rather than saw another enter the church and find a pew somewhere off to his left and behind him. Ignoring the distraction, he returned soon enough to his self-examination, just as the Jesuit fathers had taught him. Was it just pride? Or did he actually contribute to creating some order out of the chaos that was prewar Baltimore? As Addison considered this, he heard a swish of clothing behind him. Then he felt a searing pain at his throat and heard a high whining sound in his ears. The whining soared away into nothingness and his eyes popped as powerful hands held the garrote in place while the wire did its deadly work on the fat neck. The implacable images in the ceiling looked down on the scene and remained unmoved.

John English, now Enoch Stanton to anyone who asked, sipped an 1872 Adriano Ramos-Pinto vintage port from antique Waterford stemware and chuckled to himself. This wasn't the self-satisfied chortle of the average man. No sound was uttered. No change was seen in the man's scared face or in his one good eye. Rather, somewhere deep in the recesses of his mind, a connection had been made with earlier days, and the irony was delicious. He had come a long way from his days of rye and Eagle in Morgan's bar and he had paid the price. When he left Baltimore so many years ago, he had nothing except what he could extort from that fool, Davis. Then, he found Zachariah. The man had become his legs. He had become his arms, his eyes, and his ears. He had become the means by which English could make and execute plans. In return, English had fed, clothed, and educated the bumpkin. As a surrogate father, he had shown Zachariah a world outside of his whoring mother and the procession of depraved men who used him as well. English had given him a life other than one of fear and desperation. For that, Zachariah had become his tool. English knew that in some subconscious, animal way, the man loved him. It was this understanding that gave English all he needed to wield the idiot as if he were a human club. And that is exactly what he did.

Thank God for the war, he mused, peering through the crystal into the dark liquid. War had made his fortune. That is, the war and Presidents Johnson and Grant. Major conflict always offered opportunity for the quick and the bold, but the opportunities just kept coming, even after the fighting had stopped. In fact, English's business—the demolition, removal, and disposal of war damaged urban landscape— was very lucrative. This work required the hiring, organizing, and overseeing of huge, mobile labor gangs. His years in Baltimore had provided him with some previous experience with gangs of men, and cheap labor was plentiful. He took immediate advantage of the starving hoards of ex-slaves and Irish immigrants that were readily available. Many simply traded the slavery of a cotton field or a shucking house for harder, dirtier work. Pay was regular, but what there was of it went into English's company store or down the workmen's throats. As federal money poured into cities like Columbia, Richmond, Atlanta, Mobile, and New Orleans, English's ability to deliver large numbers of men quickly won him contract after contract. And he kept it all together with a carrot and a stick approach. The carrot was a paying job and the stick was a man named Zachariah. English's protégé had begun to show real promise in this field. He had even branched out into dealing effectively with competitive bidders.

Through the prisms of his glass, English noticed Zachariah waiting patiently at the study door.

"Come in, Zachariah, you may sit." English indicated a hard, straight-backed chair in front of the desk. "Report."

"Sir, he was there as expected. He was alone and I terminated him. No one saw or heard me, before or after. It will be considered a common robbery."

"Good. Thank you. I will have another from the list for you shortly. What can you tell me about the attorney, Wallis?"

"Severn Teakle Wallis is currently traveling in Europe. He is heading a trade delegation sponsored by the City of Baltimore. He's been there a year and it is anticipated that he will be there for another," reported Zachariah.

"That's too bad," commented English. "He will have to wait. What about the five names I gave you? The ex-cops?"

"Two died at Antietam and one at Gettysburg, another committed suicide in '59. I found the fifth man in a boarding house in Locust Point, near Fort McHenry. He will be discovered as the tide comes back in," reported the agent in his usual flat voice.

"Well done. Now, what can you tell me about the others?" continued English.

"Sir, James Morgan disappeared in November of 1857 after shooting two policemen. He killed one of them, a man named William Barton, known as Big Bill. Morgan does not show up on any of the standard casualty or prisoner lists for either army, there is no record of his mustering out and he has not been heard from since the day he shot Barton."

This news did not make English happy. Morgan had betrayed him and he was a loose end. His former friend must be found or his death verified. Morgan was also too dangerous a man to not be accounted for.

"That is not satisfactory, Zachariah, keep looking. Recheck the roles of both armies," ordered the older man sharply.

Zachariah had adopted a character that included a lack of outward emotions, so his frustration with the inability to trace Morgan did not show. Just the same, he had disappointed his employer and that could not stand.

The assassin continued his report. "John Vonderhorst is very much alive. He spends a lot of time in New York but returns regularly to Baltimore. He has grown very wealthy through his Eagle Brewery, railroad investments, and insurance. The brewery has gotten bigger and it remains in operation up on North Avenue. Vonderhorst's son, Henry, known as Harry, currently manages it. The senior Vonderhorst is very well connected both here and in New York and remains active in both politics and social reform. While a second son, John, lives in

San Francisco, the two local men share a large home out on Frederick Road."

"That's very good news. With this one, we'll need to be especially cautious. I will think about it and we'll talk again," replied English. "Now, for the subject of most interest. Have you completed your investigation into the child's whereabouts?"

Zachariah was not looking forward to this conversation. His patron was obsessed with a baby girl that was born in Baltimore in 1857. All the factotum could find was the hospital birth record and the release of the baby to James Morgan. After that, he had hit a brick wall. Both orphanage and court records had been sealed and access to them would be a problem. Zachariah didn't even know whether further records even existed. Inquiries in the Biddle Street neighborhood produced nothing. Adoption agencies would not talk to him, even with the sizable bribes he had offered. It seemed that the baby had evaporated into thin air, or someone had helped her to disappear twenty-five years ago.

"No, sir. I have not. I have a report of the child's birth at the Union Protestant Infirmary off of Pennsylvania Avenue. We also know that the child was last seen with James Morgan. I am continuing to talk to people who may have been connected to either the baby or Morgan. But the war or the hangman's noose has taken its toll of his former associates. Perhaps if we find Morgan, we'll find the girl," Zachariah proposed.

English exploded. This took the form of an arm sweep that sent the port flying in his man's direction. He stood using the desk as a prop, his still strong arms and shoulders keeping him steady. Leaning forward and locked on Zachariah's eyes, he spoke menacingly, "Haven't I given you everything? Haven't I changed your miserable life? I ask you for very little and now you disappoint me. I must know what happened to that baby and where she is today. Do you understand? Do you?" spat English.

As Zachariah wiped the wine from his face and shirt front, he looked down, abashed. He spoke quietly and without meeting the eyes that had suddenly come alive with near insanity. "I will find her. I will find them both," the agent said simply.

Chapter 17

Baltimore
May 1883

It wasn't long after Bernadette and her father joined Harry in the big house in Baltimore that she began to seek information on her natural father. It was all there in excruciating detail in the public record of the trial. Her relationship to the accused and her adopted father's influence also opened the court's detailed record of the proceedings to her. Additional information was available in the archives of *The Sun,* the *American News,* and *The Gazette.* There was no lack of personal stories available either. Memories are long in Baltimore and a beautiful woman can open a lot of doors and mouths.

Bernadette feverishly excavated her roots for five months. During that time, she traveled the streets and learned the neighborhoods. She walked the trail of events and talked to people involved. She could be found in City Hall, the Municipal Building, on the docks, and in firehouses. She spoke to old men in smoky corner bars and she spoke to old men sitting around ornate dinner tables. She interviewed retired judges, cops, reporters, carriage men, and former slaves.

After all of this research, Bernadette felt she had a thorough idea of what had happened. And she was appalled by it. This was a story and a place that she could not have imagined. Her European life did not create a naïf. Any innocence she once had didn't last long in the jaded world of privilege, excess, and abuse that was normal behavior among the rich and the courtiers of the old world. But at least there had been rules. In the Baltimore of 1857, men made their own rules. In the end, her reasoning found the story indecent and unacceptable. The world had come farther than that, certainly.

Just the same, her eyes were opened forever. It wasn't just the violent and antisocial life of her father, as disturbing and sad as that was. It was this city, Baltimore. It fascinated and frightened her. Constantly in the throes of fury and change, it was a living, heaving thing—a huge, angry bear in chains. She could hear the beast's soul-wrenching roar as it struggled against its shackles, twisting and shaking and baring its yellow fangs. It was an animal taunted by the crowd at a medieval fair. It was contained chaos, and its handlers played a dangerous game. But as long as the chains held, they made a living with it, some a better living than others.

She learned that her mother's full name was Henrietta Simpson English, known as Hattie to her family and friends. Hattie's parents had passed on in 1846, apparently from consumption. No brothers or sisters. Hattie's Certificate of Death listed the cause as "heart failure." The attending doctor signed it at 5:55 p.m. on April 16, 1857. Bernadette also found that her mother had been buried quietly in a public graveyard on the west side, now home to a dry goods warehouse. Relocations of the deceased were made when the building went up, but that's where the record stopped.

There was no trace whatsoever of her father. John Vonderhorst had been looking for him off and on for over twenty years without success. Bernadette got no further than her adopted father did. However, she was able to determine that there were two men who could tell her the most: former Congressman Henry Winter Davis, and a one-time associate of her father's, a man by the name of James Morgan.

Davis was John English's attorney during the trial and reportedly was the last person to see him alive. Unfortunately, Davis died a mysterious death of unknown causes in 1865 and was buried in the Greenmount Cemetery, not far from the Eagle Brewery. Inquiries at the lawyer's firm produced an officious attorney named Cooke who was part of the English defense team as a young man. But he could offer nothing to the whereabouts of his former client after the trial.

That left this specter, James Morgan. Bernadette knew that Morgan was as lawless and immoral as her father was. Together, they led the Plug Uglies street gang that had become all too familiar to her. Morgan was wanted for the murder of a policeman and the wounding of another that same awful year of 1857, and he was still at large.

The fugitive had not been seen since the shooting and no one seemed to be looking for him. So many had died in the war.

It was one of those rare nights that the Vonderhorsts had the opportunity to have dinner together. Jane, now a valuable part of the family, had taken over the management of the household and had decided that they should dress, use the formal dining room, and lay out the Kirk silverware and Spode china.

As the servants moved in and out with dishes, John, Harry, Bernadette, and Jane chatted about a range of things. Bernadette spoke of her plans for the upcoming eleventh Preakness, touting a colt named Jacobus. Harry recounted, pin by pin, the winning of his most recent bowling ribbon and, as usual, managed to make them all laugh. Jane told them of the opening of the World's Fair in Amsterdam that she had read about in *Puck*. The elder Vonderhorst offered a synopsis of Twain's new *Life on the Mississippi*. Then he rendered a less-than-enthusiastic opinion of Robert Louis Stevenson's latest, *Treasure Island,* finding it "for children." And everyone cheered the news that the younger John Vonderhorst was unaffected by the latest earthquake on the Pacific Coast.

By dessert and coffee, the conversation had turned to more serious subjects. Harry had been made owner of the brewery this past Christmas and he gave the family a brief first quarter financial report and an overview of plans for the rest of the year. In the process, he broached a topic that was still a sore subject between him and his father.

"Papa, beer sales are up fifteen percent this spring. We are selling out at every Orioles game. Ticket sales and food concessions have added another eight thousand dollars despite the fact that the team is losing."

Harry had been infected with the idea of owning a baseball team ever since a professional league had been founded in 1876. He also played the sport in school and loved testing his considerable skills and muscled frame against others like him. Among his minor regrets was his inability to hit the horsehide with any degree of consistency, despite the fact that he could go get a fly ball with the best of them. He was an unabashed *crank* and could discuss the Beaneaters of Boston in the National League or Philly's Athletics in the new American Association. He was known to be able to quote the batting average of Dan Brouthers or the runs-batted-in of Cap Anson. He loved baseball and he loved entertaining in the owner's box.

Back in January, Harry had made a decision. He had been trying for months to erode his father's opposition to sponsoring the Baltimore Orioles as a business proposition. Finally, citing the fact that he was now the owner of the brewery, and that he was responsible for all business decisions, he informed his father that the Eagle Brewery had purchased the team and Eagle's sponsorship would go forward with the start of the 1883 baseball season.

"Harry, you know how I feel about your investing in baseball. It's just a passing fancy. Those who drink Eagle, while wasting time in that park of yours, will soon be looking for somewhere else to waste time and drink Eagle. Either way, they drink Eagle. The team is five and twelve and have lost eight in a row," he observed, perhaps revealing his own growing interest in the sport and the team. "What are you going to do when they get tired of a losing team?"

"Papa, Henderson's hurt and Gallagher's been in an early slump. They'll start to win a few games. It's early yet."

But Harry's defense of the Orioles rang hollow. They were not a good team and were picked to finish dead last, even behind the woeful Alleghenies of Pittsburgh. The problems were many: porous fielding, aging pitchers with sore arms, weak hitting, alcoholism, and in general, a bad attitude. Despite this, Baltimore had a professional team and people were still coming.

While Bernadette liked attending the games, her interest in baseball was more social than anything else. Harry and his friends were fun and she never tired of observing the cauldron of human stew that filled the seats. It was futile, however, to attempt to get her excited about the sport. This evening was no different and she had other things on her mind anyway.

"Papa, you told me one time that you 'found' me with the nuns who served the priests at St. Mary's Seminary. Do you know how I got there? Do you know a man named James Morgan?" This abrupt change in the conversation signaled Bernadette's distraction and elicited raised eyebrows around the table.

"Bernadette, perhaps this is not the time. . .," began Jane.

Harry said nothing, surprised at his sister's train of thought but glad to move away from talking about the Orioles with his father.

"It's quite all right, Jane, I want to answer any questions she might have," said the elder Vonderhorst. "Yes, Bernadette, I knew James Morgan. He was close to your father. What brings him to mind?"

"Well, when I was checking the birth records from the old Union Protestant Hospital, I found that, after my mother died, I was released to someone named James Morgan. So, I started to research him. He ran the Plug Uglies with my father. He was also a rough customer. All I know is that he's wanted for killing a policeman and is now missing. Some believe that he died in the war. What I can't understand, what I can't picture, is this ruffian spiriting me away when I was an infant."

"Sweetheart, it's been a long time since I thought about James Morgan. You are right. He was as bad as they come. But there is more to the story and the man than that. Morgan was a complex character. Oddly, he was devoted to you and your mother. Not only did he get her to the hospital in time to save you, but he also buried Hattie and found a home for you with the nuns, albeit a temporary one. I know he visited you there frequently. I saw him at St. Mary's myself while I was arranging the adoption. He was not happy about it and it was worth my life to press the issue."

"Why, Papa? What was my mother and me to him?" she asked.

"I'm not sure, Bernadette, perhaps it was loyalty to English. Perhaps it was feelings for your mother."

"Then, if he was so loyal to the point of being dangerous, why did you do it? Why did you adopt me? Why did you want me? What was I to you then?"

John Vonderhorst hesitated. These were questions he had asked himself many times. Did he do it out of revenge? Did he do it out of hatred for a man who had just escaped what he believed was justice? Was it outrage and frustration over his inability to achieve both of his objectives in getting involved in the trial? None of those motives were very admirable. Could he explain himself sufficiently to his daughter so that she didn't hate him for it? He wasn't sure, but he knew he was not going to lie to her.

"Bernadette, I'm not proud of this and I hope you understand. I adopted you because I couldn't bear to see your father go unpunished.

Once I saw you, I knew that I could not let that devil of a man have you. I was playing God, I know, but I believed I was doing the right thing and I still believe that."

Bernadette sat staring, stunned yet again by something this man told her. Jane moved to her, putting her arm around her.

"Bernadette, regardless of why the adoption took place, your father loves you and has proven that to you time and time again."

"There is more to the story, sweetheart," said Vonderhorst, his voice quavering. "I said James Morgan was a complicated man."

The older Vonderhorst looked directly at Harry, then back to Bernadette.

"Just before he disappeared, he came to me at the old plant. He wanted to talk to me about you, about my adopting you. He seemed ready to challenge me. I know he was armed. You were with me, Harry, so I told you to meet me in the carriage house. I told you I would be along shortly. But the conversation with Morgan never took place. Arsonists had started a fire in the main building and it was going up like a torch. The carriage house was on fire as well. Everything was in chaos. Men were running everywhere, some were screaming, trapped in the fire. Just as I realized that I had sent you into danger, Harry, there were gunshots and I was hurt pretty badly. The next thing I know, I'm laying in the yard office, and you, Harry, are sitting next to me, crying, but alive and unhurt. The foreman told me later that James Morgan had gone into the burning barn, found Harry and carried him out. That was the last we saw of him. That night, in the hospital, I learned that Morgan had shot two policemen, killing the one named Barton. That was the last anyone has heard of him."

Harry sat at the dining table, swirling the last of his wine, lost in a hazy memory of a fire and a big man who found him in a carriage. Bernadette's eyes filled and Jane put her arm around her shoulders. The ex-nanny could only look at John Vonderhorst in wonder.

Chapter 18

Baltimore
May 1883

James Morgan stepped off the Old Bay Line's paddlewheel steamer *Eolus* and onto the Pratt Street dock in Baltimore. He stood for a long minute among his baggage and continued to feel the roll of the sea. He had been on steamers, clippers, and a variety of packet boats for several weeks as he made his way from New Orleans. He still wasn't sure that this was the smart thing to do, but his heart over-ruled his head and here he was. As he grew older, he felt the increasing demand of his roots. Even with all of his travels and all of the things he had seen in twenty-five years, he came back here. It wasn't until recently that he realized he missed Baltimore. For years, he had told himself that he had escaped a hell. But now he knew that hell was one of his own making. Maybe that was it. Maybe he had come back to see if he could make something other than a hell.

The city looked much the same to him, a little cleaner perhaps and the streets were wider. But when he directed the cabman to Barnum's, he was told that the place had been allowed to fall into disrepair and that a gentleman such as he would be much more comfortable at The Carrollton Hotel. So, his few but expensive bags were loaded and he sat in the hansom getting a new feel for his old home as they made their way to the hotel on the corner of Light and Baltimore streets.

The cabbie stopped in front of a six-story monster whose mansard roof was topped with a series of structures that reminded Morgan of siege towers. The building covered an entire city square with its rows of arched windows and ornate scrollwork. Climbing out of the cab, he amused himself by thinking that the towers must be where they put their archers.

The hotel was abuzz with activity, people moving with purpose. Two black, liveried porters immediately picked up his baggage and began walking into the columned entrance of the hotel.

"One moment there, boy. That small one stays with me," Morgan already had the man's wrist and was squeezing it.

"Of course, sir. Of course, here you are," said the bellman politely, handing Morgan what he wanted. "No offense meant," he said deferentially.

"No offense taken," growled Morgan and turned back to pay the cabman. As he turned, the porters shot each other a look that passed judgment on the latest white asshole to check into The Carrollton.

Morgan graced the well-to-do ladies in the gleaming entrance foyer with a smile and he ignored the frock-coated gentlemen populating the massive, velvet-covered lobby. That he was not quite one of their own was their impression. Thanks to the amenities aboard the packet from Norfolk, his dark, tailored suit was brushed and pressed. Under it, he wore a soft, wide-collared shirt with onyx studs and a narrow necktie, tied in a bow. The left sleeve of the suit was pinned back neatly. His hat was not one of those detestable toppers, but a Homburg with a lower crown and a wider brim. As he walked toward the front desk, his boots reflected the dustless chandeliers, hanging in a row from the high ceiling.

He must be Southern, the other guests thought. No, with that face, perhaps he was from out West. Some were sure he was an ex-reb; others saw him as maybe one of those Horse Soldiers.

"I'd like to speak to someone about an extended stay," said Morgan to a desk clerk in a waistcoat.

"Sir, do you have a reservation?" asked the clerk politely enough.

"No, I do not. But I am willing to pay you for a month's stay right now," answered Morgan, cutting the dance short.

"One moment, sir," said the man as he spun a wheel of index cards. "Yes, I believe we can accommodate you, Mister ah. . . ."

"Wells, Ulysses Wells," said Morgan as he signed the ledger the clerk slid in front of him. "I'll be paying with a draft on the Bank of New Orleans. Tell me what I owe you. Oh, and I'll be needing the use of your safe."

He had been assigned a suite on the top floor that looked north and west. The view across the rooftops was only broken by the occasional taller building and a forest of steeples he remembered from earlier days. Spread in front of him and running to the horizon were the neighborhoods of his youth.

It occurred to him that today was his sixtieth birthday and, not for the first time, he thought, *I'm running out of time.*

His life had kept Morgan fit, but his hair was an equal mix of curly black and gray. The crows feet, carved at the corners of his eyes by the sun and the passing years, were yet another sign that he was no longer a young man. While this was well-known to him, he was always surprised by what he saw in mirrors.

He turned away from the window to the glass and mahogany table that held the bottle of Sherbrook Rye that he had ordered. Pouring two fingers and adding soda, he turned back to the urban landscape and raised the glass.

"Happy Birthday, Jamie, and welcome home," he said out loud to the tarred rooftops.

The next morning, Morgan retrieved his small, locked bag from the hotel safe and walked into the spacious main dining room to have breakfast. He had an hour to wait, since the First National Bank across the street would not open until nine. Both the dining room and the lobby had been decorated in equine-themed bunting and banners, proclaiming that today was something called Preakness Day. The room was crowded and he was seated alone but not far from other guests.

"Black coffee, orange juice, bacon, eggs over easy, and toast," he said to the waiter who had inquired. "And this morning's *Sun*."

"Certainly, sir. Will that be all?" the professional said.

"Can you tell me, just what is Preakness Day?" asked Morgan, indicating the decorations. He noticed that his question elicited a giggle and some interest from two very attractive, well-dressed women in soaring, be-feathered hats. The women were sharing the table next to his.

"Allow me to explain to the gentleman, William," said one of the ladies.

"Yes, ma'am, Mrs. Tilghman," said the waiter. Then to Morgan, "I'll bring the paper and your breakfast, sir," and he was off.

Morgan turned to the women, smiled, and said, "You'll have to excuse me. I have just arrived in the city."

With that, the two modern-minded women invited him to join them and rapidly made room at the table. Their realization that he was one armed caused a moment's hesitation, but they quickly became fascinated by his deft compensation and economy of motion.

"Pardon, my asking, Mister ah. . . ." began one of the bold women.

"Forgive me for not introducing myself, ladies," said Morgan, who in truth had not had the opportunity. "My name is Ulysses Wells. I am from New Orleans and this is my first time in Baltimore," he lied.

The ladies didn't seem much for all of the "forgive me's," the "pardon me's" and the "you'll have to excuse me's" because they assessed him openly and were not shy in their conversation.

"Was it the war that took your arm? How did it happen? Was your recovery very terrible, Mr. Wells?" inquired the slightly younger of the two ladies, unable to resist a tale of heroism.

"Yes, ma'am," answered Morgan. "The Yankee artillery had its way with us at Cedar Creek."

"We're very sorry to hear that. Don't ever think that your sacrifice went unappreciated," said the other lady with an expression of sympathy.

As Morgan drank the coffee and ate his breakfast, he learned that Amanda and Rosalee were, in fact, in town for Preakness Day. The Preakness, they explained, was an annual horse race and, in the preceding ten years that it had been run, it had become a social event not to be missed. The ladies were sisters from Maryland's Eastern Shore who had been introduced by their deceased husbands, may they rest in peace, to the Sport of Kings. So, each spring, the two migrated across the Bay for the parties and to see who would win the stake and take home the Woodlawn Vase. This bit of crockery was a huge monstrosity of polished silver that the winner was punished with maintaining until someone else won the race the following year.

The event was unusual this spring because it was a two-horse race. The favorite, Jacobus, was to be ridden by none other than the famous English rider, George Barbee. The colt's challenger was a precocious, young bay called Parnell, named by his wealthy owner for Charles Stewart Parnell, the Irish nationalist land reformer.

"What brings you to Baltimore all the way from New Orleans, Mr. Wells?" asked Rosalee with interest.

Morgan continued to lie, "My business is petroleum and mining, and I'm here seeking a partner to assist in distribution." There, that should be intimidating and boring enough to prevent further questions, he thought.

"We thought you might be a southerner. A gentleman is always easy to identify," purred Amanda. "Well, you simply must come to the races with us today, Mr. Wells. The Carrollton has arranged a box for us and it would be so much nicer if a man of your distinction escorted us."

Morgan doubted if either of the two women needed escorting anywhere.

"I don't know," he said. "My wife only died a year ago and I'm not used to. . . ." said Morgan, hesitating, laying it on thick.

"That's all the more reason you should come! Now, no more arguments, it's a beautiful day and it will be fun. You'll see. The hotel will put together a basket for us. We'll meet in the lobby at eleven and take our barouche out to Pimlico," said Amanda with finality.

As Morgan walked across the street to the bank, he thought, Well, there's something new about my old town. When he left Baltimore, he had some experience with horses, of course. But, it wasn't until he had joined Mosby and ridden with the Forty-Third Battalion of the First Virginia Cavalry that he learned to appreciate them. The opportunity to watch racing horses of this caliber was rare. The opportunity to understand Baltimore at this level of society also may not come again easily. Besides, he liked the two ladies.

The tall southerner calling himself Wells entered the bank and sat in a comfortable leather chair in a waiting area while an account manager took his time arranging the paper and pens on his desk. Morgan opened the newspaper and skimmed it until an article caught his eye. The piece was talking about how the Baltimore Police, after five months, finally had a suspect in the robbery and murder of W. Meade Addison, former U.S. district attorney for Maryland. Addison had been strangled to death in a pew of the old St. Ignatius Church. The suspect was a Negro vagrant who had been seen loitering nearby on St. Paul Street. Addison, Morgan recalled, was the name of the man who had prosecuted John English.

Chapter 19

Baltimore
May 1883

The ride out to the racecourse, or Old Hilltop, as the ladies called it, was full of ghosts for Morgan. They drove north up Charles Street, nearly to Mount Vernon Square. Then turned left on Franklin, right past St. Mary's College and Seminary. Once they reached Pennsylvania, they turned northeast onto the avenue past Orchard and Biddle, the old neighborhood of the Plug Uglies, the Oyster House, and his home on Orchard. Neither the bar nor the house was still there, and the Plugs had been long gone. Improvement in the quality of housing had been made, and the smells were gone, but the rough ward and its people were much the same.

By the time they crossed North Avenue, he had grown quiet, not that he had been able to say very much during the ride since the ladies were very chatty. But, eventually, the two women turned to each other, apparently having some catching up to do. This left Morgan with a copy of *The American Turf Register and Sporting Magazine*, picked up from a hawker outside the hotel.

The carriage moved quickly and, in due course, the flag-topped, gleaming white, wooden structure of the racecourse grandstand came into view. Ultimately, they could see the box seats and the broad apron below them that stretched to the track and its outer rail. Here, there was an explosion of color and movement as the racing crowd came into view. The throng fanned out on either side of the finish line, running ten deep along the rail, from the top of the stretch to the first turn. In front of them was a meticulously raked, chestnut-colored racetrack.

This perfect surface enclosed an oval of green grass, sporting a small hillock in its center. This mound, Amanda explained, is what gives the track its nickname of Old Hilltop and is where the trainers and jockeys meet ahead of each race.

As the barouche slowed with traffic, Rosalee sang happily, "This is going to be a party! Look at the hats!" Then she laughed, "I'm so sorry, Mr. Wells, I know your interests are not in millenary."

Quickly, Amanda then said, "There are some very worthy preliminary races today, as well as the stakes, Mr. Wells. Are you a betting man?" She challenged him with a twinkle in her eye.

"Oh, must we continue to be so formal, Mr. Wells?" Rosalee asked with feigned exasperation. "Would it be fine if we just called you Ulee? I'm Rosie and she's Mandy. Tomorrow, we can worry about convention."

This sudden rush of attention stirred Morgan from his handicapping. He sat up, took his hat off, leaned forward, and said with a younger man's grin, "Mandy, I'm betting that you and Rosie don't worry very much about convention."

Morgan settled the ladies in an excellent box, one or two rows removed from the owners and the members of the Maryland Jockey Club. Much of the formally dressed crowd here knew each other and those who didn't were rapidly being introduced. He assisted the opening of chilled white wine, uncovered a basket of fresh strawberries, and made sure the ladies where getting along with their neighbors. Tucking *The Turf Register* under his empty sleeve, he left them and went to explore the facility, its amenities, and its patrons. He bought an Eagle beer, found a cheroot, leaned against a wooden column, and watched the swirling chaos. Heads with silk top hats mixed with those wearing bowlers and workman's caps. Women wore fancy concoctions of flowers and feathers and some were simply covered with a threadbare scarf. All came together in a kaleidoscopic sea of humanity. Morgan's purpose was to identify the professionals who made the whole thing go: the horsemen, the stewards, the odds makers, the touts, and the handicappers. Swarming around them was the betting public and a variety of grifters plying their trade.

Morgan spotted an odds maker working the first race of the day. He checked the *Register*, finished off his beer, and stubbed out the smoke. Shouldering his way through the crowd to the sound of a few brief complaints, he made his bet and plowed back through the mass to the boxes.

Arriving, he found the ladies fully engaged with the four gentlemen in the adjacent box. Pleasant, but cursory introductions were made and Morgan sat down, surveying the track and its infield.

The horses were out of the paddock and warming for the first race. There were eight beautiful, strapping colts, dancing and straining against their lead ponies. The warmth of the bright, beautiful day and prerace nerves drew the sweat from the animals, giving them a sheen that worked to highlight their muscular, shuddering flanks. Wild eyed, nostrils flaring, ears pricked back, the racers knew what was about to happen and were impatient to get started. The huge, deafening crowd added a further layer to the beasts' anxiety and distraction. As a result, the jockeys rode high on their mounts, working hard to keep their charges focused on the task ahead.

"Ladies, have you made your bets for this race?" asked Morgan, as Mandy poured him a glass of wine.

"Oh, no, Ulee!" they cried.

"We were chatting. Is it too late? I really like that gray!" said Rosie.

"Well, I'm afraid it is," answered Morgan, as the racers skipped and pranced their way to an acceptable standing start. "But, this must be your lucky day because I bought both of you a win ticket on the gray. His name is Ghostly and we've got him at 10-1."

The women were thrilled and gushed over him, calling him "courtly," "considerate," and "sweet." Morgan grinned to hear such words applied to him as he handed over the modest bets, which the ladies clutched as if they were already winners.

"How did you ever pick him?" asked Mandy, craning to watch her horse come into line.

Morgan was having fun, a rarity in his life. "You know what they say," he laughed. "Once a day, bet a gray!"

The women were delighted and made a very feminine sound as the flag was dropped and the horses bolted off, bumping and snapping at each other until the jockeys could get them under control and focused on the first turn.

The crowd roared the entire time, but the noise became nearly unbearable as the field reached the top of the stretch and turned for home. A large chestnut led a knot of horseflesh charging for the finish. The crowd was in a frenzy and so were Morgan's companions. Their hats, and the fancies atop them, bobbed up and down as the ladies bounced and clapped with excitement.

Morgan's research on the way to the racecourse began to pay dividends as the gray was closing on the leader. *The Turf Register* had suggested that the first race was full of horses stretching out to the distance for the first time. There had been one exception: Ghostly had already won once at the distance.

The racers came pounding past in a colorful blur, men and horses straining together. The tension among the crowd was exquisite. The big gray headed the leader, then got his nose in front on a head bob, just as they crossed the finish line.

"Did we win? Did we win?" screamed Mandy and Rosie, hopping up and down.

"I do believe we got there," answered Morgan, feeling happy and smug.

The rest of the afternoon wasn't quite so successful and their winnings had eroded. But, as Morgan explained, it's always more fun when you play with someone else's money. The ladies couldn't care one way or the other. They had managed to extend their circle to all of the boxes around them and the party was in full swing.

Morgan sat back and scanned the cream of Baltimore society all around him. There were still a few minutes before the feature race and he had already placed the women's bets. He saw no value in betting such a short field, but he wanted to see the two well-bred animals run. He was enjoying himself, but he knew too that it wouldn't last. He had unfinished business and the next day would be sobering. Tomorrow, he would start his search for English, Gambrill, Vonderhorst, and the baby girl the brewer had adopted.

Idly, he watched the crowd, occasionally focusing on a beautiful woman or following the mannerisms of a wealthy man. It was hard not to recognize the huge gulf between these privileged people and those in the Biddle Street neighborhood in which he had grown up. For that matter, the patrons of the boxes were very different from those he had known in the war, those he had traveled with over the years, and those he had left behind in innumerable towns and cities.

As his vision swept along the showy people in front of him, he noticed one particular young lady who almost seemed to glow. A wide hat of some cream-colored, gauzy material hid her face, but the animation of her conversation gave Morgan an occasional flash of an ear, a chin, a nose, or lips. Her distinguished male companions were tall and dressed in light-gray frock coats sporting two covered buttons on the back. Their stovepipes matched their coats and trousers and gave them additional height. One was younger than the other but both wore trim, Van Dyke beards.

A man who stood in the aisle in front of him abruptly blocked Morgan's view of the group. He was a thick man, well constructed, and of average height. He wore a black bowler hat and a short, dark jacket that was fastened so that the watch chain, hanging from his plain vest, showed. His shirt was collarless and buttoned to the neck. His right hand was stuffed in the pocket of his coat. He seemed better suited to the grandstand than loitering among this fashionable crowd. The two racers had just been called to the post, but the idler's concentration was on the same party that had caught Morgan's attention.

The older of the two men in the box rose, spoke to his friends and started up the aisle, apparently on his way to arrange a wager. The man in the bowler followed an aisle away, unnoticed.

Morgan suddenly started. He rose quickly, made hurried apologies to Mandy and Rosie, and moved rapidly to intercept the bearded gentleman and his shadow. His effort was in vain, however, losing both men in the crowd, now pressing to watch the main event. So, he stood at the top of the aisle, just outside of the entrance to the grandstand and waited.

Morgan could not believe it. He marveled at the coincidence. He was almost sure that he had recognized John Vonderhorst. That realization drew his eyes back to the young lady in the box. But the race was close now and the aisles were jammed with those hoping for a better view. As he swayed back and forth, trying to see around the wall of bodies, Vonderhorst deftly pushed past him and immediately was absorbed into the mass as he worked his way back to his party. Morgan looked for the man in the bowler and found him one aisle over,

attention still locked on Vonderhorst. Morgan had too much experience not to notice the signs of a weapon hidden in the man's pocket.

The world around him detonated as the flag went down and the two
thoroughbreds sprinted off, gaining speed. They raced as a matched
pair around the first turn while the jockeys took the measure of their
mounts and each other. Both had been ordered to keep the race close,
the trainers fearing that too big a lead might come back to bite them in
the home stretch. The noise lessened in the run along the backstretch,
but not by much. Morgan, ignoring the contest, wove his way against
the grain of the crowd, attempting to move over an aisle and behind
the stalker.

Now, the two combatants thundered into the turn at the top of
the home stretch in impressive time. The horse called Parnell led by a
half length, but the Englishman, Barbee, had his mount moving like a
locomotive. The all-out dash to the wire, after a mile and a half of controlled exertion, would be the ultimate test of the animals' breeding
and the trainers' preparation. The jockeys and their mounts were one
as they drove furiously down the track. These last few seconds were
what both lived for. Competitive man and instinctual horse strained as
one to answer the imperative of their dual nature: be first.

Morgan had managed to reach the adjacent aisle, but the stocky
man had moved. The noise was all encompassing as Jacobus reached
deep inside to cross the finish line a half length in front of his
challenger. The overwhelming din was now a mix of delighted shrieks
and bellowed disappointment. Morgan spied Vonderhorst's hunter,
still frustrated by the hoard of people who were now either celebrating
wildly or shaking their heads in regret.

He could see Amanda and Rosalee laughing and hugging each other
and he noticed the Vonderhorst party doing the same. As the losers
began to melt back up the aisle, Morgan propelled himself through
them as the stocky man closed on his prey. He arrived behind the
assassin just as the man's hand was emerging from his pocket. Grabbing the hand curled around the weapon, Morgan smashed it against
the iron rail of the box. A long stiletto fell to the floor and immediately
was kicked away by unsuspecting feet, shuffling up the aisle.

The knife man was quick and immediately threw a left hand at
Morgan's head. Expecting it, Morgan ducked and yanked a Henry
Sears knife from his boot. His adversary already had a pocket derringer

in hand. The people nearest them shrank back from the two combatants, but most of the crowd was unaware of the deadly struggle and
continued their march back to the grandstand. Realizing his situation,
the stocky man chose to use the close quarters to put bodies between
himself and this formidable, one-armed adversary. He stared hard at
Morgan, then turned and bulled his way into the grandstand entrance.

John Vonderhorst, sensing a disturbance behind him, turned
in enough time to see two men scuffling. He got a good look at one
who began charging after the other who was disappearing into the
grandstand.

"What was that, Papa?" asked Harry when the older man turned
back to him and Bernadette.

"Oh, nothing. Just two idiots fighting over their losses, I suspect,"
answered Vonderhorst with a disturbed look.

Morgan had lost his man and by the time he returned to the boxes,
Vonderhorst was gone as well. He walked over to Mandy and Rosie
who were saying their goodbyes, exchanging addresses, and packing
up the picnic basket.

"So there you are, Ulee. Where were you? You missed a great race
and we won!" said a happy and slightly tipsy Rosie. "Wasn't this a
great day?"

"Yes, it was," he said, "a day full of surprises." He signaled one of
the available porters to take the basket and took her on his right arm
while Mandy tucked her arm under his left sleeve. The three made
their way up the aisle and eventually out to the women's carriage.

The trip back to The Carrollton was uneventful since the
unconventional ladies took very conventional naps, brought on by
the day's excitement and the abundance of chilled Riesling. This left
Morgan once again alone with his thoughts.

There were so many questions. Who wants Vonderhorst dead and
why? It could be for any reason; twenty-five years was a long time
ago and the man certainly knew how to make enemies. Hell, the last
time he saw the German, someone had shot him in the stomach. It
couldn't be that same old feud. And who was left alive from the old
days anyway? But, Morgan couldn't help putting the afternoon's
events together with the newspaper story on the murder of Addison.

He wondered what had happened to others involved in that infamous trial. Was Henry Davis still alive? And what was the name of that other reformer whose big mouth was in the papers every day? Wallis was the name he recalled.

It wasn't long before these thoughts were eclipsed by his memory of the young woman in the Vonderhorst box. The other man looked so much like his older companion that he had to be young Harry. But the woman. Was it Bernadette? Or was the beautiful girl Harry's wife or lady friend? The two did seem close.

By the time they arrived at the hotel, the questions had multiplied. But he knew exactly where he would start to find answers. If he couldn't readily find a home or office for John Vonderhorst, he would simply go back to the Eagle Brewery and start the search there.

Morgan woke the two sleeping beauties gently, assisted them to their suite, and thanked them for inviting him to the races. Mandy, not bothering to communicate anything but the fact that she needed something for her headache, kissed him on the cheek and disappeared into the room. Rosie, in similar shape as her sister, gave him a hug and half-heartedly hinted that she might have more energy later. Morgan made a gentle excuse about a previous commitment, thanked her again, and took his leave.

Chapter 20

Baltimore
May 1883

It was late, even for a Sunday, and John Vonderhorst was the first to the breakfast table. Jane had been in and out, of course, but Harry and Bernadette were perhaps feeling the effects of the day at the races and the endless parties afterwards. Those two seemed to be spending a lot of time together, he thought idly. Pushing his half-eaten plate away, he eased back in the chair. It was raining heavily and the water was sheeting down the French glass doors that led out onto the back lawn. He was feeling every bit of his seventy years this wet morning. His head was swimming with questions and he needed to sort them out first by clarifying what he knew.

He thought, without a doubt, James Morgan is alive and back in Baltimore. And it was clear that he recognized him, as well. And then there was the happening at the Preakness that involved Morgan in a fight, who then chased someone into the grandstand. This set of sureties began to raise so many additional questions that the old man felt exhausted just thinking about them.

Harry and Bernadette appeared in the carved oak archway of the breakfast room. They were laughing hard over a shared experience from the previous night and tried to ease out of it when they realized that their father was still at the table.

"Good morning, Papa," chirped Bernadette, seemingly none the worst for wear and oblivious to the dismal weather. "Sorry I'm running a little late this morning." She kissed him on the top of his head and plunked herself down next to him.

"Me too," said Harry. He sat down on the other side and reached for the covered dish on the table, only to find that Bernadette had gotten there first.

"What a great day yesterday was, right Harry? We had so much fun! Your friends are in need of some serious counseling, my brother. I'm too old and sophisticated for that stuff they were up to," she laughed.

"Yeah, you're too sophisticated. That's it. That's why you started most of the nonsense," Harry countered.

"What nonsense?" asked Jane coming in with a fresh carafe of hot coffee. She poured the new arrivals and herself a cup, set the pot on a trivet, and joined the family.

"Oh, nothing," said Bernadette in a tattling voice. "Just that Harry was talked into a silly wager that the Orioles would win the pennant within his lifetime."

"That was your idea, Bernadette, not mine! And it's within the next ten years!" sputtered Harry. "How did I get involved with your wager, anyway? The Orioles are in last place! You should not talk to those idiot friends of mine. All they want to do is get a good laugh, especially if it's on me," he said with a mouthful of eggs.

John Vonderhorst listened to the light chatter with a fixed, half smile. It was clear that his attention was elsewhere. In fact, he was thinking of the best way to tell them that he saw James Morgan behind them in the boxes at the races. He was not going to deal with the man by himself this time. He needed other heads to consider the possible reasons Morgan might have for appearing again after so many years. He didn't know what those reasons were, but he knew Bernadette must be involved, and maybe Harry too.

"Pardon me, you two," interrupted Vonderhorst. "I need you to listen to me seriously for a few minutes. Something happened yesterday that both of you should know about. And, Jane, ultimately, this is of interest to you as well. We need to think together about what it might mean."

He had their attention now so he got right to it. "I saw James Morgan yesterday at the Preakness. I am talking about your father's associate, Bernadette, the man who took you out of the hospital the day you were born. The leader of the Plug Uglies."

"What! Morgan?" said Bernadette in mid sip of her coffee.

"Papa, are you sure?" asked Harry meaning no insult. "It's been how many years now, twenty-five? I saw him in those days too, but I wouldn't have a prayer identifying him today."

"Harry, there is no doubt in my mind. Do you remember the scuffle behind us, just after Jacobus won?" the elder Vonderhorst asked. Harry nodded thoughtfully.

"Well, one of the men was James Morgan. We looked at each other and there was clear recognition between us."

"What did he want? What was he doing behind us, Papa?" asked a suddenly very serious Bernadette. "Who was the other man?"

Just then, a servant appeared in the archway and caught Jane's eye. She rose and left the room. Momentarily she reappeared and said, "There is a gentleman in the foyer asking for John Vonderhorst. He says his name is Wells, but he also said you may remember him as James Morgan."

Zachariah sat on a hard-backed chair next to a single bed in the small room he had chosen for himself in the mansion. The bed was made with military precision and it matched the Spartan room. The space was clean, neat, and well lit. A picture of a uniformed General Grant hung on one wall and the opposite wall offered the dour President Johnson. They were there because Zachariah had heard his father, no, Mr. Stanton, tell others many times that these two men were responsible for his success.

The stocky man was carefully wrapping his swollen right hand and he feared that it was broken. He had kept it behind his back when he told Mr. Stanton what had happened at the racetrack. After that, Zachariah didn't remember much of what was said through his misery and near despondency over failing his employer and provider. He would find a way to do what he was asked to do. He would kill the man, Vonderhorst. But, now, he had a debt of his own to pay.

Upon hearing that Morgan was in the foyer waiting, the family rose from the table simultaneously. Then, the elder Vonderhorst raised a hand and stopped them.

"Bernadette, I do not want you there when I greet him. If it makes sense and it's safe, I will ask him in and then you will have your conversation with him."

"Papa, I must talk to this man." The young woman made to push past her father.

"Bernadette, I need you to listen to me now. This is not the time to act rashly. I know what I'm talking about. Please do as I say." Her father's tone stopped her, but she was unhappy about it.

"Harry, I want you to get the pistol out of my study desk and follow me as soon as you can. Keep it hidden."

John Vonderhorst then walked through the arch, down a hallway paneled in cherry, and across the broad parquet floor of the main hall and into the sitting area off the foyer. A grayer James Morgan stood, surrounded by a circular wall of dark, stained glass windows depicting bucolic scenes of Maryland. He was dressed in stylish walking clothes, a tan cutaway coat with a waist seam, matching trousers, and a collared waistcoat. A trail of water led through the door in the direction that the doorman had taken his sopping hat and slicker.

"Mr. Morgan, welcome to my home. It's been awhile since we've spoken to each other," Vonderhorst began, extending a hand.

Morgan met the handshake and said, "Yes, it has been awhile, Mr. Vonderhorst. A lot of water over the dam since then." He then glanced at the windows with a wry smile.

"Seems you picked an interesting day for a reunion," said the older man, not missing the pun on the weather. Recalling Morgan as a particularly blunt man, Vonderhorst immediately asked, "What brings you to see me after all of this time?"

"Sir, I have several things I'd like to talk to you about. I believe it may take some time. Would it be possible to speak to you now?" asked Morgan.

With that, Harry Vonderhorst entered the room and smiled at Morgan. "Mr. Morgan, I'm Harry, you may not remember me, but I believe you saved my life one time." He crossed to the visitor, took up his hand, and shook it heartily.

"Ah, yes. The young Vonderhorst. The last time I saw you, you didn't have that beard. I recall that it was quite warm that day," said Morgan, again with the wry smile.

John Vonderhorst looked at the man once more. This didn't seem like the person full of anger and sharp edges that he remembered.

"Mr. Morgan, please. I think we'll be more comfortable in my study."

"This is a beautiful place you have here," observed Morgan as the three men moved through the hall and into the more private room. Behind them, Bernadette began to descend the big, curving staircase. She entered the room just as the men were sitting, which had them all rise again.

"Mr. Morgan, this is my daughter, Bernadette. I'm not sure you would recognize her since you last saw her."

Morgan was delighted to see what the baby girl had become. He was suddenly unsure of what to say to her. He had played over in his mind this conversation with her father many times, but he had always thought hazily of her as a baby girl and had not anticipated having to actually converse with an adult.

"Miss Vonderhorst, it is indeed a pleasure to meet you," said Morgan with a slight bow and a warm smile. "I hope we have a chance to speak later."

"Mr. Morgan, if that is your name, you are about to get that chance right now. I have a number of questions for you and I am not of a mind to wait for the answers," she said rather rudely.

Morgan looked at Vonderhorst, who said to him, "I would like Harry and Bernadette to join our conversation. There are no more secrets in this house and I suspect that what you want to talk about involves them. I would also like to ask Mrs. Jane Cooper to join us. Mrs. Cooper is part of the family."

Vonderhorst waved Jane in, signaled for refreshments, and asked everyone to sit. Morgan greeted Jane cordially.

"Perhaps we should begin by allowing you to tell us why you have come to see me," Vonderhorst began. "Would you like something to take the chill off in the meantime, Mr. Morgan?"

"Thank you, no," replied Morgan. "Unfortunately, I am not here on a social call. And as long as you don't mind the family hearing it, I will be direct. A man attempted to stab you at the racecourse yesterday. I stopped him but I could not hold him," he said, indicating his empty sleeve. "I didn't recognize him. But I chased him until he used the crowd to vanish."

"What were you doing at the races yesterday, Mr. Morgan?" asked Bernadette, pointedly.

"I was there at the invitation of two ladies, Miss Vonderhorst. Seeing your father was an unexpected coincidence. Just as I recognized him, I noticed that he was being stalked by the kind of rough with whom I am very familiar."

"I'm sure you are, Mr. Morgan. But, what I want to know is, why you are back in Baltimore at all?" Bernadette pressed.

Harry shifted in his seat and explained, "Bernadette has been researching the John English trial diligently. She has a good understanding of what happened, who was involved, and why."

"Harry, please don't apologize for me. I see no need to beat around the bush with this man."

Morgan answered Harry, "Does she have a true understanding of the people involved, who they were, and why they did the things they did, or did she get her 'good understanding' from court records, reformers opinions, and newspaper clippings?" Morgan spat. He had enough of this brat.

"That is why I hope you have come, sir," she spat back. "I want to understand from the horse's mouth what happened to my natural father, why my mother died the way she did, and why you took me out of the hospital."

Bernadette glared at the visitor, disliking this man intensely. Her sense of what should be and what was were in conflict. Since Morgan personified this struggle, he offended her.

Morgan, with a bit of fire in his own eye, rose from his leather chair.

"I'll thank you for my hat and coat, Mr. Vonderhorst. I came to warn you that someone wants you dead and is actively pursuing that goal. I did not come to explain myself to rude young women, regardless of how righteous they feel." He returned the young woman's glare and moved to the door.

"I cannot believe that is the only reason you came all the way out here in the pouring rain when you could have simply sent a message. Why are you in Baltimore, Mr. Morgan?" she demanded.

Morgan stopped and turned. "You are right. That's not the only reason I came here. I was curious about Harry. But I mainly came to see you. You, Miss Vonderhorst, are unfinished business for me. So is your father. Now that I see that I need not have worried about you, or cared for that matter, I will no longer. You may be assured of that. Good day."

He strode out the study door, crossed the hallway, retrieved his things, and stepped through the front door and out into the rain. His hansom had been waiting. He gave orders, climbed in, and was gone by the time Harry reached the doorway.

The Vonderhorst family sat in stunned silence. Bernadette hung her head. Jane looked at the old man and Harry walked to the desk and replaced the pistol. "I guess we didn't really need this," he said.

Jane spoke, "He didn't seem like the stories we've heard."

"He is not the same man. Oh, it's Morgan all right. But he has changed," said Vonderhorst. "Bernadette, sweetheart, you were ready to hate that man even before he walked in. I wish you had let him tell his story."

"I asked him his story," shot back an angry Bernadette.

"You can't push a man like Morgan, honey. He doesn't move and he has a tendency to push back. I'll find out where he is staying and try to arrange to meet him again. What was the name he gave at first? Wells, wasn't it?"

"John, if what he said is true, your life may be in danger," Jane reminded him.

"Jane's right, Papa," agreed Harry. "I'm going to arrange some security here and I'll go with you when you go to see him." He then rose, scribbled a note, and left to have it delivered to the right people.

The old man nodded and looked at Bernadette, sadly. "It was a different time then, sweetheart. I don't know whether he's really changed or not. It makes no difference though, we need him right now. He may have some of the answers, but not all of them. Maybe we can form an alliance."

"You'll do what you think is right, Papa," said Bernadette, unmoved by her elder's moderating words. She rose stiffly and left the study.

"John, I agree we need to work with that man, as dangerous as he may be," observed Jane. "He has saved your life now as well as Harry's. Who knows? He may have even saved Bernadette's life."

Chapter 21

Baltimore
May 1883

When asked, the doorman was sure that he had heard the visitor direct the cab to The Carrollton Hotel. The next morning, the two Vonderhorst men first stopped at the Eagle Brewery to allow Harry to direct the day's activity, then they went on to The Carrollton, arriving just before noon. The front desk explained that Mr. Wells had gone out early, but had recently returned to his suite. A note was sent up to let the guest know he had visitors and soon the bellhop returned with an invitation to join Morgan in his rooms.

Once they were seated, John Vonderhorst began, "Mr. Morgan, my apologies for the rudeness of our welcome yesterday. My daughter was raised within very refined circles and she is heavily invested in finding out everything she can about her parents. Unfortunately, your reputation has preceded you and her opinion was formed long before your visit."

"I cannot erase the past, Mr. Vonderhorst," said Morgan simply.

"No, nor can I. But perhaps we can begin fresh in our understanding of each other. I suspect that, if we do, we can find some common ground."

Morgan nodded at this, so the older man continued, "I would first like to thank you for protecting me the other day. If not for you, I wouldn't be sitting here at this moment."

"That's true for me, as well," said Harry.

Morgan turned to Harry and said, "Is your gratitude the reason you were carrying a pistol yesterday?"

The elder Vonderhorst said quickly, "Harry had the weapon at my request."

"As a reflection of your gratitude, then," said Morgan, not giving an inch.

"Look, I will be as direct as you are. The last time I saw you, you were the one carrying a gun. But let's not continue on this line of conversation, Mr. Morgan. Let's begin with the premise that Harry and I appreciate what you have done and use that as a basis for exploring an alliance."

"An alliance?" asked Morgan.

"Yes, sir," answered Harry. "Beyond finding answers to Bernadette's questions, we don't know why someone is trying to kill my father. Your presence also raises issues around the adoption. I understand that you were not happy with it. It's also not lost on us that Bernadette's natural father, John English, has never been found. Finally, it has always been a problem for me and my father to explain why a man of your reputation would risk his life to save a little boy from a fire. To get answers, we need your help. In return, perhaps we may be of some assistance to you in whatever it is you are trying to accomplish."

"I'm not so sure of that," said Morgan.

"Well, at least let us get to know you a bit better. Will you tell us why you have returned to Baltimore after having been away for so long?" asked Harry.

Morgan hesitated. His reasons were clear in his mind but he wasn't sure how they would sound, once he expressed them.

"I told you yesterday why I came to visit you. But, your daughter was right. There are other reasons for my coming back to this city." He paused again, deciding whether to go on.

"Please, Mr. Morgan. We are very interested and I believe we are understanding men," urged John Vonderhorst. "Why don't you start from the beginning? What happened to you the day of the fire?"

Morgan looked at the two men for a long moment, and then he began his story. He explained that when he left the brewery, he was chased and shot at by Bill Barton. It's likely the cop believed Morgan was involved in setting the fire. There was already bad blood between the two and, when Barton cornered him, it was kill or be killed. Morgan admitted his regret, but he also emphasized that he knew the policeman was about to shoot him dead.

From Baltimore, Morgan fled to Richmond, Virginia, where for the next few years he worked as a barman, a laborer in a tobacco warehouse, a cigar roller, an ironworker, and a stableman. When the war broke out, he was honchoing a rather large herd of horses for a wealthy plantation owner in the Shenandoah Valley. That's where he met an attorney by the name of John Singleton Mosby. Mosby recruited him to manage the large number of horses he had just purchased for the State of Virginia.

"Not 'The Grey Ghost'!" interjected an impressed Harry.

"That was what they began to call him in '63," answered Morgan. "Most of the time before that we were just partisan raiders, riding all over hell and gone."

"Were you in on the raid of the Fairfax County Courthouse?" asked a fascinated Harry, referring to one of Mosby's most daring raids where, with two-dozen men, he captured a Union general, two captains, thirty enlisted men, and fifty-eight horses, all without firing a shot. The northern papers had been full of outrage over the incident.

"Yes, I was there. And I was in a lot of other places with the colonel as well. He was a fine soldier and we saw a lot of action. He and I became close friends, at least we were, until that bastard Custer executed seven of our men. That was in '64. When Mosby answered with three of his own executions, he and I parted company. I hooked up with an outfit under Early in the Shenandoah and we found ourselves facing Phil Sheraton at Cedar Creek. His guns took my left arm. It wasn't long after that John Mosby showed up at the hospital looking for me. Soon, I was back in the saddle, reporting to him once again.

"That next spring General Lee surrendered and the Colonel simply disbanded the raiders. Since there was a five thousand dollar Yankee bounty on his head, we left to join Johnston in North Carolina, but on the way we learned that he too had surrendered. So, we hid out around Lynchburg until word came that Mosby had been paroled by none other than Ulysses S. Grant himself."

"That is quite remarkable. To think that President Grant could show such leniency to a mortal enemy, to such a thorn in his side," observed the older Vonderhorst, shaking his head.

Then, turning to his son, he said, "Harry, we've been talking for almost an hour and I'm sure Mr. Morgan could use a break. I wonder if we could trouble you to arrange for some lunch to be brought up?"

He looked at Morgan, who gave a noncommittal shrug. Harry nodded and stepped out of the room.

Morgan realized that the Vonderhorsts had been listening intently, and he was surprised at his own willingness to tell his story. He had never even had this extended a conversation, much less one about himself. So, as Harry reentered, he decided to continue.

"I maintained contact with Mosby over the next few years primarily doing courier work out of Washington. The colonel was a smart man, but he had a wild, risky streak in him. I'm not sure how it happened, but somehow he connected personally with General Grant and even managed his presidential campaign in Virginia for him. This did not make Mosby any friends in that chastised state. As a result, he was getting death threats on a regular basis. Some were not threats. He and I stayed close during that time, and my job became watching his back. I guess I got pretty good at it, even with one arm, since the man is still alive today. In return, the colonel put me through school, taught me the social graces, and introduced me to influential people.

"When Grant won the White House, he decided that Virginia was too dangerous for his friend Mosby, and the president made him U.S. consul to Hong Kong. I went with him for a few years, but I had my own plans and wanted to get back to the states. Then I hit a stroke of good luck.

"A contact of Mosby's in California told me of a mining operation in Utah that he had to abandon. He claimed that he had left a fortune in the ground and feared that he would never get back there again. We struck a deal and, as far-fetched as it sounds, the man was right. I came out of those mountains a rich man and made the Californian rich as well. That was almost two years ago and now I am here."

"That's quite a life story, Mr. Morgan," commented Harry, very impressed.

"Hopefully, there's more of the story to come, son," said Morgan with a thin smile.

John Vonderhorst stood and stretched his back. Listening to Morgan was absorbing and time had passed quickly. "Mr. Morgan, if you don't mind, I just may pour myself a whiskey," said the older man, looking at the suite's bar with bottles arranged under an ornate mirror.

"My apologies, sir, I've forgotten my manners. What do you take with it, Mr. Vonderhorst?" He rose and walked to the bar. Harry joined him.

"If it's a single malt scotch you are offering, I'll take it neat, please," said Vonderhorst. Then, in response to a rapping on the door, he said, "That must be our lunch. I'll get it."

The older Vonderhorst opened the door to a waiter pushing a trolley cart full of oysters on the half shell and a tureen of terrapin stew. A big loaf of fresh, crusty bread and tub of butter accompanied the Maryland delicacies. Vonderhorst turned to the bar and the drink that was being extended to him.

Pushing in behind the waiter was Zachariah. He shoved the servant aside, knocking the oysters and the stew against the wall of the suite. He raised a Colt Peacemaker and shot the elder Vonderhorst in the back. Because the waiter was screaming, he shot him as well.

Morgan reacted immediately, diving for his Webley on the sideboard. The assassin followed him with his weapon, fired, and missed. Then he turned the gun on Harry, standing frozen at the bar, drink still in hand. Morgan fired a wild shot a split second before the stocky man did and took part of his ear and dug a long red furrow along the side of the man's scalp. The mirror behind Harry shattered, but the ball missed its target. Morgan fired again through the dense smoke in the room, but missed the assailant who bolted back through the suite's door.

As Harry went to his stricken father, Morgan raced into the hallway. Guests paused on the stairway and other curious tenants had begun to open doors. Morgan noticed the door to the roof just coming to a close. He dashed to it, threw it open, and stepped back, anticipating an ambush. With no shot coming, he hurled himself up the steps and repeated his cautious maneuver with the door to the roof.

Gaining the open expanse of the building's blacktopped summit, Morgan crouched, gun ready, and scanned the area. He followed a trail of blood across the roof to another door. This one led inside of one of the crenulated turrets that decorated the hotel. Thanking God for the profusion of blood that scalp wounds produce, he dashed across the roof, threw open the door, and fired two shots blindly into the small interior. A rapid peek inside produced no man, but there was a short ladder to a platform, used by hotel maintenance to climb to the top of the structure to fly various flags and pennants.

Morgan jumped inside, ducking under the planking above him. His enemy's Colt exploded again and a ball tore through Morgan's left shoulder. He fired the Webley through the flooring in rapid succession until he hit an empty chamber. Avoiding the barrage, Zachariah staggered back against the low wall of the turret, teetered, and tried to grab the stone to right himself. But his injured right hand could not hold and Morgan watched a body flash by the archer's opening in the turret. Clutching his shoulder, he slowly walked back across the tarred roof to the screams of passersby down on the street.

Chapter 22

Baltimore
June 1883

In the nine months since he returned to Baltimore, John English spent most of his time relearning a city that he once knew quite well. The city was much changed. Politics, power, business, and wealth had all shifted. Strides had been made in every area of social welfare, public services, and education. The city's culture now had a distinct German and Irish flavor. Even Catholics were tolerated, their leaders revered. Rights for women, as some would put it, was the hottest issue in social circles. Leisure time and entertainment had changed as well. There was art, theater, baseball, horse racing, bowling, bay excursions, and pleasure boating that included fishing and crabbing, none of which existed in earlier days.

Some things remained as they were in 1857, however. The thriving harbor, the cobbled streets, the soaring church spires, the public buildings, the taverns, and the ubiquitous oyster seemed unchanged. The hatred, greed, violence, fear, prejudice, and poverty in the city were incubated and cultivated in different ways now, but the diseases were the same. Baltimore hasn't changed all that much, English concluded.

Now calling himself Enoch Stanton, he was well along in his plans to pay back the people and the city that had forced him into exile. Baltimore was once his and it would be again. Very rapidly, he had managed to establish himself as a part of Baltimore's wealthy infrastructure. Heavy, but selective investments had been made in a number of key businesses and industries. Twenty-five years earlier, he had learned the value of social leverage the hard way. So, while it was expensive, he made sure that the name Stanton was a mainstay of support for charitable and cultural institutions. Large, impressive donations went into museums, the arts, schools, and hospitals.

Through all of this, he remained sequestered in his Madison Street mansion. No interviews were granted, no visits from neighbors or well-wishers were allowed, and no public official ever got past his front door. Even though he held important positions on prestigious boards, he was represented by intermediaries and votes were cast in absentia. He attended no meetings or social functions, nor did he even go out to take the air. While thought of as eccentric, this behavior was tolerated as long as the bank drafts kept clearing.

English managed his anonymity in a number of ways, but primarily through a very well paid law firm that took direction well and had little regard for what some called ethics. His personal staff had also expanded to a set of discreet house servants, a professional valet, and a private secretary. A handful of trusted agents handled odd jobs outside of the mansion.

The man spent liberally for the loyalty and silence of those he employed. But now he had a serious problem. If the authorities were able to tie Zachariah back to him, he would be in distinct jeopardy. So, over the last week, he had been following very closely the reports of the debacle at The Carrollton Hotel.

An "unequivocal tragedy" is what *The Sun* had called it. One of Baltimore's leading lights, John H. Vonderhorst, had been gunned down by a madman. A waiter and a guest had been wounded in the gunfire that had erupted in a sixth floor suite. The assailant had fallen or jumped to his death after a chase by a man whose name was being withheld by the police. The shooter himself has not been identified. Although it was speculated that robbery was the motive for the attack, *The Sun* was unable to get the marshall of police, Jacob Frey, to confirm or deny the report.

English's own agents were able to supply additional detail, though. Through hotel personnel, they identified the man who chased Zachariah. Interestingly, he had been meeting with Vonderhorst and his son when the shooting took place. The agents learned that his name was Ulysses Wells, he was from New Orleans, he was a trader in petroleum and minerals, he had money, and he was missing his left arm. This man was one of the three shot by the assailant. Frustratingly, English was not able find out anything more about the mysterious Mr. Wells. He had checked out, leaving no forwarding address. The agents had been given the order to keep looking though, including watching the Vonderhorst house and interviewing the regular cabbies working The Carrollton.

Zachariah was a fool, thought English. It could have all come tumbling down. At least that bastard Vonderhorst finally got his. Maybe it was just as well that Zachariah was gone. He was beginning to lose his effectiveness anyway. He made a complete mess of the Vonderhorst assignment and he still had not been able to trace the girl. At least the idiot had saved English the problem of his ultimate removal.

English wheeled over to the front window facing Madison and opened the shutter enough for a crack to look out of. The worst part of this is the claustrophobia, he thought, as a parasol and silk hat went by below him. He watched a series of carriages and cabs clatter across the cobbles and he wished he were in them. He had to get out of the mansion. It was time to find a way to get around out there without the risk of detection.

As he was considering his escape, a cab pulled up to the curb and stopped at his door. One of his attorneys stepped out, climbed the marble steps, and was let in by the doorman. Soon after, the man was announced and shown a chair as English swung neatly back behind the big desk.

"Well, what do you have for me?" demanded English. "I hope this interruption is worthwhile."

"Sir, I believe we have good news for you," said the man.

"Then tell me, you ass! I don't have all day. Get to it," barked the older man.

"Mr. Stanton, first, my managing partner wanted you to know that the Board of Gray Iron Works and Ship Building has approved your plan to sell the company and transfer all assets to the Norfolk buyer you identified. We are completing the paperwork for the deal and require your signature."

The attorney quickly laid a series of documents in front of English who scribbled his mark with a gnarled hand in the places designated.

As he wrote, he asked, "All assets will be transferred out of Baltimore, as agreed?"

"Yes, sir," responded the man.

"How many jobs?"

"Counting both management and labor, eight hundred," answered the attorney.

"Good," said English simply, sliding the package of documents back to the man. "Is there something else?"

"Yes, sir. You asked us to research the investments of the Vonderhorst family."

"Yes, yes. That's not important now. Just leave the information on the desk. What else?" asked the man in the wheeled chair.

"Well, sir, it was very expensive, but we believe we have found the baby girl you have been searching for."

Morgan had seen a lot of death in his time, even caused a fair amount of it. But he had never been affected by a shooting in this way. He felt responsible for John Vonderhorst's murder. Even all of the scrapes he had been in during his Plug Ugly days, his time as a raider in Virginia, and the occasions he faced the muzzle of a pistol while protecting Mosby after the war had not prepared him for this feeling. He had begun to develop a respect for the brewer, even a like. To see Vonderhorst gunned down in front of him when he knew the older man was in danger was hard to take. There must have been something he could have done.

At least Harry Vonderhorst was unharmed. He was shaken, grieving, certainly, but unhurt. The younger Vonderhorst had proven his mettle and presence of mind when, with his father lying dead and with the suite full of cops, he managed to take the focus off Morgan with a story about an investment meeting and a robbery. He described the wounded Morgan as "heroic" and urged medical care rather than questions. Ultimately, the police had their man, the story seemed plausible, and John Vonderhorst's connections prevented any enthusiasm for probing deeper.

If there had been a debt, Harry had paid it. Morgan now felt that he owed the Vonderhorst family. There would be no more animosity and he would do his damnedest to find the party responsible for the murder. He already had his suspicions.

Soon after his release from Johns Hopkins, Morgan collected his kit from the hotel where it was being held for him. He then took a cab to Camden Station and walked through the Pratt Street entrance and immediately out the Eutaw Street side door. He hailed another hack and directed it in a circuitous route to Charles Street, just below Mount Vernon Square. Sure he was not followed, he changed cabs again and went east on Franklin to St. Paul. There, he stopped at a nondescript boarding house. He woke a pimply, apathetic clerk, provided an assumed name, and paid for a week's stay.

The Vonderhorst funeral was a heavy-hearted affair. Even though Harry, John, Bernadette, and Jane were well supported by a hoard of friends and business associates, the man's death was a shock and an unmitigated and painful loss. John had been on his way back home from San Francisco only to arrive to hear the sad news. To have this kind of a reunion with young John was punishing for the entire family.

Emily Sloane hurried south from New York with her uncle, William Vanderbilt, to be with Bernadette for as long as she needed her. But Emily found her friend angry and irreconcilable. And, once the closest of confidants, she now realized that Bernadette was sharing her innermost feelings with another. Harry had become a strong, available shoulder to cry on.

The big, black-draped house out on Frederick Road saw Baltimore's political and social leaders each take their turn around the open casket. Some even cried real tears. St. Paul's Protestant Episcopal was filled to capacity for the funeral and the internment in The Greenmount Cemetery was just as well attended.

Throughout all of this, Morgan stayed away. Then, a week after the senior Vonderhorst was back with his maker and things had quieted down, he sent Harry a note asking to meet with the family.

Morgan arrived at the Vonderhorst estate in an enclosed cab and was quickly shown into the study. Although John had returned to the

West Coast on pressing business and the Vanderbilts had returned to New York, Harry, Bernadette, and Jane were waiting for him.

Harry greeted Morgan with warmth and deference. "Mr. Morgan, how is your shoulder? That was a very close call and I'm heartened to see you on the mend."

Morgan offered a thin smile and with a shrug and a wag of his head he put the concern for his health aside.

Harry continued, "I'm also very glad you've contacted us. I was concerned that we wouldn't hear from you again. We owe you our thanks for your swift action in the hotel. This is the third time you have put yourself at risk for us. I find myself in the very unusual position of owing a debt that I may never be able to repay. What's more, the Vonderhorsts still need your help. In short, we don't understand what is motivating these attacks. I believe you have some of the answers, and it was my father's hope that we could work together to understand and address the situation."

Harry offered Morgan a seat in one of the brown leather wing back chairs. Jane took the other and Harry and Bernadette sat together on a large chesterfield sofa covered in hunting print. As Bernadette sat close to him, Harry took her hand. It was obvious that the two had drawn closer in the last few months. The sad death of their father had made them inseparable, but now, Morgan could sense there was something more between them.

Once all were seated around a coffee service on a low, richly carved table of mahogany and glass, Jane spoke first.

"Mr. Morgan, we hope that you will begin to trust that we are your friends. What gets said between us will stay within the family." With a telling glance at Bernadette, she continued, "We are willing to put the past behind us. What is important is what is taking place now. Please, tell us what you think we need to know."

"Thank you, Mrs. Cooper. But, in fact, I think it is the past that is the point. First, I'd like to express my deepest sympathies over the death of Mr. Vonderhorst. In some ways, I feel like I should have prevented it and I have a lot of regrets about that. I have come today to offer you my services in whatever capacity you see fit," began Morgan.

"Mr. Morgan, every time I see you, you raise more questions than you answer. What do you mean the past is the point? Why do you think you should have prevented my father's murder?" fired an agitated Bernadette.

It was obvious that she was not completely sold on Morgan by Harry's recounting of the conversation and the events at The Carrollton. The past could not be forgotten. It was too painful for her.

"Bernadette, please. Let the man explain. This is the second time he has come all of the way out here to talk to us. The least you can do is listen to him," said Jane, clearly exasperated by her former charge.

"I realize that I've created some confusion," said Morgan, looking at Bernadette. "Some of that is because I myself have been confused. I am beginning, however, to see some things that may lead to understanding. Rest assured, one of my purposes in coming was to answer your questions as best I can."

After a slight hesitation, he went right to it. "I believe your father, John English, is still alive. I do not know whether he is in Baltimore for sure, but I suspect he is seeking revenge for the loss of his old life. Certain events, taking place over the last year, point to this. I believe these occurrences can be directly connected to the Plug Ugly street gang and John English's trial for murder in 1857."

"My father is still alive! That's absurd," said Bernadette with some edge. "What proof do you have?"

"Bernadette, please," said Harry.

"I have no definite proof at this point, just speculation and logic. But I want to get this proof, find him, and stop whatever he is doing. That is my offer to you. If I'm correct, we are dealing with the most dangerous of men. No one knew John English as I did. No one knows what he is capable of doing like I do."

"Assuming you are correct, it's been twenty-five years. Why now, after all of this time? How do we know that he's the same man?" asked Jane.

"Yes, Mr. Morgan. You want us to believe you have changed, why not my father?" pressed Bernadette.

"That's a fair question, Miss Vonderhorst. I believe that I am not the same man I was then and it is possible for people to change to a large degree. So, why not John English? In truth, I cannot say that he's the same ruthless man he was when Baltimore's streets were his to control. All I'm going on are the facts as I know them and making a few connections. There were a number of high-profile people involved in the trial and a number of others who participated in driving John English from the city. There were still others who he perceived as enemies or as friends who had betrayed him. Many of these individuals are either dead or missing, and many have died under questionable circumstances, several very recently. John Vonderhorst was primary among this group. It's very likely that I am high on the list as well."

"So, you are saying that you think John English has returned and, harboring a historic grudge, is executing his old enemies?" asked Harry with raised eyebrows.

"That's what I think, yes," replied Morgan matter-of-factly.

"Preposterous!" stormed Bernadette. "Then, explain why, coincidentally, you have returned to Baltimore, Mr. Morgan, at the same time this so-called vendetta is taking place. And why would my father want you, his best friend, dead?"

"The answers to those questions are difficult," replied Morgan. "They are difficult because they force me to face some things that are very painful for me."

Morgan looked at Harry and Jane whose expressions were encouraging him to continue. Bernadette's face, however, was covered with skepticism and rancor.

"Perhaps the best way to start is to simply say that your father and I were in love with the same woman, your mother. It was clear to me, however, that Hattie loved your father. She married him and lived with him and I was forced to accept her choice."

At this information, Bernadette swayed and sat back on the chesterfield, so Morgan, looking directly at her, continued quickly.

"John English and I were close. But one could only get so close to him. He was a violent, jealous man who believed in a cause. That cause was to preserve a neighborhood and a city in way that he himself defined. Unfortunately, that definition required a degree of chaos that John Vonderhorst, and others like him, opposed. Your natural father became a symbol of all that was wrong with Baltimore in those days. Ultimately, the city purged itself of the particular ailment that John English represented. And, while the legal system failed to convict him, it managed to destroy his plans and expel him from the city he loved. The John English I knew would not forget this. Nor would he be deterred in seeking retribution by time, whether it was twenty-five years or a hundred years."

The room was silent as Morgan paused. Even Bernadette sat staring as the story began to unfold.

"Why would my best friend want me dead, you asked. Well, I'm not sure I have a full answer to that, but I think I can speculate on the things I don't know. First, I think John believes I betrayed him and failed to support him during his trial. I think he believes I wanted the leadership of the Plug Uglies and, as a result, let him take the brutal punishment he received while they held him. Neither of these things is true. I did all that I could for him, including getting him legal support and assisting in organizing his defense. I never wanted the Plugs. In fact, I was looking for a way out of the club.

Anyway, John disappeared immediately upon release and I've had only one contact with him since then. A few months after the trial, J.W. Gambrill, another close friend of ours, received a message asking the both of us to come meet your father. I was unable to go right away, but Gambrill did. And, even though he had very good reasons to return, J.W. never came back from that meeting. Soon after, I had my own legal problems to deal with and never did meet with John."

The Vonderhorsts sat rapt, listening to the aging Plug Ugly tell the story. No one said a word, so Morgan continued, now speaking directly to Bernadette.

"There might be another reason for bad blood between your father and me. I think that he also believes I was trying to steal your mother from him when he was most vulnerable. He knew my feelings for her and he knew their marriage was painful for me. But I swear that I never attempted to do any such thing. Yes, I loved her, but I honored their marriage. When Hattie took ill late in her pregnancy, I happened to be with her. In fact, I was trying to manage the situation for John since he could not. I got her to the hospital and was there when you were born, Bernadette. I was there because Hattie was alone and I loved her. No more, no less. This is not something that John English would understand."

Quiet tears had begun to roll down Bernadette's cheeks. She sat rigidly, gripping Harry's hand. Morgan felt his voice clutch and he looked down at the design on the Persian rug at his feet. He realized that he had called her Bernadette for the first time.

With a small clear of her throat, Jane said, "Mr. Morgan, thank you for being so candid with us. It's plain that twenty-five years has not allowed you to forget either. I am beginning to see, at least in part, why you have returned to Baltimore. I sense there other reasons, as well?"

Morgan gathered himself and ran his hand through his thick salt and pepper hair.

"Yes, there are. Baltimore has always been my second love and I've missed it. I've been away a long time and I needed to come home, so I did. I knew immediately that I belonged here when I first stepped back on its docks. The timing of my return with English's vendetta I can only explain by coincidence."

Brushing some imaginary lint from his empty sleeve, he continued, "In addition to wanting to verify Bernadette's welfare for Hattie's sake, I always felt a tie to young Harry. In my travels among other people, and in the work I did, I've learned that one takes on a permanent responsibility for those whose life they have preserved. That idea is a bit philosophical, but it explains why I also wanted to see what Harry had become.

"I was able to satisfy myself that both of my 'charges' were doing quite well and in no need of me, when I started to recognize the deadly pattern that seems to be continuing. Now, I feel responsible for bringing this situation to a conclusion, for all of our sakes."

The four sat staring at the untouched coffee service. Finally, Harry spoke, "Mr. Morgan, it's plain that our lives have become intertwined. It's also clear that we have a common problem that needs resolution. What that resolution is remains unclear to me. Do you think that Bernadette and I are in any danger?"

"That's difficult to say," answered Morgan. "What we don't know is English's mind with regard to Bernadette. He could have no interest at all. I don't believe that, though. If I'm correct about his recent activities, it is more likely that he is seeking her and has not yet found her. The reason for his search is, in all likelihood, to regain something that was taken from him. That could be Bernadette herself. Or, it could be avenging the loss of Hattie by satisfying his hatred for the cause of her death, namely the child she bore."

The family received this revelation with horror. Finally, Bernadette spoke, "What about Harry?"

"I can't say. But it's quite possible that English's bitterness toward John Vonderhorst could transfer to Harry. Especially if he realizes how close you two are," said Morgan, stating the obvious, but still causing some embarrassment in Bernadette.

"I will do whatever it takes to protect this family," said Harry. "Have you thought through what our next steps should be?"

"Not completely," answered Morgan. "But I suggest that you take extreme precautions at all times, here, at the plant, and wherever you and those close to you are. In the meantime, I will work the streets and begin to hunt the hunter. I may be back to you for contacts and resources to assist my investigations."

After some additional conversation and assurances that the Vonderhorst family was at his full disposal, Morgan made his way to the door accompanied by Jane. Bernadette had excused herself with a quiet "thank you" to Morgan and Harry had immediately repaired to his desk where he began to pen a series of messages.

"Mr. Morgan, may I have a word with you before you leave?" asked Jane, indicating a small alcove off the main reception hall.

"Of course, Mrs. Cooper," replied Morgan, allowing himself to be ushered into the apse she indicated. He had wondered about this woman. She certainly was not at all hard to look at. But what was her tie to the Vonderhorsts?

Once they were seated, Jane Cooper began, "You may be wondering about my status with the family and I wanted to explain." Morgan shrugged to show her that it was unnecessary, but he also indicated his interest.

"For many years, I was Bernadette's tutor and traveling companion. John Vonderhorst and I had developed a very close relationship after I returned with Bernadette from Europe. We were not intimate, but we had come to share a different kind of closeness, one born of mutual respect. Because of that and because of my time and experiences with Bernadette, the Vonderhorst family became my own. I love her as a daughter and Harry as a son even though there is no blood relationship. I'm telling you all of this because I want you to know that I am invested in this family and that I want to play an active role in whatever plans you have. I am very resourceful and I am not afraid of the risks involved. Some time ago, my father made sure that

I was capable with firearms and I have hunted with most of the courts of Europe. So I can be very useful to you out on the street as well. In short, I want you to use me in your efforts, as you see fit."

"Mrs. Cooper, I. . . .," began Morgan.

"By the way, I am not a Mrs.," said Jane. "And I would ask that you call me Jane. I would also like to know what else I might call you."

Smiling now, Morgan said, "My friends call me Jamie. I would like it very much if you did the same. As far as your involvement goes, I accept your offer of help. English knows me and it is very likely I will need to stay in the shadows. I could use a go-between as I nose around. You must know, however, that it may be quite dangerous."

"I cannot hide in this house or anywhere else when I know I am needed," she said.

"Okay, then. Once I think through what has to be done, I'll be in touch. That will be sooner rather than later. Thank you for speaking to me," replied Morgan.

As he moved through the front door and into the waiting, closed carriage, he thought that Jane Cooper was, in fact, going to very useful. He also thought with a half smile that he would have to be careful not to let this woman with a backbone become a distraction.

Morgan's carriage was not long away from the Vonderhorst's drive when he noticed that he had picked up a tail.

Chapter 23

Baltimore
Mid-June 1883

Frederick Road was moderately busy, but as it merged into West Baltimore Street, the horses, carriages, and foot traffic began to multiply. Morgan instructed the cabman to slow down, probably an unnecessary order given the congestion, but he didn't want to lose the tail. The man was directing his buggy around slower vehicles, lying back about fifty yards. Morgan needed to lose him in a way that would allow the ex–Plug Ugly to pick up his tracker and then follow him wherever he was going. Morgan had caught a break.

The Lexington Market would suit his purpose nicely. This vast warren of stalls and irregular passageways was the food source for most of central and west Baltimore. It was the largest of five such markets dotted around the city. The market began in 1782 in a pasture on General John Eager Howard's sprawling estate, once located north and west of the harbor. The market was named to honor the Americans who had fallen at the Battle of Lexington.

Once supplied by Conestoga wagons rolling in from surrounding counties, the market now included treasures from the Chesapeake Bay and far beyond. The place was a huge, rambling, tented area, jammed with vendors selling produce, seafood, meats, fowl, dairy products, baked goods, flowers and innumerable other goods for home, and hearth. As farmers and watermen delivered their wares, they also made the return trip loaded with feed, grain, hay, tools, livestock, and almost anything else they might need or want. In various accents, merchants purchased, sold, bartered, and otherwise did whatever they could to move their goods. The place was a veritable beehive that reflected the industry, prosperity, and complexion of America itself.

Morgan knew that the market's organized chaos of stalls and eateries could be confusing to the uninitiated. But this was his home market. He had once been a boy on his uppers here, stealing apples or tomatoes from inattentive shopkeepers. So the irregular pattern of aisles was familiar and he wouldn't be distracted or disoriented by the throng of people, the unique and wonderful sights, or the market's intoxicating smells. He was betting that it would provide an advantage over his pursuer.

Morgan directed his cabby to turn up Eutaw Street and stop at the main entrance. He stepped out of the carriage and walked to the driver's box, taking his time to be sure the tail was still there. When he saw the shadow pay a black man to hold his horse and buggy, Morgan instructed his driver to take a slow turn around the block and meet him at the market's Greene Street exit.

Sure that the pad was behind him, Morgan moved quickly through the market's doors. He edged around vendors in stained aprons and shoppers toting mesh bags. He dodged a group of filthy street urchins, swearing and laughing while fleeing from a Chinese man wearing a queue and waving a meat cleaver. He sprinted past crates of ripe watermelons, pyramids of green tomatoes, fish on ice laid out in overlapping rows, and great slabs of red meat hanging from hooks. He took several twists and turns, then abruptly dropped down out of sight behind a stall selling tins of Pride of the Chesapeake shucked oysters.

The tail came quickly by Morgan, scanning the aisles and taking small jumps to see over the sea of people and market stands. When the man was well past the oyster vendor, Morgan, staying low and keeping his eye on the tracker, wended his way to the Greene Street exit. He watched the shadow pound his fist into his other hand, turn, and walk back toward the Eutaw Street entrance and his buggy. Morgan ducked out the Greene Street exit, spotted his carriage coming down the street and jumped in without allowing it to stop. The driver was then instructed to continue his circle of the block. Before long, the tail's buggy was in sight and Morgan was now the stalker.

They went east to Howard, then north to Madison, and turned right. The buggy stopped in front of a large home in the expensive neighborhood. The man got out, secured the horse, climbed the marble steps, and rang the bell. Realizing that he was well within walking distance of his own rooms, Morgan released his hired carriage. He made his way across the street and down the block a short way to a corner café. There, he could watch both the front door and the alley that served as an exit to the stables behind the mansion. He was also hoping to pick up a bit of neighborhood gossip.

John English sat listening intently to the description of the man that had been seen entering and leaving the Vonderhorst home. It had to be the same one-armed man that had been at The Carrollton Hotel. That was very interesting.

Although the idiot standing before him had lost his man, English's other agents had been more successful. First, there was the report that the baby girl was alive and had been adopted not too long after Hattie had died. It came as a real shock to him that it was none other than the late John Vonderhorst who had adopted her. This news angered and excited English. It also opened a world of possibilities. His foresight in having the family's home watched had paid big dividends. Hattie's baby girl was probably in that house, although reports had it that she had not ventured outside in several days. So it seemed that he was not quite finished with the Vonderhorsts.

Then, there was the detailed report on his old partner, Jamie Morgan. Morgan had been particularly elusive, appearing and disappearing periodically over the years before English could pinpoint him. Now, he had it on good authority that Jamie had been seen in New Orleans and had taken passage for more northern ports. He also learned that Morgan, despite losing his left arm in the war, was still a pretty nasty customer. He guessed that Zachariah had learned that the hard way.

"Get back to the Vonderhorst place. Be sure to look for a young woman leaving. If she emerges, follow her and don't lose her. Send word as soon as this happens. We will meet you wherever she goes." English then waved the man out of the study and he was alone.

There were common denominators here, English thought. Somehow, Morgan was in Baltimore and he was connected to the Vonderhorst family. How could that be? When could that have happened? Was Morgan in league with Vonderhorst twenty-five years ago, while he was in stir and the cops were using him for sport? Maybe. Or maybe the connection is the baby. He was there when she was born. What had Hattie said to him? What did he know?

More questions. But the answers were coming. It was just as well that Jamie, the girl, and those bloody brewers were intersecting. He could see the opportunity to achieve his objectives just over the horizon. That thought produced an ugly, damaged smile.

This musing was brief, however, as he thought further about Morgan. Jamie had always been his adversary, all the way back to the Mount Vernon Hook and Ladder days. the Plugs, the streets, Hattie—all things Jamie wanted that he, John English, had. Sure, he kept the man close in those days, but wasn't that the smart thing to do? There was no way in hell Morgan was getting any of those things, not then, not now. Hattie was his so the girl is his. And now he was taking it all back.

English turned back to the reports of the men attempting to find Morgan. I have to locate Jamie, he thought. He's too dangerous and smart. If he doesn't know about the girl, why has he come back here? Has he put together that I'm back in Baltimore? If he's been to the Vonderhorst home, it is likely that he's had contact with the girl.

The wheeled-chair man pulled the tasseled cord for his secretary. There was too much at stake not to take precautions. He needed to be more mobile and he needed to make contingency plans just in case he was misreading the situation. The secretary entered and stood in front of the big desk.

"Has all of the electrical work been completed?" asked English.

"Yes, sir, Mr. Stanton, and the workmen have completed the construction of the elevator to the third floor. You may test it at any time now."

It was English's idea to have one of the new von Seiman's elevators installed that would give him more movement within the mansion. But he also wanted it as part of an escape route, if flight became necessary. The elevator would lift him to the floor that was level with lower rooftops surrounding the house. There, he had made a series of bridges and ramps constructed that would carry him across the skyline and gradually down to the street a full block away from the mansion. At first this seemed a paranoiac extravagance. However, realizing the difficulty of rapid escape from the present house and appreciating the risks he was taking, he went forward with the project.

"Good, we will test the lift and the rear exit tonight, after dark," replied English. "Now, has the modified Coupe Brougham arrived?"

This vehicle was also part of English's contingency. It was light enough for speed, yet had carrying capacity. It was armored under its silk and fully enclosed for privacy. It's sides were fitted with a series of strategically placed steps and grips that would allow English to hoist himself into the passenger seats or up and into the driver's box. He wanted the option of doing either one rapidly and without help. While the vehicle would normally be kept in hired space and away from the mansion, English would use the rear exit and the carriage to get out of the house on various errands. When and if the need to retreat became necessary, he would simply send an urgent message to the driver and use the rear exit as he normally did. The carriage would meet him at the appointed location. In this way, no one would see him coming or going.

"Yes, sir. The carriage and the driver are ready whenever you are," replied the secretary.

"Fine. Now one more thing. Have the men I sent for arrived?"

"Yes, sir, they are waiting in the kitchen. Given their, ah, nature, I thought that was the best place for them."

"Did they come in the service entrance?" asked English.

"No sir, unfortunately, they came to the front door. I'm sorry," answered the contrite secretary. "They were told."

"Goddamnit! What were my instructions, you fool?" stormed the older man. "I'll deal with you later on this. Send them up here now."

The secretary gladly escaped and shortly thereafter two men stood before English. They carried themselves with the arrogance of the streets. Bowler hats still on; open collarless shirts; short, workman's jackets; and boots that looked well used in their trade. That trade would be obvious to the police and anyone else who had lived on the cobbles for any length of time. These men were the type that family men crossed the street to avoid. They were big, muscled, mustachioed and offered hard little eyes that were ringed with a slack that could only be produced by hard drinking.

"What are your names?" was English's first question.

"Why do you want to know and what are we doing here?" answered the one on the left.

"You're here because I have money to pay you and you want it, asshole," said English.

"Who you calling an asshole, you cripple bastard!" stormed the one on the right, taking a step closer.

English's left hand emerged from under the desk holding a Smith & Wesson. It was pointed at the mouthy thug's chest.

"Look, I don't have the time to play footsie with you two clowns. I may have a job for you shortly. And I pay very well."

English took from a drawer a stack of bills with a band around it and threw it in the middle of the desk.

"There's five hundred dollars there that you can take with you. There's another five hundred when and if the job is complete. I'm told you know your business and I know where to find you. Now, let's get this pathetic negotiation over with. You want the job or not?"

The two gorillas' eyes never left the pile of cash. "We'll take the job," one said simply, reaching for the money.

English's right hand flashed and a dirk buried itself in the stack of bills not quite between the man's fingers.

"Christ!" the tough yelped, pulling his hand back against his chest and looking at his bleeding digits.

"First, I want you to know who you are dealing with. I have the resources to make scum like you disappear in a puff of smoke. Don't even think about crossing me. I have a very short fuse. Understood?" English demanded.

When the two men just looked and nodded, English hit the one who was not bleeding in the chest with the wad of bills.

"Now beat it and never come back here. Wait for my word. It should come shortly. Go out the service door."

When the men had left, English rummaged around in the paper on his desk looking for a particular report. When he found the sheaf of papers on the Vonderhorst family investments, he rocked back in his chair and began to read.

Morgan sat just inside the café drinking a cup of coffee and watching the front of the brick mansion. The man he was shadowing had come out earlier, boarded the buggy, and retreated back down Madison. Morgan decided to wait a bit longer to see if anything useful would develop. In the meantime, he struck up a conversation with his elderly waiter who was limping around on bad feet. The man was decidedly sour and laconic until Morgan mentioned his war wound, soldiers in butternut, and the possibility of a generous tip. At that, the man opened up like a gaping manhole and the information he offered was of some use, maybe.

Morgan listened patiently as the war veteran, now waiter, explained in great detail how the water in the trenches at Petersburg destroyed his feet. As the conversation allowed, Morgan steered the conversation to the mansion down the block. The waiter eventually let on that the house was owned by an older gentleman by the name of Enoch Stanton. He had never seen the man and the servants who occasionally stopped by the café were particularly closed mouthed. Strange that everyone in the neighborhood knew that Stanton was very wealthy, but no one had ever seen him. The waiter finally offered that the occupant must be rich because he had just had one of those fancy elevators installed in his house, at least that's what the dray carrying the parts had said on its side. The man's memory was still good because he recalled that the installation company was the Lafferty Bros. Mechanical Contractors, Central and Holland streets.

Just as Morgan was deciding that he was wasting his time, two men swaggered past the front of the café, crossed the street, and walked up to the front door of the mansion. After a brief wait on the steps in which the two looked around at the neighborhood like wolves surveying the flock, they were let in. Morgan knew these men. In fact, he had been one of them. Twenty-five years earlier they would have been members of the Plug Ugly social club. They were out of place here. What was a wealthy man like Stanton doing associating with thugs?

Not very long after they entered, the two street punks came out of the alley a little ways down the square from the mansion's front door. Without hesitating, they walked quickly west in the direction of Morgan's old Biddle Street neighborhood. English's old neighborhood, as well, thought Morgan. He pulled a notebook from his coat, penned a brief note, found someone willing to carry the message to Harry Vonderhorst at the Eagle Brewery on North, then he left the café. He would find a cab on Charles Street that would run him over to the east side to the Lafferty Brothers' business.

Chapter 24

Baltimore
Late June 1883

Jane Cooper was getting antsy. She didn't like being cloistered in the big house and she hadn't heard from Morgan since his visit four days earlier. Not only was she worried, but she was bored as well. Harry had provided security equal to President Chester's White House, then he was forced by the press of business to leave. It was just as well because he wasn't much company, as he too waited anxiously for additional word from Morgan. Before he left, Harry had mentioned getting a note from the ex-Plug, asking for some research on a man named Stanton, but that was all. It didn't help that Harry's beloved Orioles had twenty-one losses and only nine wins and they had just dropped another home series to the Cincinnati Red Stockings. He left that morning for the Eagle plant and Oriole Park, grumbling about dropping beer sales, poor attendance, and the New York Gothams' bad idea of introducing Ladies Day, which offered free admission for women.

Bernadette too had been distant, ever since Morgan's revelations. Perhaps distant was not the right word since Jane sensed no friction between them. But her former ward certainly was introspective and withdrawn. Bernadette spent all of her time with Harry when he was home or in her room corresponding with Emily in New York. Jane concluded that Morgan had thrown the girl's convictions about both her father and him into something of a cocked hat. She obviously needed time to sort out some very conflicting feelings. Jane was glad for this because she was concerned that the headstrong Bernadette would be driven to confront her natural father, regardless of Morgan's warnings. As a result, she was relieved that Bernadette showed no interest in leaving the house, especially since no one understood John English's intentions toward her.

Jane sat down to the big desk in the study and heaved a sigh. She stared at the mound of correspondence, invoices, and notices that were hers to manage through. She had taken on the responsibility of running the household ever since she arrived in Baltimore, but with the death of her patron, she and Harry had worked out a division of labor for some of the business activity as well. John Vonderhorst's energy for work had been prodigious and his insurance company, railroad investments, and other interests had to be maintained. While Harry took on the external aspects of his father's activities in addition to his own responsibilities at the brewery and those with the ball team, Jane had begun to handle the internal facets. That meant getting up the learning curve and wading through a daily mountain of paper. She welcomed the challenge, but today, she was weary of it and could not stop thinking about Morgan and what he could be doing.

At that moment, one of the housemaids entered and handed her a message. It was from Morgan. She tore open the envelope and began to read.

"Jane, apologies for taking so long to contact you. The time has not been wasted. John English is in Baltimore and has been for nearly a year. He is wealthy, well established in the city, and goes by the name of Enoch Stanton. His dealings all have been through agents. No one has ever met directly with the man. This and other things lead me to believe his intentions are not pure. I have an idea on how to draw him out, but the details must wait. Please communicate this information to Harry and Bernadette. Impress upon them both the danger of leaving the house without security. Additional details will be provided as the opportunity allows.

"Also, I would like to take up your offer of assistance. You are needed to help put a plan of action into motion. I do not believe English knows of you. Just the same, there may be some risk. If you agree, please let the courier of this note know. Then, meet me today at 3 p.m. in the lobby of The Mount Vernon Hotel on the south side of Monument, west of Cathedral."

The message was signed "Jamie."

Jane did not hesitate. She released the courier and pulled together whatever was required to meet Morgan. Then she left a note for Bernadette and Harry. The security refused to allow her to leave the house alone, so she rode a carriage out of the grounds with a driver and a guard on the way to meet Morgan. As soon as she was out of the drive, they passed two men stopped along the road who seemed to be checking their horses' shoes. Once the carriage was past, each mounted quickly. One galloped off in a hurry and the second rode more slowly, following the carriage at a discrete distance.

Morgan chose The Mount Vernon Hotel to meet Jane because it was quiet and only a square south of the Madison Street mansion. He was convinced by the information Harry had gathered on Stanton's activities and a very interesting conversation with the Lafferty brothers that Enoch Stanton was in fact John English.

The Laffertys, as it turned out, were a gregarious pair of twins, originally from Virginia, whose father was with Stonewall Jackson when the general died after Chancellorsville. They were more than willing, over a few free Eagles, to talk to Morgan about both the war and the eccentric old man in a wheeled chair, his expensive new elevator, and the escape route over the rooftops that they had also been asked to build. They were told the old man was deathly afraid of fire.

This information led Morgan to look for and find English's back door, one square to the north of Madison. There, he waited patiently until dark. At around nine o'clock, he watched an enclosed carriage pull up, a capable looking driver with a sidearm walk into the alley and emerge, pushing a hooded man in a wheeled chair. The man lifted himself powerfully into the carriage and gave directions. The process was smooth and fast.

Morgan followed the vehicle west to a dingy oyster house and bar on Rose Street in the old Twentieth Ward, not far from the site of the bar that Morgan himself had owned. There, through the grimy front window, he saw the pathetic, gnarled reflection of the once hearty John English. A closer look told Morgan that, despite his overall wretched appearance, his old mate still had powerful shoulders and arms. His sinewy hands were those of a master bricklayer.

English sat by himself slurping Chincoteagues, sipping Baker's Pure, and staring at the scarred table in front of him. He was waiting for something. His bodyguard sat across the room facing the door. In due time, a well-worn streetwalker entered the bar and walked over to English. They exchanged a few words, and then she pushed the wheeled chair into a windowless cubbyhole off the main barroom. She had used the place before. Not much more than a half hour later, they both emerged. English signaled his watchdog and the two men rolled out to the waiting carriage and disappeared.

Morgan had watched this sad tableau intently but never saw the opportunity he was seeking. He was looking for a chance to talk to his old partner without getting into a gunfight. He wanted some answers and he wanted to straighten a few things out. Then, maybe he would start shooting.

But English had been very cautious. Undoubtedly he was armed, as was his escort. Their positions in the room allowed no surprises, and Morgan had no idea who else might take issue with his simply walking into the place. So the odds were not good. English repeated the entire trip a second night and a third, with different whores each night. Morgan realized that he would have to get at English another way. That's when he decided to use Jane. He hoped that she was a good actress.

Jane leapt from the carriage and, in a full unladylike sprint, bolted for the front door of the hotel and into the lobby. There she scanned the room with obvious urgency and found James Morgan striding toward her.

"Jamie, we have company. I was followed leaving the house. Two more men in a hansom picked us up on the way. They just shot my security man. Maybe the driver too. They're right behind me," she said in a staccato report.

"Quick. In the bar." Morgan grabbed Jane and together they flew into the lush, but empty, barroom. He had chosen the time and place for privacy. Probably a mistake, he thought. A brief look over his shoulder gave him a view of the two men who had visited English in the mansion. One of them was raising a big weapon.

"Behind the bar," he shouted and they both shambled over the mahogany plank and fell hard in various painful ways behind it. They scrambled to a crouch in a rain of shattered mirror shards, liquor bottles, and beer mugs. A shotgun or some kind of gun designed for shooting geese must have been used, given its wide pattern of destruction. They had been very lucky, for now.

Morgan acted instantly. He popped up six feet from where he went over the rail, eyed a target, and fired the Webley, immediately dropping behind the bar again. The goose gun boomed once more, but this time it was aimed at the ceiling as the shooter toppled backwards from a hole in his neck. Morgan moved again; through the acrid smoke of black powder and the shower of plaster, he crawled to the far right end of the bar, then dove out around its foot rail, seeking another target.

The second thug, seeing his partner's dead weight crash to the floor, fled to his left in a wide arc, trying for a side exit. When he saw Morgan leap out right in front of him, looking the other way, toward the lobby entrance, the assassin stopped and pointed his Colt at the unprotected back. Morgan had lost the fifty–fifty call as to where the second target would be.

He looked up to see Jane stand and fire an over/under, pepperbox revolver twice, very rapidly, at short range, and right at him. The 34-caliber balls sung past his head and imbedded themselves in the shirt of the assassin crouching behind him. The man was flung backwards as two great, red blooms formed on his chest. He came to rest in a dead, but ash-filled fireplace and the dense, sulfurous air in the room began to fill with gray motes of soot as well.

"We have to leave. Now. I can't afford to get snagged and neither of us want to try to explain this," barked Morgan.

He was up and beginning to hear the sounds of response to all of the violence. He indicated the side door that one of the assassins was looking for a minute earlier. They tore through it, down a short hallway, and out into an alley that smelled of urine. They moved in silence out to Centre, then a half of a square to Park where they hailed a hansom and rode south, telling the cabbie they were trying to catch a train. At Camden Station, they split up, bought separate tickets, one train going north, the other one south. Leaving by separate exits, they then met again on Pratt Street and strolled east to Sharp where they entered a small German eating house. Finding a table in the corner that offered a view of the street, they each ordered two drinks, downing the first very quickly.

They had not spoken since leaving the Mount Vernon. Breaking the silence, Jane offered an opinion, "This is good Schnapps."

"Is that German for moonshine?" he asked with a crooked smile.

"I've had better though," she said, ignoring his attempt at humor. "But not many that tasted this good."

He looked at her. This former nanny had been right. She could shoot. Was she really unfazed by the recent brush with an abbreviated life? No, the reaction was there, behind her eyes, but she was under control at the moment. He wondered for how long though and how tough she really was.

"Thank you for not shooting me earlier," he said.

"Good thing my aim was off," she replied.

"Good thing you were carrying that peashooter," said Morgan stating the obvious and referring to her powerful little pepperbox revolver.

"Been with me since France," she said. "As soon as I picked up the tail, it was loaded and ready."

"Funny, you don't look all that rough and ready," he said, still smiling.

"Europe forces you to learn a few things besides ballroom dancing," Jane said simply. Then she asked, "What's next? I'm scared as hell, but we have to do something. We're targets and I can't live like that." She was beginning to show a little fraying at the edges.

"Why do you think you were followed today?" Morgan asked.

"I don't think I was followed today. I think Bernadette was," she answered. "So maybe I'm still unknown to him. But as long as I'm with you, I might as well be Bernadette. And if I go back to the house, it's likely that I will be known. What's more, if I go back, Bernadette will be in greater danger than she is at the moment with me out here playing surrogate."

"That's what I think too," he said.

"English has to know it was Jamie Morgan in that bar this afternoon, otherwise you would have stayed around," she observed. "He also knows that you and Bernadette are somehow linked. His first attempt at you was botched. So he believes the two of you are together somewhere in the city. He will be looking."

"He will be looking with one eye on his escape plan," responded Morgan.

"Then we need to act quickly, Jamie. And we need to do it without either one of us getting hurt. Any ideas? You asked for my help for a reason."

"Yes, I did. But first we have to get off the street. Mind going to my place?"

Jane looked at him for a long moment. Then, rising, she said with a sardonic smile, "It's Bernadette's reputation, not mine."

Chapter 25

Baltimore
June 27, 1883

Jane Cooper and James Morgan made their way to his rented rooms on St. Paul. They were not followed and even the drowsy desk clerk in the boarding house was nowhere to be seen. On the way, Morgan explained his idea of how to draw John English out into the open. He apologized for the risk involved but, Jane, after exploring it with a number of questions, agreed that, given the situation and the need to prevent English from simply disappearing again, it was worth a try.

As soon as they were behind closed doors, Morgan made his way to an ancient writing desk. There he scribbled a fast missive to Harry Vonderhorst and took longer over a shorter note to John English. Locking the door behind him, he left to find messengers.

Jane found his quarters to be well used but clean and furnished with pieces that would have been expensive in their day. While Morgan gave the place no real notice, she supposed that the rooms must have been where the original owners of the former home spent much of their time. They were large, comfortable, and boasted a wide bay window that looked out onto the street. The various lamps around the room provided a soft, cautious light in order to reduce any possible attention from outside.

She edged the curtains aside and looked out of the window to the darkening day and the rain that had begun to fall. She was glad to have found an oasis in a city that had very rapidly turned deadly hot. Jane admitted too that Jamie's quiet competence gave her a degree of confidence that not too long ago she was in danger of losing. She started to relax a bit.

When Morgan returned, he produced some hard cheese, a baguette, and a bottle of claret. They shared the informal repast as they sat across from each other in worn, over-stuffed chairs. For the first time, he looked tired to her. He was not a young man, but that fact could be easily overlooked, given the level of energy typically coming from him. Tonight, he looked like a man who had been in a gunfight and was just now letting himself down for a few minutes.

As they sat savoring the wine and the peace, Morgan looked at the woman in the chair across from him. She was far more than he thought she was at first. He wondered again how tough she was, but the thought drifted away as he remembered the details of how she saved his life. She was a woman of surprising depth and he had never met anyone like her. Maybe it was the light, or maybe it was the aftermath of the day's excitement, but he found himself very attracted to her, even as tired as he was. It was right after this thought that she rose, walked to him, and kissed him fully.

She said, "We have about three hours before we have to go. Let's get to know each other a little better."

Morgan said nothing but stood and took her hand and together they found the bedroom.

English was sure that James Morgan now knew that his old partner was trying to settle debts. For that matter, Jamie probably guessed his intentions for the girl as well. Morgan would never leave the city, not now. No, he will come for me, thought English.

The attorneys had made the financial and other preparations he had directed. So, if the need be, he was ready to vanish. He'd be in good shape to resurface at an appropriate time. The escape route worked well and he knew where he would go—away from Baltimore.

A knock on the doorframe of his study broke him out of his reverie and his secretary stood waiting with a message. The message read:

"John,
Enough. We need to talk. Meet me alone inside The Pig's Eye at Ross and Union Street, 10 p.m. Leave your people outside.
Jamie"

English couldn't believe that Morgan would meet him alone. Jamie would be sure to have others there as well, of course. It was an obvious trap. If he went, at the very least, they'd try to kill each other. He and Jamie, finally. Or, he could play it cautious and just leave now. There was no rush. He had waited this long.

But, in the end, the opportunity to pay Morgan back was too great to miss. The feelings that English first began to nurture laying on the floor of the cell back in 1857 resurfaced with full force. He was so close. He would meet the bastard, he thought, but not on his terms. He would be there waiting for Morgan when he showed up.

English sent messages to his agents in the Twentieth Ward, telling them the time and place. He contacted his driver and told him to be ready to take a long drive, if necessary. When the time came, he loaded two revolvers, placing one in a shoulder holster and the other he would hold in his lap under a blanket. He struggled into a protective vest, covered it with a long slicker against the rain, and called for his valet to take him to the third floor.

It was 8 p.m. and neither Jamie nor Jane was able to get any sleep after they had exhausted themselves in sweet exercise. So, they had simply lain quietly together, wanting to think about what their love-making meant, but only able to think of what they were about to do.

"Time to go," Morgan said. "Are you ready?"

"I'm ready," she answered.

"Remember, simply show yourself, and then get back behind the building. Take no chances. Harry and his men will be right there. Check your revolver."

"Yes, boss," she said sarcastically.

"Jane, I have serious misgivings about this. If we didn't need a distraction, something to stop him for a moment, you wouldn't be coming," he said with some heat.

"Look, Jamie. That man killed John. He tried to kill both you and me. God knows how many others the sick monster has murdered," she countered. "I'm going."

There was vehemence and determination in her voice he had never heard her express until now. It leant such a degree of emphasis to her words that he said nothing more.

They would take a hansom the six squares between St. Paul and Richmond streets where Morgan had discovered English's escape route. If he had it figured correctly, they would be there waiting when he emerged from the alley to get into the carriage. They would have to be quick and the timing precise to avoid losing him though. English would, of course, be early for their meeting at The Pig's Eye. But, he would never get there. Morgan was going to stop him at the mouth of the alley.

Morgan needed to slow English down in the efficient escape process he had established. That was Jane's job. As she did that, he would have to first deal with the armed bodyguard, then English, who was sure to be carrying a weapon as well.

The rain poured over her umbrella and his slicker as they stepped out of the cab and walked together to the alley. It was about 8:15 p.m. and Morgan thought that they might have a wet wait. Harry had not arrived yet. As they drew near the opening, a feint rumbling could be heard from above.

"Damn! He's earlier than I thought," Morgan hissed. "Harry's not here. Get back into the doorway."

He and Jane pressed themselves into the shadows of a brick arched doorway twenty feet from the mouth of the alley. The weak emanation from the gaslights on the street bisected the white marble slab upon which they stood.

"Where? Where is he?" Jane demanded into his ear loud enough to be heard through the rain. She followed the direction of his finger to the roof above them, and then followed it to his lips.

"Okay, he's coming and will be down in another minute," said Morgan. "This is where I want you to be after you stop him. I'll do the rest. Get your revolver ready, just in case."

"Jamie, Harry and his men aren't here. This is too dangerous," she whispered urgently.

"It is dangerous, sure enough, Jane. But we may never have this chance again. He has to be stopped now."

There was iron in his voice. There was too much history between these two men. Morgan had changed but the street and the chaos was still deep within him.

Jane fell silent. Then he said, "Get ready."

She moved around him under the arch, closer to the alley just as English's Brougham pulled up. The bodyguard scanned the area and climbed down, carrying a Winchester 1876 rifle. A side arm was evident as well. He quickly moved up the alley.

Morgan had a tight grip on the shoulder of Jane's coat. "Wait, wait," he said drawing the words out. She was shaking.

"Now," he said.

Cooper shrugged off his hand and moved up the wall toward the alley, umbrella up, feminine figure outlined by the gaslights behind her. Morgan sprinted across Richmond Street, around the shielding carriage, and came up on the opposite side of the alley. English rolled out of the opening, using his own hands to propel the chair. The Winchester followed.

Jane stepped out into the open and said, "Daddy, it's me, your daughter." Then she bolted back toward the archway. Both heads turned to her and English stopped wheeling the chair.

At the same time, Morgan brought a billy down on the head of the bodyguard and put the Webley to the side of English's turned head. He kicked the rifle away and reached under his old mate's armpit.

"Hello, John. Where are you keeping it these days?" Morgan found the holstered revolver, yanked the gun, and sent it skidding across the wet street.

"Was that Hattie's girl?" was English's response. With that, his hand jerked up out of his lap in a straight line, the big Colt Navy connecting with Morgan's nose and forehead. He then dove out of the chair while firing at Morgan, who was staggering back, stunned, and bleeding from a gash in his forehead.

English's second shot took Morgan in the side and tore a gaping hole, the round passing through.

As English continued his roll away from the chair, he heard a *boom, boom,* and felt a searing pain in his chest. Looking up, he saw the woman, both arms extended, firing at him. He scuttled over the body of his guard, straightened, and fired at his assailant. She spun away from the alley, wobbled into the street, and fell with a splash into a dark puddle.

English turned quickly back to Morgan, but it was too late. Morgan was on one knee, propped against the carriage wheel that was jerking

176 *Making Our Own Order*

as the nervous horses began to panic. He was firing rapidly, wide and high. He was having trouble focusing and he was losing blood.

The crippled man, ducking the barrage, swiftly dragged himself to the front of the carriage. The vest had saved his life—for now. Using the modified handholds, like some sort of misshapen spider, he hauled his twisted body up and into the box. He then fired over the horses' heads. That was too much for the already terrified beasts. They reacted immediately by racing from the danger, down the street and away.

Harry and the Plant's security men arrived on Richmond Street to find Morgan slumped over Jane Cooper, tributaries of watery blood radiating from the bodies. The rivulets formed a confused and terrible pattern, as gravity pushed them along the cracks between the cobblestones on their way to the sewer. The men lifted both casualties, carried them rapidly down the street to carriages, and sped away into the night. It easily could have been 1857.

Part III
Civilized Substitution

Chapter 26

Baltimore
Late August 1896

It was the top of the ninth inning. The score was tied at four with one out. The Cleveland Spiders' Patsy Tebeau danced down the third base line in front of the Orioles' John McGraw who was playing even with the bag. A fly ball deep enough would score the go-ahead run.

Cleveland's slugging left fielder, Jesse "Crab" Burkett, stood awaiting a 3-2 pitch. He had already fouled off four pitches and the infield was getting impatient and edgy. Burkett was known for spoiling pitches. In point of fact, this annoying habit of his was a primary driver behind the Playing Rules Committee's decision to make a foul ball a strike. With a full count, Burkett could care less though. The barrel of his bat made tiny circles as he stood in, wagging the thing menacingly, and glaring at the Birds' pitcher, Duke Esper.

In no hurry, the Baltimore fireballer ignored the batter and stood on the mound rubbing up the baseball with his big hands. Esper needed a pitch here. The Spiders' Cy Young had held the Orioles to two runs and the Clevelands had scored twelve runs of their own in the first game of the doubleheader. The Birds needed the rubber match to fend off their National League rivals and hold on to first place. They wouldn't mind saving a little face either.

Standing on the mound, Esper towered above the infield. Hurlers had known for some time that they could generate more speed if they threw downhill. So, when the rules changed in 1893, grounds crews had begun to build small hills around the slab in the pitchers' box. In Baltimore, as was typical of everything they did, the adjustment was taken to an extreme. As a result, in joyous defiance of opposing complaints, the Orioles' staff worked from mounds of prodigious height.

All of Union Park stood on nervous, stomping feet. The crowd's voice was deafening. Leather-lunged epithets were hurled at the batter through hands cupped around mouths. The miles of iron railings around the yard were getting a good ringing. But to Esper, it was like listening to the ocean in a seashell—audible, but fuzzy and distant. He looked around at his defense. Kelley, Brodie, and Keeler patrolled the outfield, with Doyle, Reitz, Jennings, and McGraw around the horn.

In center, Brodie was yelling something obscene. Wee Willie, in right, paced off some of his unfathomable energy, and Kelley was smiling at some floozy in the left field stands. The infield kept up a steady, encouraging chatter, except for McGraw who walked purposefully to Esper in the middle of the infield.

"Duke, you need a pitch here. Crab can put it in the air. Don't be an asshole; keep it down in the zone. No fly balls," barked McGraw over the crowd noise.

"John, what the hell you doing over here? Go play third, if you can. I know what I'm doing. This guy's a sucker for the high heat," responded Esper, just as loudly.

"Foxy Ned" Hanlon, the manager, stood straight up in front of the Orioles' bench chewing his handlebar and sweating through his suit. He too was wondering what the hell McGraw was doing.

"Duke, if you let this run in, I'm going to break your arm," said McGraw to the team's best pitcher. There was no doubt that he meant it.

"You're going to have to grow some first, runt," fired back the big pitcher.

"Just do your job so you don't have to find out what this runt is capable of doing," the third baseman snarled.

McGraw trotted back into position while yelling at Hughie Jennings, the shortstop. "Stay awake now, Hughie. Check the runner before going to Doyle. Go home with it if you have to!"

Esper turned back to the three men waiting at home plate, the batter, the ump, and the Orioles' bulky catcher, Wilbert Robinson.

Robinson squatted; called for a low, hard fastball; and reinforced it with the down low sign.

Esper nodded, looked at the prancing runner, toed the slab, took an abbreviated windup, and threw the heat, high and right across the plate.

In a flash, Burkett's eyes got very wide, then very narrow as he focused on the white sphere that was entering his zone. As he strode into the pitch, his hips turned, then his big shoulders followed, bringing with them a large club. The bat took an upward slant in its arc around the batter. In a miracle of coordination, the thickest part of the bat connected squarely with the pitched ball as it entered the strike zone at the letters.

The result was a soaring drive to deep right field. Patsy Tebeau, the runner on third, trotted back to the bag to tag up in case the ball was caught. He would be the go-ahead run in the ninth.

Jennings raced out to the cut-off position, watching the back of Keeler's uniform rippling as the little centerfielder raced, balls out, to the fence.

McGraw looked over at Tebeau who was standing on third with an ear-to-ear grin aimed right at the Oriole third baseman. That was all McGraw's short fuse needed; incensed, he rushed at his tormentor. Tebeau turned to watch Keeler make an amazing, over-the-shoulder catch. The runner then launched himself toward home, using the bag for leverage. It was to be an easy run on a sacrifice fly.

McGraw arrived at the base about the time Tebeau was departing. Reaching out in desperation, the bandy-legged infielder's iron grip clamped down on Patsy's belt. The physics of these conflicting forces caused the runner's torso to stop while his feet scrabbled, seeking traction. The combination of spikes biting into the base path and McGraw's counterweight resulted in a stumble that brought McGraw down on top of Tebeau in a tangle. Using elbows and fists, the runner was up quickly enough though, and on his way home again. The relay throw to and from Jennings was perfect.

"Uncle Robbie," the catcher, on one knee just up the third base line, caught the ball low on the fly. Left shin guard up to take the slide, he then tagged Tebeau in the face, hard. The Spider flipped like he had been clotheslined and his desperate bid to score ended six inches from home plate.

The stands erupted, the dugouts erupted, and Patsy Tebeau erupted. When it was all over, the poor quality of the umpire's eyesight was firmly established and Tebeau had been thrown out of the game. McGraw stood on third and checked his manicure.

The game ended in a 4-4 tie, but the rules of engagement had been set for the two teams, and their cranks, for the rest of the season.

Harry Vonderhorst sat in the owner's box with Mayor Alcaeus P. Hooper who was snoring off a free drunk that had started in the first inning of the first game. It was a muggy Baltimore evening after a sweltering August day, and all Harry wanted to do was get home and cool off. Listening to "His Honor's" serenade, he wondered why he bothered to entertain the city's dignitaries.

Hooper sat slumped in a chair, mouth open, head back. Streaks of dribbled mustard provided highlights to the broader beer stain on his white shirt. The stain traced the outline of the man's bulbous stomach, which was testing the strength of three beleaguered shirt buttons. Vonderhorst idly watched several houseflies play with the idea of investigating the man's tonsils. He wondered whether that would even wake the slumbering ox.

Harry could have been home with Bernadette by now, sipping a gin and quinine, if not for the meeting he had arranged with his manager Hanlon. The Orioles were in first place and well positioned for their third pennant in as many years. All of that was great, but Harry knew the Birds could just as easily implode given the personalities on the team, especially one particular personality.

Harry was expecting yet another stern letter from the Rules Committee on McGraw's interpretation of fair play. He would probably hear from League President Nick Young, as well. That could mean suspension, but another threat was more likely. It was a sure bet he'd hear from Frank Robinson too. The Spiders' owner would tell Harry that he and others in the League were getting fed up. That was a laugh; Frank's own player/manager, the same Tebeau in the scrap with McGraw, had been suspended for his own shenanigans earlier in the year.

Vonderhorst didn't relish talking to the prickly Hanlon, but he wasn't going to be the one who spoke to that maniac, McGraw, and someone had to. That meant Hanlon. The brewer sometimes regretted his decision to concede total field responsibility to the skipper, but not this time.

Ned Hanlon was an odd duck, but he was also a brilliant manager. What the New York, Boston, and Cleveland newspapers called "dirty" baseball, he called "scientific." And it was, mostly. It was obvious to anyone who followed the National League that impeding runners, cutting inside second on the way to third, hiding baseballs in the outfield grass, honing spikes to points, and applying foreign substances to the ball or scuffing it were certainly well-thumbed pages in the Orioles' playbook. Opposing teams could also expect soap chips mixed with the dirt around the mound, thick infield grass and foul lines built to keep slow rollers in play. But while all of those things were employed, so were the hit-and-run, double steals, the bunt, the squeeze play, the cutoff play, sacrifices, the Baltimore chop, and a variety of other small ball tactics. And if it wasn't Hanlon and the Orioles who invented these stratagems, then they certainly were the most prolific users of them.

It was also Hanlon who assembled Baltimore's Big Four of Keeler, McGraw, Kelley, and Jennings. He also added stalwarts Robinson, Brodie, Reitz, and Doyle. Then he built the strategy of speed and deception to match the talent. It was a bold departure from the tendency of prior years to go with big men with big power. It was his assembling of this team, which was making a run at their third championship in a row, that earned him the adjective foxy.

Still, there was something about Hanlon that made Harry uneasy. Maybe it was his tiny, black, agate eyes set above a wild beaver of a mustache. Maybe it was his receding hairline that produced a billboard forehead that communicated more than he knew. Maybe it was the chain-draped, three-piece wool suit that he wore constantly, even in the hottest weather. Or maybe it was the raw way that he dealt with the most volatile players in anyone's dugout.

No one was more volatile than John McGraw. In fact, McGraw was off his trolley. To call him scrappy would be to call Niagara Falls a leaky faucet. Mean and irritable was more like it. Joe Kelley could field and hit certainly, but his swoon-causing good looks and blond hair produced as many scores off the field as his slugging did on. This would normally not be a problem except for the occasional fatigue and lack of focus. Hughie Jennings was basically a quiet country boy and a Pennsylvania coalminer, driven to league-hitting heights by the fear that one day he might have to return to the mines. Sometimes his worry spilled over into the clubhouse. And then there was Willie

Keeler, a true gentleman, who, despite his diminutive frame, could do it all and did, day in and day out, maintaining a .341 lifetime batting average. Of them all, Wee Willie was the most loved.

Despite personalities and egos inflated by success, Hanlon was clearly in charge of the 1896 Orioles. He accomplished this through an uncanny ability to know when to apply the throttle and when to ease off. He also was smart enough to work closely with the team's father figure, captain, and starting catcher, Wilbert Robinson. Wilbert was the Orioles' communicator and it was a good thing he was because Hanlon's interpersonal skills tended to be a bit sandpapery.

Harry was about to get a dose of those skills as the manager barged into the owners box with a snort and a sour look at the city's highest official, still sawing wood in the corner.

"Evening, Mr. Vonderhorst," began Hanlon. "Who's the rhino?"

"That rhino is your city's leader, Ned," explained Harry with no little irony.

"Sorry, boss," answered Hanlon. "I didn't recognize him without his hand in someone's pocket or on someone's ass."

"Yes, well, it seems he really likes our beer. Thanks for coming. You know what I want to talk to you about?" asked Harry, moving away from the political critique.

"Not really," answered Hanlon. He was going to force Harry to voice his specific displeasure with McGraw. In this way, the manager could use Vonderhorst as leverage with his problem child without having to offer his own opinion of the nonsense at third base today.

Harry was smarter than that. "What did you say to John after the game today?"

"Say to him?" hedged Hanlon.

"For Christ's sake, Ned. I'm tired, I'm hot, and I've got to deal with that before I go home tonight," said Harry, indicating the rhino. "So stop screwing around. What do I say to the Rules Committee?"

Hanlon cracked, "In a game with rules, bending them becomes the game."

Then in response to Harry's curdled look, he sighed and said, "Tell them you don't know what they're talking about. Tell them that players get tangled up on the bases every day. Tell them that's why they pay umpires—to sort that crap out. We had an ump today, didn't we?"

Harry stared at Hanlon for a moment and thought about finding a new, more respectful manager. Then he said, "Tell McGraw, no more. That's it. Tell him that if his foolishness continues, not only will the League decide to add another ump on the field, but his bony rear will be getting splinters on the pine for the next month."

"You want me to tell John McGraw that?" asked an incredulous Hanlon.

"Ned, do I look like I'm bullshitting?" responded Harry. "Just do it and do it now."

It was Hanlon's turn to stare. Then he said annoyingly, "You're the boss." He turned for the door.

"Just a minute. There's another thing," said an irritated Vonder-horst. "One of my contacts in New York tells me that you were shopping Duke Esper to the Spiders. Is that true?"

"Everything I have, except my family, is for sale at a price," said the manager caustically and truthfully.

"Maybe, Ned. But without talking to me, you're selling something that isn't yours," said Harry, biting back. "Esper is an innings eater. You know that. The Spiders already have Young and Cuppy and they're breathing down our necks. Why would you even consider doing that?"

Hanlon shrugged, the conversation was over as far as he was concerned. Harry was not happy with his manager. There is something else here, he thought, but he let it go for now. He was tired and he wanted to go home to Bernadette.

Chapter 27

Baltimore
Late August 1896

B ernadette was waiting for him on the veranda in the rear of the big
house on Frederick Road. Ancient oaks, mountain laurel, and hon-
eysuckle surrounded the terrace while a trellis of rambling rose provided fragrant protection from the lingering heat of the day. The home
perched alone on a rise and the retreat behind the estate was designed
to create a sunset view of rolling hills. Stretching away to the west were
patches of cleared meadow, interrupted by bands of dark wood.

A surprising and welcome breeze had arisen, pushed by oncoming,
roiling clouds. Low rumbling followed the occasional distant flash of
heat lightening. A white wicker table, surrounded by matching chairs,
held a clear, cold drink with a large hunk of lime floating in it. Along-
side of the sweating glass, a message from James Morgan, marked
"Chicago," was waiting for Harry as well.

As she watched the storm approach, Bernadette could not miss the
metaphor. Years had passed since her father had disappeared for the
second time, leaving the stain of hatred, death, and fear behind him.
The uneasiness she was feeling this evening was reminiscent of those
first months after his departure back in 1883. Losing Jane was awful
enough, but not knowing where John English was, while fully understanding his intentions, was a wretched way to exist.

But Bernadette had been able to live in fear for only so long. Time
and her husband eventually did their work in helping her to put it
all away, at least for a while. Tonight's anxiety, however, managed to
resurface all of those loose ends in her history.

Harry had been a rock the entire time. He was everything that she had hoped he would be when she married him, and far more. They shared everything, both the good and the bad. And now, finally, they would share a child, she thought, as she rubbed below her navel where she had just felt the kick.

Together they had many blessings, but they had also weathered a series of personal and business trials that included economic depression, the failure of their insurance company, devastating railroad strikes, and the burning down of Union Park, the Orioles' home field. But, of those difficulties, their brother John's death in a San Francisco earthquake the year before was the most painful. It had been heartbreaking to learn that, with loving help in Baltimore, he still died penniless and in debt. Through it all, she had changed; she had been forced to grow up.

Thank God for the Orioles though. A wry smile emerged as she thought of that silly bet so many years ago. The team had already won two pennants and they were expected to win a third this year. Aside from the normal ulcers that owning a team of bad boy prima donnas produced, the Birds had been a lifesaver. They were the source of the Vonderhorsts' passion, joy, social life, and celebrity. They even continued to sell a lot of Eagle beer. The only blemish in the last three years had been the shocking news that John had sold his minority share in the team to pay off creditors. This seemed to have no effect, though. Harry's unexpected partner was a large business conglomerate, which up to this point had shown no active interest in its investment, even in the championship years. They assumed that the Orioles were a minor part of a major portfolio.

Bernadette looked at the unopened message from Jamie. It was addressed to the both of them. Her smile faded and, for the second time, she decided to wait for Harry before opening it.

She thought of Jamie Morgan. When was he home last? She tried to remember. No man his age should be on the road. She knew what drove him, of course, and a little wag of her head revealed her wonder at how she could have misjudged him. He was no saint, certainly, but to have questioned his intentions toward her and the Vonderhorst family reminded her of how wrong one could be. Once he had recovered from his wounds, he had dedicated himself to finding John English. And over the years, each time a new lead had surfaced, Jamie gathered himself and was gone.

"There you are," said a tired Harry, as he came out onto the terrace, kissed her, patted her stomach, then flopped into one of the chairs.

"We may get chased back inside in a few minutes," she warned, handing him the drink. Then, "We've heard from Jamie."

Harry took the beaded glass, rested it on the arm of the chair, and sat staring at the inky sky for a moment. "I think this storm will be a nasty one," he observed.

"He's in Chicago," she said, handing him the message.

Harry took it and held it without opening it or even looking at it. "Do you think this will ever be over?" he asked, not expecting a reply.

"Harry, we have to get Jamie home," said Bernadette.

"Yes, we do," he answered. "But he won't stop until he finds English; we both know that."

With a sigh, Harry tore the envelope and read silently, then wearily extended the note to Bernadette. She read Morgan's surprisingly high-wrought, old-fashioned hand. After the preliminary inquiries as to their health, he had written:

"I am convinced English is alive, but he is not in Chicago. I have identified a law firm here that I believe he uses. Through means that I will not explain, a bit of correspondence also has come into my possession that is very promising. I am on my way back to Baltimore and I will provide you details when I see you both. If I remember, the manager of your baseball team is a man named Hanlon. Be very cautious in your dealings with him until I see you."

There was little after that.

"I feel like it's starting all over again," said Bernadette sadly.

"It has never stopped," Harry replied. "But maybe this is the beginning of the end," he added hopefully. Then, as the first heavy drops of rain began to spatter the veranda's stonework, "What the hell does Hanlon have to do with this?"

The Diamond Café was John McGraw's pride and Wilbert Robinson's retirement plan. The two stars had become partners off the field in the creation of something Baltimore had never seen before. For the first time, the city's male population had its favorite poisons packaged under one roof. Sports and vice, two close bedfellows, were the bill of faire. This idea was so popular that Howard Street, north of Franklin, became the center of the Monumental City's sporting universe, outside of Union Park and Pimlico, of course.

When The Diamond first elbowed its way in among North Howard's theater establishment, there was a lot of sniffing. But it wasn't long before the local impresarios recognized a kindred spirit and a symbiotic partner in the business of entertaining Baltimore.

The bar offered three floors of sports, food, drink, and male bonding. It was a palace of leisure, boasting a modern saloon, bowling alleys, a gymnasium, showers, lockers, and a billiard parlor. Upper rooms were reserved for cards, private meetings, and reading. Nowhere else could a gentleman find the latest editions of the world's sporting news and those wishing to discuss it. The Diamond's electronic scoreboard offered patrons a way to follow the Orioles, whether the team was home or away. Its bowling alleys boasted automatic ball returns that drew the best tournaments and the best keglers from all over the city. Even the Birds' owner would show up on occasion, ready to take on all comers.

The saloon itself held a massive bar that was reflected in a world of mirrors, making the entire room seem cavernous. Over the bar was a larger-than-life reclining nude whose classic dimensions had the Ladies' Abstinence League all a-cluck. Oak was everywhere and the saloon's flocked wallpaper was covered in memorabilia pilfered from locker rooms around the National League. In the off season and sometimes after games, visitors might even have a chance to drink their fill while rubbing elbows with the Orioles' Big Four.

The place was a melting pot, drawing clientele from all economic strata. This suited McGraw and Robinson nicely and they kept the beer cheap, as long as it was Eagle you were drinking. There were thick steaks for the well heeled and oysters for everyone else. Free pickled eggs, pretzels, and sandwich meat could be found on the bar more often than not. There was a wide spectrum of smoking choices and cigars were what you paid for them.

Women, although never employed by the house, were welcome as long as they behaved themselves and were not too overt in their intentions. Racing bookies were regulars, but their business was not sanctioned, nor was it particularly discouraged.

In sum, The Diamond was heaven to those whose piece of the Gilded Age was limited to living vicariously through baseball stars hitting above .330.

John McGraw sat at the bar with Steve Brodie. They were having a drink waiting for Hughie Jennings. The rest of the saloon's patrons left them pretty much alone. This was because no one ever really wanted to rub elbows with McGraw a second time. The exceptions, of course, were his roommate Hughie and the rest of the Orioles. Uncle Robbie was down at the end of the bar, leaning into a group, telling some moldy baseball story.

"Brodie, what I'm sayin' is that your swearing has lost its effect. You've worn it out. It has no impact any longer. You might as well find some other way to express yourself," suggested a helpful McGraw.

"What the fuck you talkin' about?" inquired Brodie.

"See, myself, I'm very selective when I use the F word," lectured the third baseman. "That way, when I want to get thrown out of a game or I want to distract a runner, it means something. The way you use it, it's trite, expected."

"John, why do you have to be an asshole as much as you are? That's something maybe you should cut down on a little bit." Brodie had spent a lot of time with McGraw and knew how to sweet talk him.

"That goes for your use of other words, as well," continued McGraw, ignoring the outfielder. Now, for instance, take the word s—" A slap on the back signaled Jennings' arrival and before he could climb the stool next to McGraw, a foamy Eagle awaited him.

A long draught later, Hughie said, "Willie's not up for cards tonight. And Kelley's got a date, but Reitz is in and with Robbie that makes five. Did you hear what Patsy said to the guy from *The Herald*? Man, what a bastard!"

"Careful, Hughie, McGraw here doesn't like cussing," warned Brodie.

Jennings gave Brodie a strange look, then said to the Orioles' third baseman, "Tebeau claims you held him, then tackled him."

"That's not right! I saw it. John tackled him, then he held him," cracked Brodie.

"That's not exactly how it went," began McGraw.

Jennings continued, "Said the next time it was going to be you eating dirt."

"Is Patsy still crying about Johnny grabbing his belt and tackling him?" Robinson had joined the group and was mopping up the wet rings on the bar.

"That's not. . . ." attempted McGraw again.

"Yeah, and at the end of the story, he called you a 'plug ugly nutcase' and the dirtiest player in the National League," concluded Hughie.

"Wait a minute," demanded Brodie. "John McGraw is not that ugly. I bet there are a lot of ball players uglier than him."

"Fuck you, Brodie," said McGraw half-heartedly, without much impact and forgetting his earlier lecture. "You fools should know that aggressiveness is the main thing in baseball."

"Well you sure do have the aggression part down," observed Hughie.

"Besides, Patsy's dirtier than I am," complained McGraw. "Ask Reitz about turning the double play with Tebeau comin' at him."

"Ask me what?" Henny Reitz had joined the players.

"Tebeau, Patsy Tebeau," explained McGraw. "Who's dirtier, him or me?"

"I don't know about that, John, but I do know that those guys are real unhappy with you, with us."

"With us? What did I do?" whined Brodie.

"Great team spirit, Stevie," said Uncle Robbie. Then, "So what are they going to do about it?"

With that question, four members of the Cleveland Spiders swaggered into the big saloon, found a table, and began to look around. Patsy Tebeau was among them. All of the Orioles had noticed.

Robinson spoke first, "Now look, you idiots, no fighting. Do not cause any damage in my place," he warned, shaking his fist.

"Yeah, no nothing in here. Hughie, if you want to fight, take it outside," said McGraw facetiously.

"I don't want to fight anyone, John, I'm going upstairs. Let's play cards," said Jennings who generally excused himself from McGraw's extracurriculars.

"Me too," said Reitz. "My hands are fine instruments and should not be punching anything." He and Jennings stood and climbed the stairs to the card rooms.

"John, why don't you go upstairs too," suggested Robinson.

"I will Uncle, I will," said McGraw gazing over at the table of Spiders.

"I've always wanted to smack that guy, Childs," Brodie informed his friends.

"Brodie, I said no fighting," Robinson warned again. "Besides, Cupid's a Calvert County man, a Marylander.

"Just another tobacco spitter to me," said McGraw, grabbing the tray of the waiter making his way to the Cleveland players' table. "I'll take this order, Jimmy."

"Oh, no," said Robinson, hurriedly trying to work his way around to the other side of the bar.

As McGraw arrived at the table, all four Spiders players stood at the sight of the combative Orioles' third sacker.

"Gentlemen, no need to stand for me. Please be seated. What can I get for you? Milk? A slice of humble pie on the side? They tell me the crow is good tonight."

Childs stepped toward McGraw with a black look, but Tebeau's arm held him back.

"Take it easy, Cupid. Before you get to dance with Muggsy, here, I have a few things to say to him myself," said Patsy, using the nickname McGraw hated. Childs was the Spiders' second baseman and the scars he had from base runners like McGraw made the round-faced infielder nasty and dangerous.

"Patsy, I'm surprised that you have the energy to say anything, after shooting your mouth off to *The Herald*," observed McGraw. "And, Clarence Algernon, does your mother know you hang in saloons?" The abrasive third baseman couldn't resist twisting Child's tail with the name his mother had hung on him.

"You're a prick, John," said Tebeau, "but before we bust you and your place up, I just wanted you to know that once we win the pennant, we're gonna take the Cup again and laugh as the world realizes that the great Baltimore Orioles couldn't win the big one. Again."

Now these were clear fighting words. The Temple Cup was some owner's idea of a championship. Once the pennant was won, the first place team had to play the second place team for the Cup. Although the Orioles had won the season-long pennant by three games in both '94 and '95, they had yet to win this cursed trophy, losing the four-game series first to the Giants and then to the Spiders last year. Tebeau's weighty, roundhouse comment landed squarely on McGraw's ego.

McGraw had come to the table expecting to pick a fight. So he was willing and ready. Patsy's pronouncement was the spark.

McGraw swung the thick, wooden waiter's tray hard into the face of Childs, then back swiftly to catch Tebeau's ear as he was ducking. The edge of the tray came up again with force under Child's chin and he went down. Tebeau and the other two Spiders leapt on McGraw, fists flying. A knot of thrashing men rolled on the floor.

Tables and chairs flew in all directions and nearby patrons, grabbing their mugs of beer, scrambled to get out of the way. Suddenly, Brodie was in the pile, hammering away at Tebeau who was busy with a spitting and kicking McGraw. Robinson weighed in, swung a billy at a Spider and pulled another off the Oriole infielder. Tebeau stood, slipped a punch from Brodie, then grabbed a half-full pitcher of beer from a teetering table and swung it against the Oriole outfielder's head. Brodie staggered away, dazed and wet.

In short order, Uncle Robbie had a bloody, flailing McGraw in one hand and the billy planted in Tebeau's chest. "That's all for tonight, Patsy. You and your boys made your point. You don't want this to overshadow your interview, do you?" asked Robinson who had noticed two baseball beat writers sprinting for the door.

"Okay, Robbie. It's your place too, I guess," conceded Tebeau, rubbing his skinned knuckles and watching McGraw warily. Like the rest of the league, the Spiders' captain held the Orioles' veteran catcher in high regard, despite the face tag on his slide into home just the day before.

The confrontation was over, satisfaction achieved. "I'll see you on the base paths, John," Patsy said, leading the Clevelands out the door. They went peacefully, tucking in shirts, smoothing back hair, and glaring at their enemy over their shoulders. There would be another day, another game, and probably another fight.

The next morning, both *The Sun* and *The Baltimore American* carried the story. "McGraw and Tebeau In Bar Rematch" was one headline. The other picked up on Patsy's idea, "Orioles in Plug Ugly Riot!"

Chapter 28

West Virginia
September 1896

Morgan watched each ancient, round-shouldered mountain slowly melt away behind the Chesapeake and Ohio train as it made its way through the Allegheny passes to the Greenbrier Valley and the West Virginia town of White Sulphur Springs. There, hidden among a verdant, rural world of hollows, dirt roads, and tumbled down log cabins, was the exclusive Playground of Presidents. That's what they called the resort, its spa, its private cottages, playing greens, riding paths, fishing streams, and hiking trails. Tucked away, deep below sheltering ridges, covered in hardwoods, now turning red and yellow, the very wealthy escaped the noxious city. They came to take the curative waters and breathe clean air. And maybe it was also a place to hide.

Was this where he would finally find John English? It was an unlikely place to disappear. Travelers had been stopping here since Washington's time. Even Britain's Prince Edward VII had stayed in one of the luxury lodges. But there just might be something to hiding in plain sight, Morgan thought. With a new name, who would know English? Many came here looking to ease their infirmities. His former friend would need care and he could afford whatever amount of it was required. So maybe White Sulphur Springs made sense.

Regardless, whether it made sense or not, the lead was too good to ignore. When he was in California tracing another thin tip, Harry had asked him to look into his brother John's sale of his interest in the Orioles. That led Morgan to a faceless syndicate of investors, which, in turn, led him to a law firm based in Chicago. Inquiries there were met with averted eyes and a clear message that his questions would not be answered.

Morgan wanted to provide Harry with something more substantial, so he identified the firm's most junior associate and followed him after a workday. When the young man detoured into a nearby bar, Morgan took the stool next to him. A few drinks and a lot of lies later, he knew he had learned something interesting.

Talk of baseball led to a bragging admission that the law firm indeed had a client who owned a piece of the champion Baltimore Orioles. No, it wasn't a syndicate; it was a single client. Sorry, he didn't know the client's name. But the young man's grandstanding got more interesting when he let on that the firm and its unidentified client had been involved in the negotiations that brought stars Joe Kelley, Steve Brodie, and Willie Keeler to Baltimore. Then, with a wink, he told Morgan that the law firm even worked with the team's famous manager, Ned Hanlon. Morgan knew this would be news to Harry even though Vonderhorst had given the team operations over to Hanlon in '93. Perhaps the absentee minority owner had not been so absent.

Morgan's thoroughness would not let him return to Baltimore without uncovering the minority owner's name. That's when he met Mary. Mary Jeter was a charwoman in trouble. Beaten by her alcoholic husband, now in Joliet Prison, she was working to support her unmarried daughter who was pregnant with her second child. The cleaning lady was willing to help for a price.

For two weeks, Mary delivered the firm's paper trash to Morgan's rented walk-up. Just as he was about to give it up as a bad idea, he got a real surprise. A crumpled envelope offered an address:

Mr. Isaac B. Pettibon, Esq.
White Sulphur Springs
West Virginia

Then, within the address, his eye caught the following: "Attention: Hanlon Project."

This information set him pawing through the latest pile in search of the envelope's contents. He didn't find a letter, but he did find a torn scrap that must have been part of someone's draft response. The Chicago attorney had written:

> "...certainly frustrating and so the plans for Mr. Esper have been terminated.
>
> On a different matter, be assured that the underlying negotiations surrounding the failure of the Fidelity Insurance Company have finally been concluded. All assets have been liquidated, and as requested, we have taken all precautions to keep your client's involvement completely confidential.
>
> Please let your client know that we have always appreciated his business, and that we hope to be of assistance to him for another ten years.
>
> Yours truly."

The letter was unsigned.

Once again, Morgan began to fill in a few gaps. Pitcher Duke Esper, Hanlon, and the Fidelity Insurance Company had a common denominator–Harry Vonderhorst. The Chicago law firm was working through an intermediary whose client was taking great pains to remain anonymous. Putting those facts together spelled John English to Morgan. And so he found himself on a train wending its way through the mountains of West Virginia.

As he listened to the clacking of the rails, he thought of Harry and Bernadette. It had been good to see them again. The three had become close during Morgan's very difficult and extended recovery from that violent night on Richmond Street a dozen years earlier. Jane's death also knitted them together in an inseparable, painful, emotional way. As a result, each was dedicated to the preservation of what was left of the Vonderhorst family, a family that now included him.

Bernadette was not happy to hear that he planned to remain in Baltimore a mere week before leaving again. But after they had discussed what Morgan had discovered in Chicago, the arguments ceased. It was obvious that he had to go. What was not obvious to Bernadette or Harry, for that matter, was why he felt he must go alone.

This was not something that Morgan wanted to explain. Not that it was difficult, just that he didn't want to say it out loud. Simply put, he was going to kill John English. This didn't come from some high sense of justice. It came from Baltimore's Twentieth Ward where savagery was a way of life. It had never left him. He had chained it up and contained it, letting it loose on those occasions when he needed it. To protect those he loved, he would let it loose one more time. Then, it would be over.

It was a short carriage ride from the tiny train station, through the resort's gates, to an enormous, pillared, alabaster hotel that stood in the center of radiating footpaths and macadamized roads. Morgan stood on the top step of what they called The Old White Hotel and surveyed the bowl in which the resort rested.

Women in white strolled leisurely with smart gentlemen over flowered lanes and shaded byways. Perhaps they were on their way to play tennis or golf or to find the riding stables. Others strode more purposefully as they made their way across a manicured lawn to a Greek revivalist structure. This building employed a set of gleaming, Doric columns to support a perfect dome. The dome itself was of copper and served to enshrine and protect the storied White Sulphur Spring.

Beyond and all around the spring, he could see a series of well-kept cabins and larger cottages that rose in tiers, some extending well up the steep ridges that ringed the resort. The higher these buildings climbed, the greater degree of privacy they enjoyed. He turned and followed his bags in to the reception desk.

Check-in was extended by the desk clerk's enthusiasm in explaining every detail of the resort. Half listening, Morgan gazed around at a riot of colors in the soaring lobby. Carpets, curtains, wallpaper, upholstery, and huge sprays of blooms in crystal vases worked together in their contrasts to create the general impression of standing in a garden. Dead American war heroes and European nobility stared out at him from the uncountable paintings that hung on the walls. Armies of helpful, gracious bellmen, clerks, waiters, maids, and maintenance men moved deftly among the expensive looking guests in restaurants, ballrooms, bars, and lounges.

Morgan followed his baggage down endless marble corridors and up at least two sets of broad carpeted stairs, finally arriving at a big, comfortable room on an upper floor. He was satisfied with the space, but he also wondered facetiously whether the busy, floral wallpaper that picked up the hotel's motif would let him sleep. The black bellman placed his valise on a rack, opened the double window, asked if there was anything else the gentleman needed, then waited that one more second as Morgan fished for his gratuity.

He kicked off his boots and stood at the open window. A cool breeze with a hint of the coming fall pushed the gauzy curtains at him as he looked out and down at what the clerk had called the Spring-house. His eyes rose up the surrounding ridge to the cottages beyond and he could see a nurse pushing an empty wheeled chair along one of the pathways. Somewhere up there, he knew he would find English.

Moving to his bag, he found the reliable, old Webley wrapped in oilcloth. He tossed it on the bed, then sat, and unfolded the guest map that he had been given. The grounds were vast and the accommodations both in the hotel and outside of it were legion. He would need to be patient, methodical, and discreet. But he had a good place to start: the attorney Isaac B. Pettibon. If that didn't bear fruit, he knew the spring was the facility's heart and there was a good chance that English would use it. He would find him there. Now, with some idea of how to begin, he rolled over on his side, ignored his innumerable aches and pains, and fell asleep.

Chapter 29

Baltimore
September 1896

It was Willie's turn to deal. The poker players in The Diamond card salon included Kelley, Brodie, Jennings, Reitz, and the hard-throwing rookie, Joe Corbett. The team had just completed an amazing thirty-one game home stand with a sweep of the Philadelphia Phillies. They had amassed a league-leading record of eighty-nine wins, thirty-seven losses, and three ties. The next morning would see the Orioles on the train to New York where they would play out the final three games of the season against the Giants. Cleveland, their closest rival, was ten games back in the standings and the players were feeling happy and cocky.

"Willie, c'mon, give me some cards; I've got a mortgage to pay," whined the losing Reitz, reflecting his normal situation. Not every player in the League was flush, given the owner's unofficial salary limit of twenty-four hundred dollars. The second baseman was particularly pinched since he had been nursing a leg injury and had sat for a few games in the last month. It was a particular thumb-in-the-eye that the League's Baseball Trust had decided not to pay injured players.

"Screw your mortgage, Henny. You'll be buying a new house with your six-hundred dollar Cup winnings," predicted the profane Brodie. As soon as he said it, he wished he hadn't. The Temple Cup was the Orioles' monster under the bed.

As Keeler shuffled and distributed the cards with his usual flair and wizardry, young Joe Corbett asked, "How many times do you think Young will start against us?"

He was referring to Denton True Young, or Cy to professionals and cranks alike. Cleveland's ace would be the main obstacle in winning the Cup. Young already had twenty-eight wins and led the majors in strikeouts, saves, and complete games. He was everyone's nemesis and the main reason that the Spiders had four more wins than losses this season against the Birds.

"Shut up, Joe. Don't worry about it," said Kelley. "Nobody hits and runs like we do. Hell, the team is hitting .328 and this is September."

Kelley himself was sporting a gaudy .364 batting average and leading the league in stolen bases.

"But good pitching always beats good—" began Corbett.

"Yeah, yeah, yeah, we've heard it before. Change the subject," ordered Brodie.

As the group studied their cards, Hughie Jennings asked Corbett, "When's that brother of yours going to defend his title? He knocks out the great John L. Sullivan, then sits on his laurels," complained Jennings.

"Boy, I would have loved to have been there for that bare-knuckler," mused Reitz.

"Well, Jim tells me that they're talking to some Brit champion. Somebody named Fitzsimmons. This spring, maybe, he says," answered Corbett.

"Let's all get tickets for that one," suggested Willie Keeler. "Gentleman Jim doin' the dance one more time! It'll be great."

"I open for a buck," said Kelley.

The others anteed up and fingered the cards they would keep for the draw. Keeler replaced their discards and Kelley immediately pushed them with a fiver.

"Christ!" said Reitz. 'I'm out." And Brodie followed him.

The game played out but Corbett's worry about the Temple Cup had infected them all. When the hand was over and Kelley was collecting, Keeler stood and indicated that he was finished. The rest felt the same and the game broke up with Jennings saying that if he didn't get home, his "wife" would be angry.

"Give McGraw a kiss goodnight for me, Hughie," cracked Brodie, never missing a chance to tease the two roommates about how close they were. Jennings didn't care; he owed McGraw, ever since his feisty friend fixed his swing that winter up at St. Bonnie's.

Kelley caught Keeler's eye and mouthed, "One for the road?" Willie nodded and the two very dissimilar friends made their way downstairs to the bar.

"You nervous about the Cup?" asked Kelley, running is hands through his blond hair that was parted in the middle.

"Not really," Keeler said honestly. Not much made the five-foot, four-inch outfielder nervous after holding his own against the League's best for the last few years. "You?"

"I think about it but, no, me neither," answered Kelley. Then, "Willie, what do you think about Hanlon? You think he's straight with us?"

"Yeah, I think so. What's on your mind, Joe? You're not still mad about the contracts last spring?" asked the little hitter. The Big Four all had had contract disputes with Hanlon in '94 and '95. Kelley again in '96.

"Well, yeah, that's on my mind, but no, I was just thinking about something else. Something a reporter said to me," answered the left fielder.

"Oh, man! You know better than that," groaned Keeler, assuming it was about his buddy's love life. It usually was.

"No, no, it wasn't just about me. It was you and John and Hughie too."

"What did this flack have to say?" asked a now interested Willie.

"Well, I was sitting having a beer with this guy, Chadwick, from *The New York Herald*. And he asks me if I really thought Hanlon was a genius. I told him that I don't know what a baseball genius is. It sounded kind of funny."

"Oxymoronic," offered Keeler.

"Yeah, moronic," agreed Kelley. "Then he says that it was a freak of nature that we were contending for our third pennant. That winning was never in Ned Hanlon's plans."

"What the hell does that mean?" asked Willie.

"He told me to think about it. When Silent Ned took over in '93, he inherited an eighth place team of drunks going nowhere."

"Yeah, then he built a world champion with brilliant roster moves," crowed Keeler, "they call him Foxy Ned now."

"No, Chadwick says it was just the opposite. He says that Hanlon kept a few shaky players, then filled the team with Punch and Judy hitters and fielders who couldn't field."

"What? What are you talking about?" asked a confused Keeler.

"Listen, Willie. This scribbler says that in '93, Hanlon's first season, a lot of strange things went on. First, the team holds on to Robbie, who we all love, but he would tell you himself that he's at the end of his career."

"Wait, Joe. You're talkin' about a guy who's hitting .350. He went seven for seven against the Browns. Our leader," argued the right fielder.

"Just listen, Willie. Next, he promotes McGraw, a utility man. Then he forces him to switch to a base he never played before. John's hitting was bad enough, asking him to learn a new position, wasn't going to help it. It wasn't going to help his charming personality either."

"Okay, so what? Maybe Hanlon had a longer term plan," suggested Willie.

"No, you aren't getting it. There's more. He planned to play Hughie at short. Jennings was a rookie who hadn't even hit his weight in the beer league! Reitz was okay, but no star. Then he added me. I was as raw as they come. No fundamentals, just guts. I was hitting .240 with the Pirates and Hanlon trades VanHaltren, a .300 hitter, for me and two-thousand dollars. Does that sound like someone trying to win a pennant?"

Keeler had begun to think about his own history with Hanlon.

"And what about you?" asked Kelley. "Let's be honest here. You were a throw-in in the Brooklyn trade. We gave them a solid hitting outfielder with a great arm for that sot, Brouthers, and you, a left-handed third baseman who was about to be released by a seventh-place team."

"Now, don't be saying that about Dan. His slugging average led the League and he's a good man," said Willie, unoffended by the description of his own signing, and taking up for someone else. That was just how Willie thought.

"Okay, that was harsh of me," admitted Kelley. "But, do you see? Hanlon was no genius, he was just goddamned lucky!"

"Or unlucky, if I follow your point. You're saying that Hanlon was trying to build a losing club on purpose. Okay, why would he do that? You know him; you know how intense he is. He could never do that," said an unconvinced Keeler.

"I think that's just it. It got away from him and I think he got wrapped up in us personally. We hit .330 as a team that year; the arms became live and our fielding got pretty darn good. Who knows how it happened? Hanlon certainly didn't expect it. How could he?"

"Joe, what difference does it make now? Who cares what his motivation was in '93? No one questions his fire today. We're about to win our third pennant in a row with Hanlon at the helm. How many clubs can say that?" reasoned Willie.

"Yeah, but—" began the left fielder.

"There's another way to look at all of that, you know," said Willie. "Just think about what a good guy Hanlon is because he gave a flake like you a chance to be part of this."

"Yeah, I know," sighed Kelley. Then, after a pause, "Maybe he is a genius after all."

Chapter 30

Baltimore
Early October 1896

The Cleveland Spiders' Cy Young was throwing flame as he warmed for the first game of the best-of-seven 1896 Temple Cup series against the Baltimore Orioles. Surprisingly, although Union Park was loud, it was not as full as Harry had expected it to be. Maybe it was the crisp weather or maybe it was the twenty-five cent increase in the price of a bleacher seat. Or maybe it was just that the cranks didn't put much store in this championship. The Birds had already won the pennant easily and many thought having to play the second-place team for bragging rights was insulting. Clearly, the Orioles had more to lose than the Spiders. They had experienced the pain of not finishing out the last two years.

Harry, Bernadette, a sober Mayor Hooper, Governor Brown, and other Baltimore notables jammed the owner's box and those seats around it. Harry was determined to solidify his place as everyone's favorite host. But he was also nervous. After all, they were facing the best pitcher in all of baseball and playing for a meaningless trophy that just could not be lost this time.

Bernadette read her husband perfectly. She turned to him, away from some weak witticism from the governor about her pregnancy. Taking Harry's hand, and resting her other on her growing abdomen, she said, "Doesn't the flag look grand?"

They both looked at the new, twenty-five foot, blue and white pennant, snapping sharply as it clung to a pole in centerfield.

"How do you like the ump's broom?" asked Harry, indicating the orange and black sweep he had bought for the occasion.

"Cute," she pronounced inappropriately. "Hoffer looks sharp today," she added, watching the Orioles' twirler warming.

She was trying to build Harry's confidence, not really knowing what "sharp" looked like.

"Uh huh," answered the owner absently.

Harry was watching Hanlon try to organize the team for a pregame photograph. Kelley was talking to a reporter, McGraw had Jennings in a playful headlock, Brodie was yelling something to the Spiders, Wee Willie was doing jumping jacks, and Doyle was refusing to join the group.

"It would have been nice to have Jamie here for this," observed Bernadette. "Any word?"

"What? Uh, no," said Harry, as they all stood for the playing of the National Anthem by the local German-American marching band. "That's another thing I'm worried about."

The Baltimore cranks in the stands sung the anthem's words with a religious seriousness until the point where Francis Scott Key wrote: "O say does that. . . ." The crowd screamed particular emphasis on the "O" in the line to let the world know that the Orioles were their team and they were proud of it.

With the song completed, the crowd settled in and began to clap and buzz as the gong sounded to signal a start to play. "Get at 'em!" could be heard echoing around the park.

The Orioles rung runs out of every opportunity that game. They did it early and often, finishing strong, as they got to an unusually vulnerable Young. The hurler gave up thirteen hits on the way to a 7-1 Baltimore romp. Jennings did most of the damage with Keeler and Kelley chipping in and running the bases with abandon.

In the fourth inning, Bill Hoffer threw a very nasty curve ball to Patsy Tebeau, who at first wanted to bail out, then decided to thrash at it. The result was a graceless hack that wrenched his back to the degree that he stepped out of the batter's box in great pain.

"Hoo haa!" yelled McGraw from third. "Did you even see that one, Patsy?"

Then, from Doyle, doing a sort of jig on the first base bag, "Screw you, Tebeau. Don't be a baby. Stand in there like a man!"

The comments brought a "damn you" and a shove of Doyle from the Spiders' first-base coach. Doyle overreacted with a punch to the solar plexus of the fat, out-of-shape veteran. The man doubled up and went down on one knee. Spiders boiled out of the dugout and Orioles flew to the fight. Many of the Birds remembered last year's Temple Cup in Cleveland when Kelley had to fight off a gang of cranks who had climbed out of the stands; Willie had been hit by a bottle and the Birds were regularly pelted with stones and potatoes.

During the chaos, amid kicks, punches, and bites, Patsy Tebeau, the Spiders' leader, hunched quietly and painfully back into the clubhouse, grabbed his duffle, and took a hansom back to his room at The Carrollton. The Spiders' player/manager was finished for the series.

The cops, Hanlon, and the ump eventually restored order. The fans sat back down, the benches returned. and the fielders took their positions. The Clevelands went quietly after that. All in all it was a good day for Baltimore and the paying customers got a little extra for their additional quarter.

West Virginia

There was no Isaac B. Pettibon registered at the hotel now or in the recent past. Those who managed the rental housing around the resort were very circumspect and wouldn't say whether the attorney was a resident or not. After a few unsuccessful days of watching the Springhouse, Morgan decided that, if English were here, he didn't use the mineral baths.

All he learned by looking over the top of his newspaper in various gathering spots was some good sporting news. The Orioles had won the National League pennant and the Temple Cup series against the Cleveland Spiders.

Talking to maids and waiters didn't pan out either. The black men raking the fall's first leaves could offer nothing. But after speaking casually to various medical personnel he encountered, he thought he might have something. Yes, there were several elderly gentlemen that used wheeled chairs. And, yes, at least one of them lived in a cottage on the ridge.

The nurse he was talking to knew this because, on one occasion, she had been asked to push the patient all the way up one of the paths to an overlook that provided a view of the Greenbrier Valley. "Lovers' Leap" she called it. The woman would never do that again, she emphasized. No, she didn't have the gentleman's name, but she recalled that he was staying in Copeland Hill Cottage, pointing up to a thin roofline that could barely be seen through the changing trees.

Morgan climbed the macadam path of Copeland Hill. Passing a row of lodges lower down, he reached a small rest area with a bench that was intended to give the guests a breather in their ascension. Trees and brush hid him from view as he watched the front door and gallery of Copeland Hill Cottage, thirty yards further up the path. He sat down quickly as he saw a small, bald man, dressed in a vest and shirtsleeves, step out onto the porch, lean over the railing, and look his way.

"Thomas, you're late. It's almost three o'clock. Hurry now, Mr. Cheeks is waiting," called the man.

At that, Morgan, now sitting on the bench, watched a large man, dressed as an orderly, trudge slowly up the incline past the rest platform. He either didn't see Morgan or ignored him as he commented quietly to himself, "Mr. Cheeks can wait for all I give a damn."

The man proceeded to the cottage, up a ramp to the gallery, and went inside. He emerged shortly after, pushing a wheeled chair with a gnarled old man in it. They descended the ramp, and with a grunt from the man pushing, the two began to climb further up the ridge.

"Have Mr. Cheeks back before sunset, as usual, Thomas," reminded the small man.

"Yes, Mr. Pettibon. I'll have the gentleman back the usual time," answered the orderly.

Morgan had found the man whose return address was on the letter to the Chicago attorneys. But was the old man in the chair John English? Pettibon closed the door to the cottage and walked briskly down the path, past Morgan without seeing him, to the resort below.

The cottage seemed empty. So Morgan tried the door and, finding it unlocked, entered. Through the door, he found a neat but very busy office on the left and a large well-lit sitting room on the right. A narrow stairway led to a second floor, but its steps were cluttered with heavy boxes. At least one of the boxes was marked "Baltimore." Rooms beyond were being used for storage and sleeping. A large bathroom with its door removed could be seen as well.

Stepping into the sitting room, he saw the debris of an invalid, pillows, blankets, medicines, and various apparatuses for moving someone who needed help. But there was nothing of particular interest in the room. Back in the hallway, Morgan would have liked to have scanned some of the paperwork he saw on the desk in the office, but that had to wait. He walked into the old man's bedroom next. The room, its smell, and the fact that it might be where English slept repulsed him. He found nothing identifiable there either. Then he checked the nightstand and received a shock. Looking out of the drawer at him was the tintype of a ghost. After nearly forty years, Hattie Simpson English was old fashioned, but still very beautiful.

Morgan replaced the picture, left the cottage, and began to climb the path in the direction that the wheeled chair had taken. The narrow lane soon turned to dirt and he could easily follow the tracks created by the chair. He took a left at one fork and a right at another, following a small wooden arrow with the words "Lovers' Leap" carved into it. Arriving at a clearing, he stepped back into the shadow of a thick tree.

The open, grassy, space stretched for about fifty yards, ending in a horizon of mountaintops and blue sky. Perched at the lip of the precipice was the man in the wheeled chair. Morgan looked for the orderly, but instead he heard one short snore off to his right. The attendant was sitting on a shaded bench pushed well back from the edge. His feet were stretched out, his arms were folded, and he was fighting off sleep.

Morgan quickly processed the possibility of pushing the old man off the cliff. The prospects were not good. It might not even be English, he reasoned. The orderly was a factor as well. He then remembered the last time he encountered John English in a chair. The Webley was back in the room. So, he watched the unmoving figure on the ledge and fingered the old scar on his forehead.

Before long, the medical attendant rose and slowly walked out to the seated man. As he bent to speak to the patient, Morgan moved deeper into the dark of the mountain woods in a position to have a clear view of the invalid as he regained the descending path.

As the chair came toward him, Morgan had a good look that improved as the vehicle moved past him. At one time, John English might have been thought of as a handsome man, even with his scarred eye. This was no longer even a remote possibility. A stroke had finished the job that the cops had started all those years ago. The left side of his face looked like melted candle wax, leaving his eye protruding and weeping something that was not tears. His left arm was shriveled and he held it like a dinosaur would hold its smaller fore claws. The arm shook involuntarily. His head was hunched down and cocked. It seemed to be supported by the collar he was wearing. Thin greasy strands were all that was left of his hair and hoary stubble covered what was left of his chin. He was now the monster outside that he had always been inside.

Baltimore

Bernadette had been taken to Hopkins in plenty of time and in no real frenzy. Harry arrived shortly thereafter and was promptly asked to calm down and wait in the designated lounge. In due course, Bernadette delivered a large, healthy baby boy that she and Harry named James.

With his wife and son sleeping in the safest of hands, Harry felt sure some celebration was in order. Not only was there another Vonderhorst in the world, but the Orioles had won the Temple Cup. They had swept the series four games to none. There was only one place to be tonight, he thought, so he headed there.

The Diamond sparkled like its name. Its bright, exterior electric lights illuminated a large, happy crowd celebrating their heroes by waving orange and black pennants and dancing to the band playing inside. The interior was even brighter, lit by rows of blazing chandeliers and reflecting mirrors. The revelers who made it through the front doors of the saloon found themselves surrounded by a throng of tipsy, backslapping, howling baseball fanatics. For a native Baltimorean and Oriole crank, it could not get any better.

The traffic around the building was utter confusion, but Harry's carriage managed to get close enough for him to step out and push his way to the door. He stood under a huge black and orange banner proclaiming his Orioles to be "Champions of the World!"

Cigars seemed to be the order of the day since the proprietors of the sports palace were handing out Oriole Brand perfectos. Harry pulled a Henry Clay Sobranos Havana out of his pocket. He had been saving it and now was the time. He clipped the end of the cigar, then struck a Lucifer match. Holding the Cuban at a downward angle, he slowly turned the foot of the cigar just above the flame to ensure an even burn. He toasted the fine smoke for five seconds, just as his father had taught him, then took that first long, gentle draw, continuing to turn the cigar to create a uniform burn. The old man was right when he said that the procedure was the only way to fully realize the flavor and bouquet of a resinous smoke like a Henry Clay.

Harry stood outside near the door for a few minutes, leaned against the wall, and watched his hometown celebrate. He loved his team, not just because their success was his, but also because their success was the city's. The Orioles were a galvanizing force that gave those who cared to look a glimpse of what Baltimore could be. He knew his team's reputation; he also knew his town's reputation. That's why they were the perfect match. The thought brought a smile to his face.

He listened to the band playing *Happy Days in Dixie* before segueing to a new George M. Cohan tune. The throng around him seemed to know the music already and had no trouble dancing with abandon to the piece. At one point, Harry was forced to step aside to avoid flying human refuse, as two hired apes forcefully ejected three drunks. In their wake, he squeezed through the door and struggled his way through howling revelers to the bar. Standing on the marble plank was John McGraw, distributing stogies from a paperboard box.

"Look who it is!" yelled the third baseman over the din. "The bowling champ is here!"

With that, he threw the box into the crowd and jumped down. Clapping Harry on the back, he said, "Glad you could make it. We played great, didn't we? What do you drink? I'm buying. Anything you want."

McGraw muscled a spot at the bar rail for he and Harry, then bawled to get his partner's attention. Uncle Robbie, working hard behind the bar, came right over with a big smile on his face.

"Mr. Vonderhorst, we're very pleased to have you here. Has John offered you a drink?" Wilbert Robinson was a happy man. The Diamond was a winner and so were the Orioles.

"Mr. McGraw here said I could have anything I wanted. Right, John?"

"Right you are, Harry my man, anything," said McGraw with the familiarity of a friendly drunk. Then he grabbed the team's owner around the shoulders and gave him a congenial shake.

"Then I want champagne!" said Harry. "But only as long as you let me do the buying. Bernadette and I just had a baby boy tonight!" he announced loudly and with considerable pride.

"What! A boy? Why that's great Mr. Vonderhorst!" boomed Robinson. McGraw began hooting and slapping his back again.

"Congratulations to you and the missus," said Robbie in Harry's ear. "Let's get away from these yahoos in here. There's a bunch of the team upstairs. We'll open the bubbly up there. John, you take the boss up and I'll get the wine and be with you in a wink."

In fact, the Orioles had an easy Temple Cup series, four straight games won in their usual fashion. No more jinx, no more questions about who was the best. In game two, Hanlon pitched young Joe Corbett who had begun to show the first glimmer of his future stardom. The Birds' bats were active and their creative aggressiveness on the base paths made them no friends outside of Baltimore but produced a 7-2 victory.

The third game of the series was a classic of Baltimore's philosophy of intentional chaos. With tickets returned to their old prices at Union Park, the fans filled the seats and any open space that could be found. The game was close until the eighth inning with the two dirtiest teams in baseball going at it hammer and tong. Then Cleveland lost control of it.

It started with a Robinson double and McGraw picking up the RBI with a bloop single into right field. Willie Keeler and McGraw then worked the hit and run to perfection and the Orioles occupied first and third. Hughie Jenning's deep sacrifice fly scored McGraw. On the next pitch, Wee Willie stole second. The catcher's throw was good and there was a nasty collision at the bag as Keeler came in hard and safe, knocking the ball out of McKean's glove. Joe Kelley stepped to the plate, watched a couple of pitches, then smashed a scorcher off the glove of a diving Chippy McGarr, Cleveland's third baseman. By the time McGarr retrieved the ball near the dugout, Willie was sliding home with the third run. With Hoffer pitching as well as he did in the first the game, the Birds had all that was needed. The game ended with the Orioles scoring six runs to the Spiders' two.

The last game took the team to Cleveland, where a small but very hostile crowd found little to cheer about. Corbett threw a shutout on three days rest and the Orioles capped the series with an easy 5-0 win. The Temple Cup would reside in a happy Baltimore for the next year.

A cheer went up as Harry, accompanied by a screaming McGraw, stepped into the private room that held most of the team. When the partiers heard that there was a new, little Vonderhorst to celebrate as well, the noise reached epic proportions.

Robinson arrived and began to pass out bottles of champagne. It was Kelley who discovered that the big, ugly, silver Temple Cup, displayed on a table in the middle of the room, could hold no less than seven bottles of bubbly. Passing it around became a sloppy game, but it created the momentum for a party that would become a part of Orioles' lore.

Chapter 31

West Virginia
October 1896

Morgan lay in his room thinking about John English. There were no second thoughts; he was just working out the details of what he had to do. English's neurotic need to stare out over Lovers' Leap every day made it simple. Eliminate the orderly and he would have a free hand.

The attendant was a problem though. Morgan had no desire to harm a man who was just doing his job. He was engaged in a well-deserved execution, not a slaughter. So, somehow he would have to find a way to do it without the orderly.

He thought about the questions his enemy could answer. Why had English seemingly ceased the effort to murder he and Bernadette? What role had he played in the Vonderhorst's financial difficulties over the last twelve years? How was he connected to the demise of the Fidelity Insurance Company? What had he been up to with Hanlon, the Orioles manager?

Morgan's desire to simply walk up and wheel English out and over the rock face was powerful. But there were too many questions that would go unanswered if he did. There would be loose ends that would haunt his new family forever. He must have some time alone with English before he acted.

After spending the morning working out details, Morgan dressed in a suit, making sure that the Webley was well hidden under the folded and pinned sleeve of his missing left arm. He packed his few belongings, checked out of the hotel, and arranged to have his bag waiting for him at the rail station prior to the scheduled departure of the 4 p.m. northbound train.

He found the administrative offices of the hotel and asked to speak to the manager. When he was ushered into the office of one of the assistant managers, he engaged the man in asking about leasing one of the cottages on the grounds for next season. When the hotel man left the office to find the resort's leasing agent, it took no time for Morgan to rummage through the man's desk and find a spare, brass nameplate that read "Assistant Manager." Taking the badge, he left the office.

Morgan strolled the paths of the resort until just before three. The weather had shifted overnight. The fall now was descending upon White Sulphur Springs and the air was crisp with a building breeze. Trees all around shuddered. Red and yellow leaves whipped through the air and chased each other down paths and across lawns.

When Morgan saw the orderly, Thomas, making his way up toward the cottage on Copeland Hill, he followed him. He hung back as the attendant collected English and he listened to the attorney, Pettibon, issue the same admonition to have the patient back by sunset.

Morgan watched the lawyer once again leave the cottage and descend the path to the resort. He then walked into the cottage and into English's bedroom. There, he found the picture of Hattie in the nightstand and put it in his pocket. *John won't need this any longer,* he thought.

He then followed the wheeled chair up the path, through small cyclones of swirling leaves. Above him, the increasing wind swayed the heavy limbs of oaks. The air was full of sound that rose and fell with the gusts that found the trail on the ridge.

Once English was settled on the lip of the precipice and Thomas was again dozing on the bench, Morgan pinned on the nameplate and approached the sleepy attendant.

"This is not how we provide our guests superior care," began Morgan sternly. "What if something should happen to Mr. Cheeks out there? Sleeping on the job is a good way to lose your position here."

The orderly jumped up from the bench and stood up straight. "I wasn't sleeping, Mr. . . . ah,"

"I saw you. You were about to nod off," countered Morgan. "Never mind that now, we'll discuss this later. You are needed down in the infirmary immediately. I'll take care of Mr. Cheeks. Now go."

Thomas thought this a bit odd. Why would they need him in the infirmary? The threat from this assistant manager was enough, however, that he obeyed the directive. When Morgan was sure the orderly was well down the hill, he tossed the nameplate into the woods and strode out to John English.

Morgan approached the chair from its right rear. The wind whipped his jacket open and he checked that the Webley was loose in its holster. English sat looking out over the October valley, watching leaves blow out into the ether, then drift slowly down, only to be picked up by the breeze again.

"Hattie would have thought this beautiful," said Morgan, hoping to surprise and disorient his enemy. Then he reached quickly to the blanket covering English's lap. A yank of the cover revealed two empty, shaky hands and no weapon. The blanket was thrown aside.

The seated man gave a start. Then slowly he turned his head and stared at Morgan without speaking.

"It's taken me a while to find you, John, but it's over now."

"Thought...you...dead," English slurred out of the side of his mouth. It was clearly a chore for the man to speak.

"No, you bastard. I'm not dead. And neither is your daughter," spat Morgan.

English's bulging eye widened. His forehead creased with pain and anguish. Morgan's comment was aimed to hurt and it did. It was difficult to determine exactly why it hurt, but a moan made its way out of the man and he hung his head.

"I know you've been attempting to sabotage the Vonderhorst family," Morgan stated. "What I don't know fully is how and why."

English lifted his head and gave his former friend a baleful look. He gathered himself to speak, and finally uttered, "Hattie...loved... you...not...me."

This comment paralyzed Morgan. Then English squeezed out with a gleam in his eye, "The baby. . .yours. . .not. . .mine."

"What? What did you say?" demanded Morgan.

English was exhausted and for a moment Morgan thought the wretch was going to collapse. Then his old partner managed a few more words. With an evil glint that Morgan immediately recognized, he uttered, "She...told...me."

Morgan felt dizzy. The roaring in his ears was not just the wind. His world spun and he staggered a step toward the cliff, as if English had punched him. She loved me? Why then did she marry him? How much could he believe? Morgan's thoughts swirled like the leaves in the air.

Then, he thought, Bernadette is my daughter? The son-of-a-bitch knew this all along? He knew Bernadette is mine?

This was a level of hatred and psychosis he had not expected, even from this foul bastard. Morgan reached for the chair.

The air had now begun to whip the two men's clothes, and English's blanket tumbled away across the clearing. The swaying oaks above them added to Morgan's feeling that he was standing on the deck of a rolling ship. Grabbing the wheeled chair, he began to push English toward the drop.

As Morgan resolutely strode toward bringing just a little more order to the world, an explosive crack split the air. The sky was suddenly filled with a dark, rushing presence. Without warning, a massive oak limb crashed down on the pair. The stout branch, snapped by the gusting wind, destroyed both the chair and the man in it.

Morgan was slapped away by lesser branches, the main weight of the bough missing him by inches. He was alive but buried under smaller limbs and their leaves. He felt new pain in a number of places, a rib or two were surely broken, and his face and neck were covered in cuts and scrapes.

He extracted himself with considerable effort, then stood over the remains of John English. His nemesis was dead. The wind and the tree had done precise and conclusive work.

Morgan peered up through the bending trees to the blue sky above and listened to the hissing of the leaves. Okay, maybe it's just as well that ordering the world be left to God, he thought.

Baltimore

Morgan sat in the solarium of the big house on Frederick Road. A weak morning sun shown through the windows and in among the lush ferns, potted trees, and flowers that Bernadette tended so lovingly. It had been a week before he was able to gather his thoughts and deal with the physical pain and emotional confusion he felt. Harry and Bernadette were shocked at the state in which they found him standing in their foyer. But they had left him alone. They simply tended to him and were determined to let him come to them when he was ready.

"I see you are up," said Bernadette, coming into the room with a watering can in her hand. "Would you like some coffee?"

"A cup of coffee would be great, thanks, Bernadette," said Morgan, smiling at her. "Has Harry left for town, yet?"

"No not yet. I won't go until later today," said Harry Vonderhorst coming into the bright room. Then adding, "I have a meeting with Ned Hanlon at the Park at two."

"Good," said Morgan. "I'd like to talk to you both. Do you have a few minutes?"

Harry and Bernadette had been waiting for this and the wait had been excruciating. Although Jamie had looked terrible when he arrived, they noticed that, despite his injuries, he seemed more at peace than they had ever known him to be. Clearly, something had happened in West Virginia.

The three sat in the sun-dappled room sipping coffee. After an initial awkwardness as Morgan seemed to be ordering his thoughts, he began in his typically blunt way.

"John English is dead. He will no longer threaten anyone, neither you nor me. He is now just a bad memory."

Waiting for this conversation had been particularly hard on Bernadette. She had never been one with much patience. "Jamie, what happened? Tell us. Did you. . . .?"

"No, he died in an accident," said Morgan.

He provided them the whole story. The tale was unvarnished and held no hint of triumph or arrogance. His recounting did, however, include a sense of awe for the way English died. It was also obvious that Morgan was humbled and mystified by the sparing of his own life.

Harry's first comment reflected this. "There seemed to be some other forces at play up on that ledge."

Morgan nodded thoughtfully. Then said, "I spoke to him before he died."

This set the itchy Bernadette off again. "What did he say? What did you ask him?"

Morgan set the coffee cup down, seemed to gather himself, and leaned toward Bernadette. "He told me that he was not your father. He told me that I am your father."

Bernadette had had a few shocks in her life, not surprising, given her start in the world. But, perhaps the fact that this was the third time someone claimed to be her father, she took the information with an uncomprehending blink.

Sensing her confusion, Morgan continued quickly, "English was told by your mother that I was the father. He kept that information within himself for forty years. He knew it even when we were supposed to be friends."

"Jamie, you are my father?" The information was beginning to sink in to Bernadette.

"My God! That would explain his actions in large part. That's a lot of poison to carry around," observed Harry.

Morgan said nothing at first; he reached into his breast pocket and produced the tintype of Hattie Simpson English. He handed it to Bernadette. She took it in two hands and stared at the mother she had only dreamed about.

"Bernadette, I loved Hattie and I never stopped loving her. I should have fought for her, but I didn't. John English was someone who could protect your mother in a way that I guess she felt I couldn't or wouldn't. It was the biggest mistake of my life."

With that, Morgan did something he had never done before. He hung his head, hunched his shoulders, and let out a tearless sob. It was a releasing of years of pain, and it had an elemental strength and pitch to it. It was a sound of the anguished streets in which he was still firmly rooted.

Bernadette rose and went to him. One hand held the photograph to her heart; with the other hand, she lifted his head, then knelt and enfolded him in her arms. Silent tears started.

"My little girl," is all James Morgan could say.

Harry Vonderhorst waited for his meeting with Hanlon in his office at Union Park. The Temple Cup sat hulking on a corner table, surrounded by three orange and black pennants proclaiming the Orioles as champions for the last three years. Through a large window, he could look out onto the diamond and the green outfield beyond. As hard as he tried to fill the stands during the season, he enjoyed it now, empty and waiting quietly for the Birds' spring assault on the '97 pennant.

He reflected upon Jamie's revelation of that morning. It was not lost on him how often things failed to work out the way one thought they would. He had not foreseen the depth of base emotions that had driven both Morgan and English. He had not guessed that it would have worked out the way it did. Jamie Morgan as a father-in-law had not even entered his mind. In fact, most things seemed to be different than he had anticipated them to be. His investments, his team, even Bernadette, as much as he loved her, was not the woman he married. There was one exception to this combination of myopia and impermanence—the beer business.

A knock on the door brought him back to the matter at hand. Once Morgan had collected himself, he also mentioned the other questions he had planned for English before he died, including his tie to Ned Hanlon. But fate stepped in before the answers were forthcoming.

It was a puzzling coincidence that the Birds' manager wanted to talk to him. The season was over, the celebrating done, and player contract negotiations were not due to start for a couple more months.

"Come in, Ned, have a chair," said Harry amiably. "To what do I owe the pleasure of this visit?"

At least he could start pleasantly enough, although that's not how his conversations with this prickly man always ended.

Hanlon was as formal as he always was whether it was in an office or in a dugout. His five-button, wool suit sported a plain, white pocket kerchief and covered a starched shirt. Above the stiff collar and neatly tied cravat, his thick black mustache twitched. Hanlon sat and stroked his bristles before he spoke.

"I have something I want you to know," said the manager. Harry nodded and waited.

"I may not have ever told you this if it wasn't for Joe and Willie," said Hanlon, referring to Kelley and Keeler, maybe the team's two biggest stars. "They convinced me to talk to you."

Harry ignored the implication that Hanlon could care less if he ever spoke to the team's owner. He continued to nod to encourage the laconic man.

"Well, you probably should know that I am the minority owner of this baseball team," said Hanlon matter-of-factly.

This got Vonderhorst's attention. "What do you mean, Ned? There is a minority owner but it's an investment consortium out of Chicago."

"It used to be an investment consortium; at least that's what the former holder of the stock wanted you to believe," said Hanlon with a bit of smugness.

Harry leaned forward on his desk and looked at his manager. "Why don't you just tell me all of it?" suggested Harry, now annoyed by Hanlon's arrogance.

"Back in '93 when you brought me in, I was approached by a law firm in Chicago. Their client had a minority share in the Baltimore Orioles that he was willing to let go. This client, who I have never met, was willing to sell his holdings to me at a discount, if I met one condition."

Harry's mind was churning rapidly. Was this English working against the family? It was Jamie's opinion that the bastard had been involved in a number of the Vonderhorst financial misfortunes over the years. Was English also responsible for John Vonderhorst's problems in California?

"And what was that condition?" asked Harry, just barely holding in his anger.

"The condition was that I field a team that had no chance whatsoever of winning a championship," answered Hanlon.

"Something here doesn't fit, Ned," said Harry. "I fly three banners over this field and they all say 'championship' and I've got a damn big Cup taking up too much of my office. I have the team to thank for both of those things."

Vonderhorst was proud of the twenty-five-foot red, white, and blue burgee pennants and loved to hear their tails crack in the breeze. The Temple Cup was something different again.

"Well, it's true enough that I didn't meet the condition of sale," observed Hanlon. "But it wasn't from lack of trying, at first. That '93 team was awful on paper and that's what allowed the deal to go through, signed and sealed. There is no question that I'm your partner." With that, the manager and part owner laid a folder of documents in front of Harry.

"Why are you telling me this now?" asked Vonderhorst without opening the file.

"It was Willie who threatened to leave if I didn't come clean with you. He said he didn't want to play on a team that had this kind of a secret. Said it would eventually tear us apart," answered Hanlon.

"So, if Keeler hadn't threatened you, you never would have told me?" asked Harry with a sneer.

"Look, Harry, I feel like I can call you that now, I would have told you eventually. But what difference does it make today? Nothing changes. My intentions changed back then as soon as I realized what I had. Even with that, I can't explain how the team accomplished what it did. It defies explanation, really, given my roster moves that year."

"What you did was unethical and maybe illegal, Ned," answered Harry. "How am I to trust you in the future?"

"I would challenge you on legality and win without a doubt in my mind," said Hanlon. "What's more, there is no record of the condition of the purchase. As far as unethical goes, have you been watching us play for the last three years? We've broken every rule we could get away with and you are as proud of the results as anyone is," said Hanlon, gesturing to the pennants on Harry's wall.

"As far as trust goes," continued the manager, "you never trusted me anyway. At least now you can trust that I will protect my investment."

"Hanlon, playing baseball and being ethical in business are two different things," said Harry lamely. He was angry and frustrated with the man's logic and didn't think very hard about his own.

"Are they?" asked the manager. "What makes you think that?"

"This is not how I planned to win championships," said Harry, ignoring the question.

"Funny how things don't always work out the way we plan, isn't it?" observed Hanlon.

Epilogue

Union Park, Baltimore
July 1899

The reporter had gone, leaving the old man with his memories, some fond and some not so fond. In the three years since the Orioles won their last championship, their fortunes had waned. Star players came and went, certainly. But the charisma and character of that great team was gone forever.

The rule makers made sure that baseball was no longer organized chaos. And in the process, they destroyed a great deal of the individuality, the excitement, and the unpredictability of the game. Now, only on occasion, could one see the fury that lurked below the rules in the current deportment of these businessmen/players. He missed the anarchy, just as he missed his youth.

Morgan sat in the hard, wooden seats of the park's boxes and looked out over the scoreboard to the increasing number of houses and buildings surrounding the field. He remembered when North Avenue was the northern limit of Baltimore.

The city he loved mirrored the game. The growth that occurred during the middle of the century had now tapered off, with many enterprises merging or being sold or moved to larger economic centers in the country. Baltimore clearly had been tamed from the chaotic days of firehouse gangs and riots. While never quiet, civilization had come to most of Mobtown's streets along with sanitation, education, and art. It was a much better, safer place to live these days.

Even with that, Morgan couldn't help but think wistfully of the times when he and Gambrill, and even English, were running the streets, full of Eagle and full of themselves. It brought a smile to his face and a bit of an itch too. I guess I haven't changed much, he thought.

"Jamie, are you ready to go?" asked his daughter, Bernadette, sitting down in the seat next to him. "Harry's home for dinner and your grandson is waiting for you. He says you promised to go fishing this evening."

He smiled, nodded, and began to stand with some effort. His physical life and the trials within it had begun to take their toll.

"How are you feeling?" asked Bernadette, reaching to help him up.

"Oh, I'm okay," he answered. "I'm just feeling a little restless these days."

She looked at him, squeezed his arm, and laughed. She had never known him to feel any other way.

THE END

Author's Note

Plug Ugly Ball is a work of fiction. Just the same, I have attempted to create an accurate picture of the City of Baltimore, its residents, and their activities between the years 1857 and 1899.

Most of the book's main characters lived in Baltimore at the time they appear. However, a number of liberties have been taken with individual personal histories for the sake of the story. James Morgan, John English, J.W. Gambrill, John and Harry Vonderhorst, Severn Teakle Wallis, W. Meade Addison, Henry Winter Davis, and others all may be found in the legitimate historical record. Each member of the Baltimore Orioles and Cleveland Spiders baseball teams mentioned in the book also were very real people, and although some of their actions in the novel are fictional, others are not.

Morgan, English, and Gambrill are names that repeatedly surface in the history of the city's police, courts, and legal proceedings during the 1850s. The record is riddled with their brutal antisocial behavior. Each of them also seems to have held leadership positions in the Plug Ugly American Club, which was associated with the Mount Vernon Hook and Ladder Company on Biddle Street near Ross. The Plug Ugly social club was, in fact, established by John English out of his saloon next to the firehouse.

The three men actually began their active street lives running with the New Market Firehouse, the Mount Vernon Hook and Ladder's hated rival. When Mount Vernon was established in July of 1854, English, Morgan, Gambrill, and others shifted their alliance over to the newly established house on Biddle Street. This desertion did not sit well with the New Market adherents, especially when they soon found themselves competing for fires with their old mates. When Mount Vernon aligned itself with the nativist American Party, and the

Market with the Democratic Party, it became all-out warfare between the two firehouses.

Like many of the Plug Uglies, Morgan, English, and Gambrill owned and operated saloons. John English's bar, with its proximity to the Mount Vernon firehouse, drew the young men of the area and became the center of the street gang. James Morgan's bar was located not far away at Ross and Eutaw streets and was known as The Mount Vernon Restaurant. For the purposes of the story, the author has renamed the saloon and oyster bar after its owner and centered some of the action in this location, rather than at English's tavern.

Eramus "Raz" Levy was one of the key members of the Rip Raps social club that operated out of the west side's Fourteenth Ward. The Rip Raps controlled the streets just south of the New Market's Twelfth Ward. Levy was as violent and as antisocial a man as could be found at the time. In addition to his role in the Rip Raps, he kept a saloon at No. 11 Holiday Street in downtown Baltimore. There he hosted much of the leadership of the American clubs, including John English, who seemed to spend a great deal of time there when he wasn't in the Twentieth Ward.

Augustus Albert was, in fact, the president and driving force behind the preeminent New Market Firehouse in 1857 and served in that capacity until the company went out of existence with the formation of the Baltimore City Fire Department in 1859. The author has given him the nickname of "Bully" for reader interest only. He was not murdered by John English and was no relation to W. Meade Addison, the U.S. district attorney for Maryland.

The Vonderhorst family (often seen written as Von der Horst) was in fact a very prominent Baltimore family, owners of the Eagle Brewery and Malt Works, investors in railroads, and the original owners of the early Baltimore Orioles. John Vonderhorst was not murdered in a room in The Carrollton Hotel. The respected businessman was a pillar of Baltimore's German–American community and died of cancer in 1869, leaving two sons and a daughter. Some liberty has been taken with the transfer of the brewery's ownership from the senior John Vonderhorst to his sons, Harry and John. The description of the ownership of the Orioles is generally accurate, with some adjustment in support of the story.

The characters of Hattie English, Bernadette Vonderhorst, Jane Cooper, Bill Barton, and Zachariah are fictional and were created for their interest and key roles in the plot.

Ned Hanlon was in fact the Hall of Fame manager of the World Champion Baltimore Orioles of 1894–1896. His part ownership of the team and how he gained that ownership is the result of my imagination. The actual deal that brought Hanlon to Baltimore from the Pittsburgh Alleghenies in 1893 granted him total field responsibility, some amount of stock, and the presidency of the club. Although it is true that Hanlon managed to assemble an extraordinary team that had five eventual Baseball Hall of Fame players on it (McGraw, Keeler, Kelley, Robertson, and Jennings), my premise that his initial intentions in gathering these men were less than ethical is pure speculation. I have attempted to capture the personalities of each of the ball players as they have been drawn in a number of respected baseball histories.

A sincere effort has been made to be accurate with the generally accepted understanding of historical events and the evolution of the city. This includes Baltimore's rise as a port city; it's connection to the world by iron, steam and rail; its development into a manufacturing power; and its transition through consolidation and acquisition to branch office status. The city's mid-to-late 1850's society, its class divisions, its population of freedman, and its influx of German and Irish immigrants are all historically accurate. Baltimore's politics and its fire, police, and judicial support systems have been presented as they were in this mid-nineteenth century urban environment. If anything, the violence and general lawlessness in the city, resulting from the marriage of politics and hooliganism, has been understated.

I believe the description of Baltimore politics and the social issues faced by the city's leadership to be accurate. The tooth and nail fighting between adherents to the Democratic Party and those of the fading nativist American Party (Know-Nothings) is well documented. The philosophies, principles, and tactics of these parties in the mid-1850s also are well understood and hopefully presented in an accurate way.

The frictions arising out of the transition to demographic diversity in the city are captured accurately. The changes in power at the state, city, and the street levels due to the influx of German and Irish immigrants was a very difficult time for Baltimore. Added to this was the issue of slavery, which was already in a nationally explosive state on the verge of the Civil War. Baltimore, as a haven for the largest community of black freedmen at the time, it's key role in the Underground Railroad, and the dangers that slaves and ex-slaves faced in its streets, is also accurate and very probably understated. Throughout the book, blacks are depicted in a series of menial and low-status jobs. This is by intent and reflects the facts of the time, rather than any statement by the Author. The fight over the transition from a volunteer system of fighting fires to a municipally controlled system was very real. The birth of the street gangs out of hangers-on to the volunteer fire brigades is also accurate.

There is no evidence that John Vonderhorst and Severn Teakle Wallace were friends or worked in concert to eliminate the volunteer fire companies and their social clubs. And, although the Baltimore Reform Association existed, my speculation on its membership and activities are also part of the fiction. Congressman Henry Winter Davis was a well-known political player of the time and his ties to former President Millard Fillmore were well known. However, the novel's use of the character and his ties to political violence are also fictional liberty.

The names and locations of the parks in which the Orioles played can be confusing due to various fires and rebuilding efforts over the years. The first mention of a formal facility that collected admissions to watch a team from Baltimore was Newington Park where the Lord Baltimores of the National Association played in 1872. Ten years later, Harry Vonderhorst bought the city's professional team, joined the American Association, and moved the Baltimores to Oriole Park at Greenmount and 25th Streets. By 1884, the team had also picked up the name Orioles. (At this time, two other professional teams were also playing in the city: the Baltimore Unions of the Union Association used the Belair Lot at Forest and Gay streets in Old Town, and the Monumentals of the Eastern League played on grounds at Druid Hill Avenue and Whitelock Lane.) In 1889, a new and bigger Oriole Park was built at York Road (now Greenmount Avenue) between Barnum and Homewood avenues (28th and 29th streets). In 1891, the year before the American Association merged with the National League, Harry Vonderhorst built the first double-decked grandstand in Baltimore and christened it Union Park. The new location at 25th and Barclay streets was the home of the championship Oriole teams and the scene of the baseball action in this novel.

The Diamond Cafe (sometimes referred to as The Diamond Tavern) existed and was owned and operated jointly by Wilbert Robinson and John McGraw. Although McGraw eventually sold his interest in the enterprise at 519 North Howard Street, Robinson continued to operate the saloon well after his retirement from baseball in 1902. According to the Maryland Historical Society archives, the building had multiple owners over time, but was always operated as a tavern in Baltimore's old theater district until its demolition in 2004. Unfortunately, with the exception of a few newspaper articles, there is little in the known historical record about the business. Photographs of the building's exterior or the interior of the place have been described by collectors of such things as "the Holy Grail" of Baltimore photographs. Although the bar's description is fictional, the activities and entertainments offered by The Diamond are not. It also may be of interest that the invention of duckpin bowling, a uniquely Baltimore sport, is credited to one of the tavern's managers who was said to have cut down damaged ten pins in an effort to save some money. The credit for the name "duckpins," however, is laid to none other than McGraw and Robertson. The story goes that, sometime around 1900, the pair came up with the name while hunting ducks on the Eastern Shore of Maryland. Evidently, the action of the pins, when struck, reminded them of ducks rising from a pond at the sound of a shotgun.

Pimlico Race Course opened in 1870, seven years after the start of New York's Saratoga Race Course, the oldest organized sporting facility of any kind in the United States. Old Hilltop is, of course, still in operation after 141 years. The description of the tenth running of the Preakness was drawn as accurately as possible from the historic record. However, the Author, being a lifelong fan of thoroughbred racing, realizes that no writer could ever fully capture the true excitement of two evenly matched horses pounding toward the finish line, especially when he has bet on the horse on the front. The Tilghman sisters are likely to remind readers of people they know, but although their name is quite familiar on Maryland's Eastern Shore, they are the creation of the Author's imagination.

The description of White Sulphur Springs, West Virginia, and its exceptional and historic resort, The Greenbrier, comes directly from

my personal experience there. Although the resort continues to maintain exacting standards of modern excellence, the Author found it very
easy to imagine what it was like over one hundred years ago. That, for
me, is a big part of the resort's compelling charm.

Finally, James Morgan's activities during the American Civil
War are fictional. The descriptions of the actions and history of his
supposed mentor, Colonel John S. Mosby, CSA, including Mosby's relationship with Ulysses S. Grant, are accurate, however.

The Author's hope was to entertain and to offer readers a sense
of the time. There was no intent to offend or establish this novel as a
historical record, especially in relationship to the characters within.

John Thomas Everett

Sources and Suggested Readings

Baseball Almanac Web site. http://www.baseball-almanac.com. (A privately held Web site)

Bennett, D. H. 1988. *The Party of Fear: From Nativist Movements to the New Right in American History.* Chapel Hill, NC: University of North Carolina Press.

Bready, J. H. 1998. *Baseball in Baltimore: The First Hundred Years.* Baltimore, MD: The Johns Hopkins University Press.

Dozer, D. M. 1976. *Portrait of the Free State: A history of Maryland.* Cambridge, MD: Tidewater Publishers.

Felber, B. 2007. *A Game of Brawl: The Orioles, The Beaneaters & The Battle for the 1897 Pennant.* Lincoln, NE: University of Nebraska Press.

Freeman, D. S. 1998. *Lee's Lieutenants: A Study in Command.* New York, NY: Simon and Schuster, Inc.

Gordon, J. S. 2004. *An Empire of Wealth.* New York, NY: HarperCollins Publishers, Inc.

Hagberg, D. 2011. *Baltimore Baseball and Beer: Baltimore's Brewers and Their Early Ties to Beer.* Online article.

Hipp, S. F. 2011. *Old Line Divided: Maryland in the Civil War: Volume I: Antebellum to 1862.* Baltimore, MD: The Baltimore Bookworks, LLC.

Hounshell, D. A. 1984. *From the American System to Mass Production, 1800–1932: The Development of Manufacturing Technology in the United States.* Baltimore, MD: The Johns Hopkins University Press.

Lewis, T. A. 1988. *The Guns of Cedar Creek.* New York, NY: Harper and Row.

Longacre, E. G. 2002. *Lee's Cavalrymen: A History of the Mounted Forces of the Army of Northern Virginia.* Mechanicsburg, PA: Stackpole Books.

Mantell, M. E. 1973. *Johnson, Grant and the Politics of Reconstruction.* New York, NY: Columbia University Press.

Melton, T. M. 2005. *Hanging Henry Gambrill: The Violent Career of Baltimore's Plug Uglies, 1854–1860.* Baltimore, MD: The Press at the Maryland Historical Society.

Mosby, Col. J. S. 1917. *The Memoirs of Colonel John S. Mosby.* Boston, MA: Little, Brown, and Company.

Rayback, R. J. 1959. *Millard Fillmore: Biography of a President.* Buffalo, NY: The Buffalo Historical Society.

Scharf, Col. J. T. 1874. *The Chronicles of Baltimore: Being a Complete History of "Baltimore Town" and Baltimore City from the Earliest Period to the Present Time.* Baltimore, MD: Turnbull Brothers.

Scharf, Col. J. T. 1881. *History of Baltimore City and County: From the Earliest Period to the Present Day.* Philadelphia, PA: Press of J. B. Lippencott & Co.

Solomon, B. 1999. *Where They Ain't: The Fabled Life and Untimely Death of the Original Baltimore Orioles, The Team That Gave Birth to Modern Baseball.* New York, NY: A Main Street Book, Doubleday.

Stiles, T. J. 2009. *The First Tycoon: The Epic Life of Cornelius Vanderbilt.* New York, NY: Vintage Books.

Stinson, D. B. 2011. *Deadball: A Metaphysical Baseball Novel.* Chevy Chase, MD: Huntington Park Publications, Inc.

CITY OF
BALTIMORE
MARYLAND.

PUBLISHED BY J.H. COLTON & Co. Nº 172 WILLIAM ST. NEW YORK.